HOT HONOR

Hostile Operations Team® - Strike Team 2

LYNN RAYE HARRIS

All Rights Reserved. This book or any portion thereof
may not be reproduced or used in any manner whatsoever without the
express written permission of the publisher except for the use of brief
quotations in a book review.

This is a work of fiction. Names, characters, places, and incidents either
are the products of the author's imagination or are used fictitiously. Any
resemblance to actual persons, living or dead, businesses, companies,
events, or locales is entirely coincidental.

The Hostile Operations Team® and Lynn Raye Harris® are
trademarks of H.O.T. Publishing, LLC.

Printed in the United States of America

First Printing, 2023

For rights inquires, visit www.LynnRayeHarris.com

HOT Honor
Copyright © 2023 by Lynn Raye Harris
Cover Design Copyright © 2023 Croco Designs

ISBN: 978-1-941002-80-3

Chapter One

LAS VEGAS, NEVADA

ZANE SCOTT WOKE SLOWLY, trying to remember exactly where he was. He could hear water running. He had an impression of a crowded bar, laughter, and voices.

His little sister's twenty-first birthday.

She'd wanted to celebrate in Vegas, and he'd flown out to meet her and her friends because she'd asked. His parents were there too, but they'd bowed out long before the evening ended. He remembered drinking tequila shots, thinking there was no way Mia was old enough to drink, and scowling at the random dudes who came by to chat with Mia and her friends.

Her friends were all around the same age, and they flirted outrageously with him. He didn't mind. He knew better than to bang any of them, no matter how drunk he got.

He had a sudden impression of skin on skin, hot sex, and the satisfaction of at least two orgasms. He'd definitely banged someone last night. But had it been one of Mia's college friends? A shudder rippled through him.

God, he hoped not. They were pretty enough, but they were kids. He was thirty-one, a full ten years older than his baby sister. No way would he have let down his guard enough to fuck one of her friends. Would he?

The water stopped running. He pushed upright slowly, his head aching. He didn't usually drink so much, but it'd been a long few months and he'd welcomed the break from work. All his teammates were married. Some of the wives were pregnant, or soon would be. It was downright domestic at HOT HQ these days. He was the only one still up for spontaneous bar hopping or for darts and wings at Buddy's Bar & Grill.

The guys still went to Buddy's, but they tapped out early, saying they had to get home to their women. Zane sighed. It was a lonely business being the last unattached operator on the team.

He told himself to snap out of it. He *liked* being single. Banging a different woman every night if he wanted. Not being tied to a schedule for going out or coming home. He reached for a bottle of water on the bedside table and drank it down. He set it back on the table when something glinted on his left hand.

He blinked. Stared. Spread his hand to stare some more.

There was a ring on his left hand. He lifted it to stare at it a bit closer. Gold, smooth, encircling his ring finger. As if he'd gotten married.

The chill that shuddered through him earlier became an ice storm.

Married. Oh, shit.

He'd gotten married. It'd happened. He remembered standing in front of Elvis, saying vows to a woman with red hair and luscious lips that he'd wanted wrapped around his cock.

"Oh Jesus," he groaned. Of all the stupid fucking things.

He'd married a woman he didn't know last night. For some hot sex and a blow job.

Fucking hell…

———

TWO DAYS EARLIER…

"DUDE, don't do anything stupid out there in Vegas," Mal McCoy said, throwing a towel at him. Zane caught it and wrapped it around his neck. Strike Team 2 had just finished a grueling workout at the gym and were heading for the showers.

"Who do you think you're talking to? Yourself? Naw, man, it's my baby sister's birthday party. I'll be looking out for her and her friends, not pulling a Mal and getting shit-faced."

Mal managed a look of mock offense. "I'll have you know I do *not* get shit-faced."

"Scarlett won't let him," Noah "Easy" Cross said with a laugh. "Not since that last time."

"And Jenna lets you?" Mal shot back. "Scar is not the boss of me."

The guys within earshot laughed. "Not what I heard," Ryder "Muffin" Hanson said. "Besides, you gotta admit that standing on the table at Buddy's last month and serenading her with *You Are So Beautiful to Meeeeee* was the straw that broke the camel's back."

"Well, she is beautiful. And it was heartfelt. Not my fault you bozos gave me that bottle of Jack for my birthday."

"Yeah, but you didn't have to drink it all in one night," Cade "Saint" Rodgers said with a laugh.

"I might have been a bit happy," Mal acknowledged. "And my judgement was off. But I didn't drink the whole bottle alone. You people helped."

"We just helped ourselves to a lot less than you did," Zane replied.

Mal twisted the taps in the walk-in shower and turned to point a finger at Zane. "Yeah, well, remember that when you're in Vegas, buddy. I sang off-key to my woman and had a headache the next day. You can get into a lot worse trouble in Sin City."

Zane twisted the taps to his own showerhead and stepped under the spray. "I'll be fine, Mal. Thanks for the concern though."

The guys showered, making jokes and razzing each other, then dressed and attended a commander's call briefing. After that, it was time to leave work. Since it was a Wednesday night, they were heading home to their women instead of out to Buddy's Bar & Grill for pool and pizza. Zane missed those days when at least a couple of the guys were still up for it. But with Muffin marrying Alaina this past summer, he was the last single guy on the team. Not that he didn't hang out with some of the guys from other teams, but it wasn't quite the same as hanging with your brothers from your own team.

Everyone said goodbye in the parking lot, and Zane climbed into his RAM truck and fired it up. He loved that truck. Solid black, Night Edition, which meant blacked out badging and black wheels in addition to black paint. It worked, and he loved it because it was tall and he could see everything as he rolled down the road.

He drove home, stopping to pick up a pizza on the way, and parked in the drive since the truck was too big for the garage of his rental. His phone dinged with a message as he walked to the front door. Everything inside him tightened up like someone had pulled a brake handle on the DC Metro.

Juliet: *Hey, haven't heard from you in a few days.*

Zane gritted his teeth as he unlocked the door and went inside. Every time Juliet messaged or called, he let himself get sucked in again. He knew he shouldn't, but he did.

He dropped the pizza and his keys on the counter, then thumbed a response. *Been busy. How about you?*

Three dots indicated she was typing. He knew from experience it'd take a while, so he set the phone down while he unbuttoned his camouflage uniform shirt and shrugged out of it. He kept the rest of the uniform on—jump boots, pants, T-shirt—and flipped the pizza box open.

Mmm, pepperoni with extra cheese. His favorite. Zane grabbed a slice, folded it in half, and took a bite while he went to snag a beer from the fridge. The kitchen was small but serviceable, and the house was older. One day he'd like to buy his own place like Muffin had done recently, but he wasn't there yet. Since his dad's business partner had embezzled company funds a couple years ago and drove the business into the ground before killing himself, his parents' finances had been tight. Tight enough that Zane was the one financing his sister's college education these days.

Not that he minded. Mia was worth it. He hadn't been ready for college when he'd graduated high school, so he'd joined the Army instead. But Mia was sharp as a tack, and she'd be a damned fine accountant when she was done.

Zane took the beer to the counter where he had a couple of bar stools and sat down. Juliet's latest message slipped across his screen.

Same. I just don't know what to do sometimes, you know? I just want this divorce to move along, but Daniel is being such an asshole about it. He fights me about everything. And the dog! He's never cared that much for Sweetie but now he claims he loves her and wants to share custody. I mean Jesus, Zane. Why did I marry this guy? Why did I let you go? I was such an idiot.

Zane's gut twisted when she said stuff like that. At one time he'd thought Juliet was his forever girl. They'd been high school sweethearts, each other's firsts, and he'd been crazy for her. She was a cheerleader, prom queen, and an honor student. Not just beauty and personality, but brains too. They'd planned to get married, though the ring had to wait until he could afford one. They'd talked about it often. Where they would live, how many kids they would have and when. The parties they would throw, the lives they would lead.

But when he'd gone into the Army, something changed. Not at first. They'd kept calling each other, texting, emailing, and video chatting. Her replies started taking longer to arrive, and she never found the time for video chats. Too much schoolwork, she'd said. Too many demands on her time. She'd chosen to go to a college only half an hour from home, so she did a lot of driving to visit friends and family.

And Daniel Brentwood, apparently. Zane only found out she'd been cheating when he went home for Christmas and Juliet dropped a bomb that she was in love with Daniel. The engagement ring he'd finally managed to buy for her had burned a hole in his pocket while she'd said she was sorry, but she'd been too young when they'd promised to get married and love each other forever. She wanted to experience life, wanted to date and have a good time before she settled down. She didn't want to marry an Army guy and move around the world on short notice.

They'd made the plan together, but the joke was on him. Especially when she married Daniel the next summer and started enjoying her life as a country club wife.

Zane picked up the phone again. Juliet was the reason he was a serial dater. The reason he'd erased the word forever from his vocabulary a long time ago. He needed to remember that, no matter how much she twisted him up inside.

It's what you wanted, Jules. You couldn't know it'd go wrong. Hell, we might have gone wrong too. Maybe it's a good thing we broke up.

Her reply was swift. *No, it wasn't. I was young and dumb and wowed by Daniel's flash and his family's money. I want to try again with you, Zane. I want to erase the past few years and start over. We were always good together. We had such plans!*

His heart squeezed. Yeah, they'd had plans. And she'd ruined them all. *You've been saying that, but I think you're confused and hurt, and you need time to figure out what's right for you. I think you're making us better than we were because of the situation you're in. Jumping from a marriage into a relationship isn't the right way to go.*

He hit Send and growled to himself. Part of him wanted the rosy picture she painted. Wanted to fold her into his arms and see if the spark was still there and if the ache in his chest that she'd created would go away.

But another part of him sent up warning flags like crazy. They weren't the same people anymore. They were older, different, and Juliet was unhappy. She was projecting her idea of the perfect life on him, viewing her choices with a critical eye, and convincing herself *if only*.

It wasn't enough. He'd watched his teammates and their women, and he *knew* it wasn't enough. He wasn't going to pretend they could take up where they'd left off or that the past eleven years hadn't happened.

But he'd gotten sucked in again, at least a little bit, and he'd been messaging and talking to Juliet for the past couple of months. He should have never engaged when she sent the first email to him after years of silence, but he'd been curious. And maybe a bit lonely since Muffin had just found Alaina and Everett, effectively ending his bachelorhood and leaving Zane the last single guy on the team.

Juliet: *Can you talk soon? I really want to hear your voice. I would have called, but Daniel is in the other room and I don't want him harassing me.*

Zane closed his eyes and blew out a breath before he typed a reply. He knew the answer he should give, but he was somehow still incapable of it. Dumbass.

Yeah, I can talk. How's Friday morning?

Chapter Two

One day ago...

EDEN HALL WAS GOING to be late. Her stupid fake eyelash was stuck in her hair, the other one looked like a drunken caterpillar, and her hair wasn't behaving. As usual. She looked at the red mass in the mirror and wanted to burst into tears.

Abby walked into the bathroom then, her beautiful face that was so similar to Eden's own—though without the rusty freckles that literally covered Eden's face and much of her body—looking much more polished and put together. Whereas Eden had wild red hair that refused to be tamed, Abby had sleek reddish-blond locks that were always perfect. Smooth, creamy skin that Eden would have died for considering she didn't have a single patch of unmarred skin on her face or neck. They were twins, but not identical. If they had been, Eden was certain Abby would have pulled off the brick-colored hair, mottled skin, and awkwardness without fail.

"Oh, Eden," Abby said as she caught sight of the stray eyelash in Eden's hair. "I think you've been attacked."

"Tell me about it," Eden grumbled.

"Let me help."

Eden dropped her arms to her sides and Abby pushed her onto the chair nearby. "You shouldn't be helping me get ready. It's *your* bachelorette party."

"All I need to do is slip into my slinky black dress and I'm good to go. Speaking of slinky, I want you to wear my other dress."

"It won't fit, Ab. You're much smaller than I am."

"First of all, I am *not* much smaller. Second, it's stretchy and I know it'll look amazing on you. You have to at least try it. Okay?"

"I'll try it. But what's wrong with my dress?"

"You mean the one that covers you from neck to knee? It's not a party dress, Eden. It's something you wear to a funeral. Now tilt your head back and let me fix you up."

Eden sat patiently while her sister unstuck the eyelash from her hair. Then she did as she was told while Abby applied the lashes to her lids. After that, Abby insisted on doing her makeup. Eden didn't wear much makeup. Not only because she was hopeless with it, but also because whenever she'd tried to cover her freckles, she ended up looking like a clown with pancake makeup. She'd given up trying. Abby, however, wielded brushes like an artist.

Eden studied her sister while she worked. There were bigger things to worry about. Finally, Abby frowned and stopped what she was doing. "What?"

"Nothing."

Abby swirled the brush in the shadow again. "You think I'm worried that Trevor's going to come looking for me now that he's been released, right?"

Trevor Hagan had been released two months ago, and Eden worried about it every day. "You aren't?"

Abby's expression tightened. She flicked powder off the brush and applied it to Eden's face. "No. He was in prison for five years, and things have changed. I left Chicago and moved back to Maryland to be near you. I'm marrying the best man I know. Trevor doesn't know where I am and even if he did, he won't risk his freedom. He's probably intent on making another fortune and taking over the tech industry again. Coming after me for some idea of revenge is counterintuitive and unproductive. Besides, *I* didn't send him to prison. That was the tax fraud."

"You're right," Eden said with a sigh. "I've watched too many Lifetime movies."

Abby laughed. "Exactly. Trevor isn't interested in little ol' me these days. He'll find a new girlfriend to boss around and get on with his life. There, done. What do you think?"

Eden looked in the mirror. She'd avoided it while her sister worked, but now she was a little bit stunned by the woman looking back at her. Smoky eyes, red lips, pink cheeks. Her freckles were still there, but they'd been muted somehow.

Abby grinned like a kid on Christmas morning. "See? You just needed my expert help is all."

Eden's hair wasn't sleek, but it was manageable now, curling over her shoulders and falling almost to her ass. Eden usually wore her hair in a ponytail or a bun, but she liked the way it looked when her sister styled it for her. Too bad she couldn't ask Abby to fix her hair every day.

"Thank you. At least I won't embarrass you now."

Abby lightly tapped her on the shoulder with the hairbrush. "You never embarrass me, girlie. You're gorgeous. I don't know why you think you aren't."

Eden smiled shyly. Her sister was her cheerleader, but she was also biased. "I am when you help me. But you know I'm no good at makeup and hair. Or talking to people," she added.

Abby threw an arm around her shoulders. "People love you. You just have to learn to let go a bit more."

Eden nodded even though she knew her sister didn't get it. Abby was the outgoing one, the one who found everything so easy when it came to people. Their mother had always told her she needed to be more like Abby. But how was she supposed to do that? Abby always knew the right thing to say, the right thing to do. She was a natural, whereas Eden felt awkward when she had to converse with people she didn't know. She felt like they were staring at her freckles, judging her for not always knowing what to say.

She also felt awkward with people she did know sometimes. Like her boss. A wave of despair crashed over her. Mitchell Shaw was tall, handsome, outgoing, and good at everything. She'd been working for him for two years now as a legal assistant, and she'd had a crush for most of that time. Watching him argue cases made her heart race. Having him smile at her across the room when he knew he'd nailed a closing statement had the power to render her speechless. She'd spent hours imagining how a romance with him would go. Silently urging him to ask her out. Wondering how to be more interesting and prettier so he would.

None of it mattered anymore. Not since the instant Abby had walked into the office eight months ago and Eden introduced her to Mitchell. What happened next was probably inevitable. Mitchell had fallen for the vivacious, beautiful, confident sister. Now they were in Las Vegas, celebrating Abby's upcoming wedding to Mitchell. Which Abby deserved. After the hell she'd been through, she was due some happiness.

Abby's phone buzzed. Her face lit up as she grabbed it and walked out of the bathroom. "Baby! I miss you so much!"

Eden's heart sank like a stone as guilt and despair overwhelmed her in equal measure. *Be happy. Be happy. She deserves this.* She stared at her reflection. If she was more like Abby, maybe she'd be the one getting married to her dream man in two months. Maybe Mitchell would have taken one look at *her* and fallen head over heels long before he'd met Abby.

But he hadn't, and it was too late. Not that she wanted to steal her sister's happiness for one instant. She would never do that. Everything came easy to Abby and always had, but she'd also paid a price for her beauty and for her open and outgoing nature that Eden could never know.

Abby was hopelessly in love with Mitchell, and she *deserved* this. Yes, Eden had resented her sister over the years for how easily she made friends and attracted boyfriends, how people always loved her and included her in their gatherings, how their mother praised Abby's beauty and told Eden she needed to be more like her sister, and she'd felt guilty for it too. It wasn't Abby's fault she was beautiful and good at everything Eden wasn't. She just was.

Same as Eden was good at details, like doing legal research and organizing wedding prep. In fact, yesterday she'd ordered three hundred personalized wedding favors for Abby and Mitchell's guests. Because she was *good* at shit like that.

Eden stuck her tongue out at her reflection. *Them's the breaks, kid.* If she'd told Abby she was crushing on Mitchell before they'd ever met, this wouldn't be happening. Abby wouldn't have gone out with him. But Eden hadn't done that because she knew her sister would've urged her to be bold and ask Mitchell out. The thought gave her hives. There was no way she could've been that brave. The end.

Now she was going to put on Abby's dress, go downstairs, hold her chin high, and have a good time with Ab and her friends. Eden would be outgoing and vivacious tonight even if it killed her. Hell, she might flirt with a stranger if the opportunity arose. This was Vegas, and what happened here stayed here.

She could be someone she wasn't. At least for one night.

"HAPPY BIRTHDAY, MIMI," Zane said, catching his little sister as she barreled into his arms.

He'd arrived an hour ago, checked in, showered, and changed into black jeans, boots, and a black Henley. Five minutes ago, Mia texted to ask if she could come to his room. Now she was here, and he couldn't get over how grown up she looked. He'd seen her just a few months ago, but somehow she seemed more mature than she had before. Probably just him fixating on her being twenty-one.

Mia looked up at him, her smile wide. "I'll forgive you for the nickname tonight, Zany, but don't you dare say it in front of my friends."

"Not a chance, kid," he replied, kissing her on the forehead. "You're gonna behave this weekend, right?"

Mia rolled her eyes. "I'm twenty-one, not twelve. And it's not like I haven't had alcohol before. I just get to order it for myself in a bar tonight. I promise not to get too crazy. Besides, Mom and Dad are here, so that kind of puts a damper on table dancing."

Zane laughed. "God, please, no table dancing."

She elbowed him in the ribs. "If I'd planned on real craziness, I wouldn't have asked you and the parents to join me now, would I?"

"Probably not."

Mia eyed him up and down. "Still not adding color to the ensemble, I see."

"Black's my style."

"You could wear some navy every once in a while. Branch out a bit."

"I wear camouflage most of the time."

Mia gave him a serious look. "Okay, so I missed you like crazy, and I wanted to see you first. I did see you first, right?"

"On my honor. I just checked in. Haven't told Mom and Dad I'm here yet."

"Good. I just wanted to see you before you meet my friends. They are going to go nuts over you, but I also wanted to ask you to please, *please*, not bring one of them back here tonight, okay?"

Zane's brows arrowed up. "You really think I'd do that?"

"No, I don't." She managed to look contrite. "But you're kinda handsome for a big brother, and my girls go after what they want total ho-bag style."

Zane snorted a laugh. "Ho-bag style? Isn't that term a little out of date for you?"

Mia giggled. "I heard Mom saying it about one of those *Real Housewives* shows when she was telling Dad what was happening. Then I told her there's nothing wrong with being a ho-bag and going after what you want. Girls have needs too, and I'm all for scratching itches, etcetera. She agreed, but she still uses it. I think it's funny."

Zane held up both hands to stop her from saying anything else. "I don't want to hear about needs and itches from my baby sister, okay? Jesus, Mia, you're still in pigtails to me. And I don't want to have to strangle some guy."

"Well of course I don't mean *me*," Mia said very seriously. "I am a nun. A veritable nun! Not interested in the big D at all."

"The big D—oh crap, don't even say it. I know what the big D is." Zane wasn't the kind of guy to blush, but he thought he might if he kept having this conversation with his itty-bitty baby sister. *Not so itty bitty anymore.*

"*Any*way, no giving the big D to any of my friends, no matter what. Because, eww, my brother and my friend. No, can't happen."

"Babe, it can't happen anyway because, eww, you're all kids to me."

She nodded. "I'll accept that if it means none of those girls will end up doing the walk of shame from my brother's room." A second later, she grinned. "You're going to like everyone, I promise. I don't pick shitty friends. I already told them that, A, my brother is off limits and, B, it's for the best because you'd just break their heart anyway. But I just needed to clarify with *you* that you won't go there when one of them inevitably drinks too much and starts to think you can't be all that bad."

Zane blinked. "How do you know I'd break someone's heart?"

"Seriously, Z? You've got the whole broody-alpha-male thing going with the black ensemble. You do some badass shit in the Army which you won't tell me about. And you haven't talked about *any* woman, or brought any home, since Juliet Northrup broke your heart. Which means you're the heartbreaker now."

Zane's gut tightened. "What makes you think Juliet broke my heart?"

"Please. She was all you talked about until that Christmas when you two broke up. I was ten and I remember it well. You even had an engagement ring."

"I didn't think you were paying attention back then. Yeah, it was rough, but that was years ago. Just because I haven't brought anyone home doesn't mean I'm breaking hearts."

Because he didn't stay long enough to break a heart. Short-term, sex-only relationships were his deal. The second a woman started making plans or getting clingy, it was over.

He thought about his conversation with Juliet that morning before he got on the plane. She'd done a complete one-eighty from a few days ago. She thought maybe she was being too hard on Daniel. Maybe they weren't done after all. Zane didn't know what the man had done, but whatever it was, it had Juliet's pendulum swinging in his direction again. And Zane had whiplash from it.

Hearing her say she wanted to give Daniel another chance had hit him harder than he'd thought it would. Not because he still wanted her, or maybe he did, but holy shit, it'd brought up all those old feelings of hurt and rejection. He was a twenty-year-old kid again, standing in front of the girl he loved with a ring in his pocket while she told him she loved someone else. The whole thing pissed him off. He'd known better than to start talking to her in the first place, but he'd let it happen, and now he was pissed he'd let her in again. Listened to her talk about her marriage and the mistake she'd made. Hell, if he were honest, it'd stroked his sense of justice that she'd been so certain she'd made a mistake, that she shouldn't have given him up. It was a nice *told ya so* that he no longer got to enjoy because, once again, she'd yanked the rug away.

Just went to prove that he was right to keep his heart out of the mix when dealing with the opposite sex. Sure, it was lonely sometimes, especially when he watched his brothers on the team with their happy families. But not everyone got that happy family, did they?

Mia slipped her arms around his waist and hugged him again. She and his mom were the only women in his life who had his heart. That was enough for him.

"I'm so glad you came, Zane. It means a lot."

"I wouldn't miss it for the world."

"I should take you to Mom and Dad's room. They'll be so excited to see you. Then I'll slip away and get dressed and meet you all for dinner as planned. You dressed, or did you need to slip on a black mask?"

"Ha-ha, brat. I'm ready. Lead the way."

Chapter Three

"Wow, look at *that* guy," Hannah, one of Abby's friends, shouted. All the women at the table swung their gazes toward the man in question. They were sitting in the dance club, and the music was pounding. Eden had been watching the drinks while the others danced, but they were back now, gulping drinks and talking about the guy who'd just entered the club.

"Damn, that's a hot man," another said. "Too bad you're getting married, Abby. Bet you could have him if you wanted."

Abby laughed. "He's hot, I'll grant you, but Mitchell is hot too."

"Mitchell is definitely hot," Hannah replied. "But that guy is next level. Look at those muscles. Rawr!"

Eden looked at the man who'd strolled over to the bar. He was tall, with a broad chest and arms that looked like he must work out. He wore black from head to toe, and his hair was the same shade. He had a strong jaw and looked more than a little dangerous. Like one of the criminals that Mitchell defended. *Alleged criminals.*

Mitchell took all kinds, and some of them were definitely not upstanding citizens, but everyone had the right to a robust defense. Innocent until proven guilty. Eden believed that, but there'd been some people who seemed more guilty than others. Not that this guy looked guilty of anything other than making women swoon. He also looked like he might be willing to break some rules if necessary.

Still, when she went to law school and got her degree, she hoped to be a great defense attorney like Mitchell. Which meant not judging someone for how dangerous they appeared at first glance. Or how hot.

The man turned to the side, surveying the crowd in the bar. His gaze slid over their table, then back again. Eden's heart skipped. She felt like he was looking right at her, but of course he wasn't. He was looking at Abby or one of her friends. Eden was the least likely person he'd make eye contact with.

She dropped her gaze to her drink and told herself she looked good tonight but not *that* good. A man like him could get any woman he wanted. He wouldn't be looking at a freckled redhead in a form-fitting dress and thinking *she* was the one he wanted to take back to his room.

"I dare you to go talk to him," Hannah said to willowy Kate. Next to Abby, she was the prettiest one there.

"Okay, I will."

Kate stood, took a gulp of her drink, and grinned.

She weaved a little on her way over to the bar, but she made it, climbing onto the stool beside the guy, who looked her up and down appreciatively. After she ordered a fresh drink, she turned to him. Eden watched as they started to talk. Of course Kate would be successful. She was stunning, with long blond hair, sparkling eyes and a figure that could wear anything and look good. Unlike Eden with her big breasts and hips. If she chose the wrong clothing, she looked awful in it. Though not Abby's dress. Her sister had been right that it looked good on her, but it was clingier than she was used to and made her a bit more self-conscious about her curves than usual.

"She's totally going to bag him," Hannah said.

"Totally," Abby agreed.

"But will she bang him in a bathroom stall, or will she get him to take her to his room?"

"Oooh, hot bathroom sex could be exciting."

"But getting naked with him in a bed would be *so* much more satisfying," Naomi purred. "Then she gets to see everything and not just a glimpse of his dick before she starts sucking it."

"Wait a sec," Darcy said. "There's a woman headed directly for him."

A dark-haired girl approached the man and slipped an arm around his waist. He put one of his around her shoulders and she leaned into him. She was gorgeous, but she looked a little young. Almost like a teenager, really. Then again, at the ripe old age of thirty, Eden thought everyone under about twenty-five looked like a kid. Funny how your perspective changed as you got older. When Eden was twenty-five, she'd thought everyone over thirty looked so much older.

The man continued to talk to Kate, then the waiter brought over some drinks and he and the girl grabbed them before heading toward the other end of the club. Kate made her way back to the table and plopped down.

"Taken," she said. "But polite."

"All the good ones are taken," Darcy said morosely.

"Including Mitchell," Hannah added.

"Especially Mitchell," Abby cried.

"I'll drink to that," Kate said.

Eden lifted her drink with the others, and they all took a swallow. The alcohol burned going down, but she didn't mind. She really kind of needed it tonight. Mitchell had never been hers, but a stubborn part of her insisted that she'd known him first. And she had, but that didn't change the fact he'd fallen for Abby. She'd had months to make him hers. She never had. He simply hadn't looked at her that way. Ever.

The thump of the beat changed into something more up-tempo. Abby squealed and grabbed for Eden. "Dance with me, sissy!"

Eden shook her head. The room spun a tiny bit. "No, it's okay. You go ahead."

Abby stood and kept pulling. Someone else started to push. "You've only danced once, Eden. Come on! It's my party, and I want my sissy to dance with me!"

"I'll watch the drinks," Kate said. "You go."

Eden didn't have any choice but to do as her sister wanted. Abby dragged her onto the floor and started gyrating to the music. She was, of course, beautiful doing it. Eden stood awkwardly, worried about how she looked to everyone watching, but then Abby put her hands on Eden's hips and started to move her. Eden gave in. When nobody laughed or pointed—as if they would because everyone there was an adult and not a high school kid—Eden eventually let herself slip into the moment and have fun. She wasn't there to impress anyone, and it didn't matter anyway. She was there for Abby.

They danced to three more songs and then headed back to the table to grab their drinks. Eden ordered water when the waitress came by again. She was hot, the dress clung damply to her body, and her head swam.

The hot guy and the girl he was with hit the dance floor, and Eden watched them enviously. They seemed very comfortable with each other. Companionable. He spun the girl and dipped her, and she laughed uproariously. Once, he looked over at Eden's table. Their eyes met, and Eden jerked her gaze away, her heart pounding. She told herself to calm down, that he hadn't been looking at her, that she was being ridiculous. She'd imagined their eyes meeting when it was impossible to tell in a crowded room who someone was really looking at. Like when you waved at someone waving at you, but it turned out they were waving at someone else entirely.

So embarrassing.

When Eden looked up again, the hot guy and his girlfriend had gone back to their table to join a group of women. He didn't dance with any of the other women, which meant he was definitely with the dark-haired girl.

"Let's hit another club," Darcy said. "Party all night!"

Everyone agreed, but Eden shook her head. "I think I'm done for tonight. I'm going back to the room."

Abby's skin glowed with moisture, and happiness danced in her eyes. "You sure, sissy? We're just getting started."

"I'm sure. You go without me. We've still got tomorrow, and I need to catch up on sleep. It's been a long week."

Mitchell was preparing for a case involving a man accused of having his wife murdered, and they'd pulled long hours working on the defense. It was a wonder Eden had gotten away at all, but Mitchell had urged her to go because Abby wanted her there. Between the long hours and getting ready for the trip, plus the flight today, she was starting to feel every bit of the exhaustion that'd been chipping away at her all day.

Abby nodded, though the light in her eyes dimmed a little. She knew that Eden sometimes got overwhelmed in crowds and needed down time. Abby didn't understand it as an extrovert herself, but she knew it was a thing for Eden. Still, Eden hated to disappoint her. Maybe she'd hang in there for a while longer, force herself to go.

Abby squeezed her hand. "I'll let you know where we are in case you change your mind, okay?"

Eden hoped the relief she felt wasn't showing on her face. "Sounds good."

The bill came. Before Eden could pay her share, Naomi paid for everything and declared it her treat.

Eden thanked her sister's friend, and they got up to make their way to the exit. The club was in the hotel they were staying in, so all Eden had to do was go upstairs. Still, she went to stand outside with the others while they got one of the taxis waiting to ferry passengers between casinos. After they piled into a long white limo, giggling and snapping pics, Eden waved and went inside again.

She was alone at the bank of elevators when a man approached. She didn't pay him any attention until he threw an arm around her. "Hey, baby. How you doin' tonight?"

Eden stiffened and tried to push him away, but he held on tighter. "Let me go. I don't know you. I think you've got the wrong person."

"Nah, I don't. You don't have to know me to have a good time, sweetheart. And you look like you could use a good time. Pretty girl like you? Come on, let's go up to your room and get to know each other."

"What? No!" Eden pushed again, but the man wasn't budging. For the first time, she noticed how big he was. How strong. His hand clamped on her waist, holding her tight. "My friends are waiting for me. I need to go."

"You mean the friends who just got into that limo?"

Eden shuddered. He'd been watching them? Watching her? "My husband is upstairs in our room. If I-I don't show up in the next five minutes, he'll come looking for me."

The man laughed. "Babydoll, you're a bad liar. Cute

though. Great tits, too. Come on, I don't bite. I just want to hang out."

Eden's head was still swimming, but not as much, and the sweat that'd cooled on her body was back again. Not from dancing this time. She swallowed and tried to think. The elevator dinged and the door slid open. There was no one inside. Panic flared as the man pushed her in.

Scream.

The voice in her head was too late as the doors started to slide closed. The man gripped her harder, his fingers digging into her waist, pushing her into the wall to keep her from trying to get away.

SCREAM!

Eden obeyed, screaming as loud as she could as the doors closed. Fear slammed her heart into her ribs. The man clapped a hand over her mouth and shoved her against the wall. Her head bounced off it.

The doors slid open again and another man stood there. Tall, handsome, dressed in black from head to toe. His jaw was as strong as she'd originally thought, and his eyes were the color of a rainy sky. He did not look happy.

Eden didn't know what happened next but the man holding her wasn't there anymore. She huddled against the back of the elevator, unable to speak, as the black-clad man from the club dropped her assailant to the ground. She didn't know what he'd done, but the only person screaming now was the man on the floor.

"You okay?"

Eden couldn't find her voice. She nodded.

A security guard appeared and then another. "What's going on here?"

The tall man turned. "This asshole was in the process of assaulting the lady. I put a stop to it. Better call an ambulance. His arm is broken in two places, and he's going to need some stitches."

"Ma'am," one of the guards said, "is that what happened?"

Eden's heart was in her throat. But the man stood patiently, confidently, as if certain she would back him up. And why wouldn't she? She'd watched him in the club with his girlfriend earlier, and she felt like he was a good guy based on the way the woman had laughed and hugged him. Plus the fact he'd just rescued her from a potential rape and/or murder.

"Y-yes," she blurted. "Th-this man saved me."

He held out a hand. "Zane Scott, ma'am. United States Army."

Army. That explained why he had Jason Bourne moves. "E-Eden Hall. Thank you."

"Do you want to press charges, ma'am?"

"N-no." It wasn't going to be worth the time or the effort it would take, not when her assailant hadn't done anything more than shove her into an elevator. She'd worked in a defense attorney's office long enough to know what kind of defense this guy would get, and how it would cost her more in time and money than it was worth. Besides, when she flew home on Sunday, she'd never have to see him again.

"You should file a police report anyway," Zane said. "In case he's done this before."

"Y-yes, of course." She knew that, but it was hard to think when shivers rolled up and down her body.

Zane held out a hand. "I'll stay with you, Eden. You don't have to do this alone."

She hesitated, and then she looked into his silvery eyes and felt something inside her shift and tighten. *Really, Eden? He's spoken for. And he's just being nice anyway. He's not interested in you.*

"I, um, thank you, but I'll be fine. You shouldn't leave your girlfriend alone. I saw you together in the club," she added when he looked puzzled.

He laughed, a rich sound that made her insides tingle. "You mean my little sister. Dark hair, blue dress, big smile?"

"Yes."

"My baby sister, Mia. Not that she'd appreciate me calling her a baby. Her twenty-first birthday was Wednesday."

He was still holding out his hand, so Eden put her palm against his. A tremor ran through her at the touch of his skin. Not that she was surprised. He was gorgeous, after all. He didn't tighten his grip, didn't do anything to make her wish she'd refused. He held her lightly as he escorted her to the security office where they waited for the police to arrive. It didn't take long for her and Zane to give their statements about what had happened, and then it was over, and they emerged into the cool, ornate interior of the hotel again.

She'd calmed down a lot in the last half hour or so. She wasn't shaking anymore. Nothing had happened to her. The man who'd assaulted her was stopped, and she was fine and whole. Which she owed to the man standing with her now.

"I'll take you up to your room. Make sure you get inside," he said. "Unless you don't want me to."

"No, I want you to," she blurted. Though she felt safe now, she couldn't stand the idea of riding up to her room alone. Not that she thought the same thing would happen again, but this was Vegas, and anything was possible. The idea made her shiver anew. But so did the idea of being alone with Zane—though not in a bad way. Still, she had to be smart about this. "I, um, I should text my sister first."

"Of course. Tell her my name. Want a picture of my ID?"

"You would let me do that?"

"I don't want you scared of me, too. Here." He held out his hand and she handed him her phone. He took a picture of the ID he'd pulled from his pocket and then handed the phone back. "Send it to her. Tell her you're with me."

Eden blinked as she read the details. "You live in Annapolis."

"Yeah. I'm stationed at a post near there."

"I work at a law firm in Annapolis. B-but I live across the bridge."

Why are you telling him where you live? He doesn't care. It's irrelevant.

So was the fact she lived on the Eastern Shore because it was cheaper. Mitchell paid her well, but if she wanted to go to law school someday, she needed to save everything she could. Even with the scholarship from the firm she hoped to earn, she'd need her own money to supplement it. Abby had lived with her, splitting rent, but she'd moved in with Mitchell four months ago, and that made things tighter. Not that Eden had said anything to Abby.

"Then I guess it's meant to be. Send that to your sister and I'll make sure you get back to your room safely."

Eden considered it a moment longer. Abby would freak. So would Kate. They all would. She let herself feel the absolute thrill of the moment when her sister and friends realized she was with the hot guy from the bar. It wasn't anything beyond a bit of kindness on his part, but they didn't know that. And she didn't have to explain a thing. Let them think *she* was the one going to his room to have wild sex in his bed. They'd be so envious. Not a thing she was accustomed to anyone feeling about her. She wanted that satisfaction, at least for a few hours.

Do it!

Eden sent the photo before she could talk herself out of it and then followed with a quick text because she had to tell her sister what was happening. *I'm with this guy. His name is Zane. He's escorting me up to the room because there was a weird guy on the elevator. Oh, and that was his sister, not his girlfriend.*

Abby's reply was swift. *What? Are you okay? Do I need to come back?*

Eden: *No! Do not come back. I'm fine. Zane took care of it. The man is gone.*

Abby: *Okay. But I will if you want me to. And if you* *don't, maybe talk to this guy for a while instead of shutting yourself up in the room. Go get a drink or find a quiet corner of the casino. What do you have to lose?*

Eden: *A good night's sleep?*

Abby: *Sissy, you've been given a smoke show of a man. Be careful as always, but at least try to enjoy yourself for a bit.*

She loved that Abby actually thought she had a chance with him. She didn't, because he was so gorgeous and she wasn't, but it was sweet. Still, what did she have to lose?

Eden: *I'll try. Tell the girls I bagged the hot guy.*

She ended the text with a laughing emoji.

Abby: *Oh, believe me I will. They're gonna be so jelly!*

"Sorry," Eden said, tucking the phone away. "I had to explain a few things first."

"That's all right. Everything okay?"

Eden nodded. "Great. Thanks."

"You ready then?"

She thought back to the moment when she'd stared at herself in the mirror earlier tonight and said she was going to be somebody different. Maybe it was time she tried. Even if he shot her down, at least she could tell herself she'd actually done it. She could be bold for once, prove to herself it was possible.

"Sure. But, uhm, do you want to get a drink? I'm too keyed up to go to bed just yet."

Oh my God, what was she doing? This would never work.

"But it's okay if you don't," she added, her words tumbling over each other like bingo balls. "I can just go to my room and drink from the minibar. I probably should anyway, really. You aren't here to keep an eye on me, and you need to get back to your sister."

Eden clamped down on her tongue as the heat flaring in her cheeks went nuclear. Way to word-vomit all over the guy.

His gaze roamed her face, making her insides tingle and tighten. He was still smiling. That was a good sign, right?

"My little sister and her friends have reached the part of the night where they're giggling about girl stuff and going on about the men they've slept with or plan to sleep with. Way too much for me, I gotta admit. So yeah, Eden Hall, I'd love to get a drink with you."

Chapter Four

DAMN, HE LIKED THIS WOMAN. SHE WASN'T FLIRTING with him or trying to get in his pants. Not that he'd mind if she did.

Zane sat with her in a quiet corner booth of a quiet bar as she spilled her guts and they downed tequila shots. He'd noticed her in the club earlier when he was drinking with Mia and her friends. She was sitting at the table with the woman who'd approached him at the bar. That woman was attractive, but she'd reminded him of Juliet, and he'd been repelled.

Plus he'd just gotten to the club with his sister, after his parents had gone to their room for the night, and he wasn't ready to ditch her or her friends. He'd noticed the women at the table, though.

They were clearly celebrating a bachelorette party since one of them wore a sash that said *Bride To Be* on it. They'd been animated, pretty, but only one had caught his attention. The shy looking one who had to be coaxed into moving her hips on the dance floor. She had a mane of red hair that gleamed under the lights, and her dress had caressed every amazing curve of her body. Her skin was covered in freckles. He found himself wondering about the parts he couldn't see. Would she be freckled there too?

She wasn't so shy now, but he assumed that was the tequila talking. He focused on what she'd just said. "So your sister's marrying the guy you love, and you're okay with it?"

She nodded, the move exaggerated. "Mitchell was never mine. I just wanted him to be."

Zane licked salt off his hand, downed a shot, and followed it up with lime while she did the same. "Mitchell sounds kinda clueless to me."

He had a pleasant buzz going. He'd had it for a while now. Things were a little fuzzy at the edges, but he remembered how they'd gotten there. Remembered heading for the elevator and hearing a scream. He'd bolted for it and jammed his hand into the crack before the doors closed completely. They'd slid open again to reveal the pretty redhead and a man who stood too close to her. She'd looked terrified, and it had pissed Zane off enough that he'd gone in strong when he neutralized the threat.

Still, he supposed the guy should be happy Zane had only broken an arm. He could as easily have crushed the dude's windpipe. That would have definitely gotten back to Mendez, and he'd be explaining himself to a general on Monday morning. Hell, he might have to anyway, though the Vegas cops didn't seem inclined to hassle him for what he'd done.

"Noooo, not clueless," Eden said, her words the tiniest bit slurred. "He's brilliant. And I never spoke up, did I? I could have asked him out, but I never did."

"Then your sister met him and that was it, right?"

"Uh-huh. Abby is everything I'm not. Outgoing, pretty, always says the right thing. Everyone wants to be her friend. Nobody wants to be mine."

Zane put his hand over hers. She lifted her gaze. He could see how people might overlook her for her sister, but they'd be missing out if they did. Her eyes sparkled and her freckles were fascinating the way they scattered over her face and down into the scoop neck of her dress. "You're pretty, Eden. And maybe you aren't outgoing, but so what?"

She sighed and dropped her gaze again, shaking her head. "You're just being nice. Thank you, though. I know I'm too freckly. People stare sometimes. It was much worse when I was a kid, though."

Zane put a finger under her chin and made her look at him. She had green eyes to go with all that red hair, and her skin was like golden wheat beneath the freckles. The little black dress she wore clung to all the right spots, emphasizing her lush breasts and curvy hips.

"Not being nice, sugar. You're pretty hot, and you deserve a guy who can see that. A guy who'll do whatever it takes to make *you* happy. Mitchell isn't the guy. And if people stare at you, it's because you're so lovely they have to."

Her tongue darted out to sweep her bottom lip. Zane's groin tightened.

"You're a charmer, Zane Scott. I like that about you.

But I suck at dating so it's never going to happen. I'm going to die a bitter, single hag surrounded by my twelve cats. I only have one right now, but the rest will happen. It's inevitable."

He wanted to laugh, but he didn't. She was serious and it astounded him. "It's not possible."

Her nod was exaggerated. "It is. I haven't been on a date in over a year now. And that one was so awkward that he didn't even try to kiss me at the end. He did ask if my freckles were everywhere, though. I didn't answer. He didn't deserve to know if he didn't want to kiss me."

Zane wanted to know about those freckles too, but he wanted to find out himself. See if her pretty skin was adorned with rusty freckles in all the places he wanted to touch. He stroked his thumb across her bottom lip. Lush. Pretty. He imagined those lips wrapped around his cock, and the hard-on he'd been fighting flared up in full force.

"I'd like to kiss you, Eden. I'd like to do a lot more than that if you let me."

She looked stunned. It wasn't the reaction he expected, and it pissed him off. Not at her. *For her.* What kind of idiots had she been dating anyway? Men who couldn't appreciate how gorgeous she was, clearly. Then there was this Mitchell Shaw idiot who'd had her under his nose for two years but chose to marry her sister instead. And Eden hadn't said a word about how much it hurt to either one of them.

"I want you to kiss me. Before I lose my nerve."

Zane thought maybe he should unpack that statement, but his blood was buzzing, and she needed to know she was desirable. That her beautiful, banging body was turning him on big time. He dragged her closer, lifted her legs to drop them over his lap, and wrapped one arm around her body while the other went to the back of her head. Her breathing quickened, but she put her arms around his neck, giving him permission to continue.

Zane dropped his mouth to hers, softly, sensing she needed him to be gentle rather than devouring. That could come later. Her leg brushed his cock, and he bit back a groan. She smelled like heaven, a mixture of vanilla and peaches, and he wanted to eat her up. Instead, he kissed her as sweetly as he could, being gentle and slow.

But she was impatient, or turned on maybe, and she ran her tongue along the seam of his lips. He opened to her instantly. When their tongues met, he felt the jolt down to his bones.

Probably the booze, but he didn't think he'd ever wanted a woman as much as he wanted this one right this minute. He needed to bury his cock in her sweet heat, needed to hear her panting beneath him as he drove her over the edge. And he really needed those lips wrapped around him. Like, needed it to breathe. To forget his anger and helplessness in the face of yet another rejection from the only woman he'd ever loved.

Fucking Juliet and her fucking manipulative bullshit.

"Mmm," he said, breaking the kiss and pushing Eden's thick hair over her shoulder. "What do you think about taking this somewhere more private?"

Somewhere he could explore every inch of Eden Hall's lush body.

"I want to. Yes, definitely."

A voice in his head told him to consider this a little more in depth. She was a little drunk, and he wasn't much better. But he knew what he wanted. She seemed to know, too.

He stood and held out his hand, swaying only a bit. She took it. Before he could pocket his phone, it buzzed on the table. He could see Juliet's name flashing as she tried to call him. It was almost like he'd conjured the call by thinking about her. What the hell did she want now? Why did she think she could just call him whenever she wanted and expect him to drop everything?

Anger burned into him as he silenced the phone. Eden studied him with a little more concern now.

"Are you married, Zane?"

"I'm definitely not married." He sucked in a breath, then told her what he never told anyone. She'd shared with him, so it was only right he give something back. "That was my ex. The woman I'd planned to marry eleven years ago, until she dumped me and married someone else. She's having marital trouble, and she's been calling me after years of silence."

Eden stroked her fingers down his cheek. The gesture made his skin tingle. "I'm sorry. Do you still love her?"

"No." It shocked him to say the word aloud, but he knew he meant it. He didn't love Juliet anymore. Didn't mean she didn't still get to him, though. The old feelings of hurt were still there, and Juliet seemed to know where to press on the nerve to make the pain throb to life.

"That's good. Still, we're the ones who have to watch someone we love marry someone else. Well, *had* to watch in your case, whereas I will be a dutiful maid of honor in two months with a front row view of the entire thing."

He hated how sad she looked in that moment. The defeat written on her pretty face. What if he could take that away? What if he could make her smile instead? Make her forget? Make him forget, too. Because, why not? Didn't he need that? He'd show Juliet she wasn't the only one who had someone else.

He tugged Eden against him and tried not to groan at the feel of her body plastered to his. "I have a crazy idea."

She leaned against him, grinning. Her arms went around his neck and her breasts flattened against him. "How crazy?"

"We're in Vegas, baby. Let's get married."

She blinked. Then she started to giggle. "That would blow those girls away if I showed up at the wedding with *you* as my husband. Oh my God, they would freak. Nobody would ever believe it."

His sense of justice flared. Why wouldn't anyone believe her? She was gorgeous, and he was the lucky guy who was going to spend the night showing her how beautiful she was. The tequila buzzed through him, spreading warmth and dopamine through his body. One of those happy hormones, anyway. Why not get married? Then he could be like his teammates.

Coupled. Happy. He wouldn't be the last guy left standing anymore. And Juliet would have to stop calling him. He pictured the moment he told her he was married, her reaction.

Yeah, this was a fucking marvelous idea. Why hadn't he thought of it before?

"So let's do it. What do you say?"

"Do we get to have sex after?" she asked with a giggle.

Zane nibbled her bottom lip until his dick was rock hard and she moaned. "All the sex you want. I promise to make you see stars."

She shivered and laughed again as she flung her arms wide. "Let's get married!"

Chapter Five

THE MORNING AFTER...

EDEN'S HEAD THROBBED. Her mouth was a desert. She opened her eyes and the room spun. What the hell?

Abby snored nearby. Eden hadn't heard her come in because she'd been sleeping so hard. Or was it because she'd been so drunk? Maybe...

But wait, Abby didn't snore. Eden stared at the ceiling and waited for it to stop spinning. When it did, she pushed up on an elbow and turned toward the sound.

A few things hit her a once. First, she didn't have any pajamas on. Second, a man lay in bed with her. Third, this wasn't her room. Fourth, there was an ache between her legs. Not unpleasant, but it definitely hadn't been there yesterday.

She stared at the man as memories of last night

dropped in her head. How they'd gone for drinks and hammered back tequila shots, how she'd blabbed about Abby and Mitchell, and how her skin had been on fire whenever he touched her. How they'd gotten married in a twenty-four-hour chapel with Elvis performing the ceremony.

What the hell?

Of all the stupid, impulsive, *out of character* things for her to do! Eden Hall was dependable and methodical. She did *not* marry a strange—though extremely hot—man after only a couple of hours in his company.

She most certainly didn't have wild sex with him before passing out cold and sleeping like the dead.

Except that's exactly what she'd done. Eden slid from the bed and groped for her phone. When she found it, she saw it still had a charge but barely. There were messages from Abby that had landed on her phone only an hour ago.

Are you out of your mind? Where are you? Is this for real?
Eden?
Eden?
If I don't hear from you by nine, I'm calling the police.

Eden scrolled back to the picture she'd sent Abby at 1:20 a.m., though clearly Abby hadn't seen it then. It was of Eden with a bouquet of flowers and a veil, grinning like an idiot at the camera while the man beside her did the same.

Good Lord, he was breathtaking. And she was still herself. Still freckled and awkward. Ugh.

Except none of that was the point. The point was she'd gotten married, and they'd only just met.

"Oh crap," she whispered before thumbing a reply. *I'm fine. I'll explain everything. See you soon.*

The man in the bed—Zane—didn't wake as she tiptoed toward the bathroom, collecting her clothes as she went. She had never done the walk of shame in her life, but she was about to. Except she needed a shower first. Eden locked the bathroom door, which was ridiculous considering she'd spent a good part of the night having sex with him—letting him see her body and all its imperfections. She twisted on the taps, downed one of the bottles of water that was sitting on the counter, then stepped in the shower and scrubbed her skin, wincing a little at the beard burn on her thighs, though she also remembered how she'd gotten that burn.

Eden shivered. She wasn't someone who had a ton of experience, but she'd had sex before. Just not in a long time, and definitely not like that. Though maybe that was the tequila talking. She'd had a lot of alcohol and so had he. Not enough to make her pass out, but enough that her inhibitions had *poofed* into nothing. Clearly.

She had a mental picture of riding him in that bed, all the lights on while he stroked her body and told her she was beautiful. He'd seen it all. How her freckles were thickest on her face and shoulders, how they grew lighter on her breasts and belly. How her legs and butt didn't have many. He hadn't been repulsed at all. Instead, she remembered him flipping her over onto her back and driving into her while she made sounds that were more fitting in a porn film.

"Oh God," she said, shoving her face under the

water. This was not her. *That* wasn't her. Eden Hall didn't have hot, porny, *unprotected* sex with a stranger, no matter how gorgeous he was. It displayed a serious lack of judgement on her part that made her queasy.

She finished the shower, dried off, and found a blister pack of Tylenol in the basket of complimentary supplies on the counter. Thank heavens. She downed it, swigged some water, and dressed in the only clothes she had, feeling way more self-conscious in them than she had last night. Abby's dress clung to her in ways her own had not. Why had she let Abby talk her into borrowing it? Maybe if she'd worn her own sensible dress instead of one that showed too much leg and too much cleavage, she'd have gotten into that elevator unmolested. As soon as she thought it, she was mad at herself because it wasn't her clothing that had made that man target her. He would have done it regardless. But if the man hadn't chosen her, Zane wouldn't have had to come to her rescue. Which meant she wouldn't be here now, panicking over the absolute mess she'd gotten herself into. Everything was the fault of a complete stranger.

Except it wasn't. It was hers for drinking too much and flirting and letting her hormones get the best of her. This was *not* how a future defense attorney behaved. It wasn't logical.

She stood at the bathroom door, sucking in breaths, telling herself all she had to do was tiptoe across the room and out the door. Then she could rush back to her room and change clothes. And she wasn't leaving the room tonight, no matter how much Abby begged. Eden was done with Las Vegas.

But what about the husband? You can't just run away from that.

"Shit," she breathed. She'd have to get in touch with him when her stomach wasn't in knots and she could face him without her skin feeling like it was going to melt from the heat of embarrassment.

She tugged the door open as quietly as possible then crept into the room to grab her tiny purse and get the hell out of there. She'd leave him a note on hotel stationery. They could figure out what to do later when she didn't feel so hungover and embarrassed to her core.

Eden stopped with a squeak when she hit the bedroom. Zane was sitting up in bed, frowning hard at her. Was it wrong of her heart to thump a little faster at the sight of all that glorious muscle? The sheet draped around his waist, revealing the expanse of his chest. He had a tattoo sleeve in black and gray that went from his shoulder to his elbow. She'd noticed it last night when he took his shirt off, and she'd studied it in fascination. There was a dragon with skulls, a rose, and a name. *Juliet.*

She knew it was the ex who'd come back into his life recently. It had made jealousy flare and burn inside her for some stupid reason that also wasn't logical. Still did, which alarmed her to no end.

Zane shoved a hand through his dark hair, and she practically whimpered at the play of muscles that bunched and flexed as he did so. Mitchell didn't have muscles like that. She'd seen his arms when he rolled up his sleeves at work. They didn't look like he could crush cans just by bending them.

"I, um, I was going to leave you a note."

"I think it's a little late for a note, don't you?"

Eden swallowed, hard, but couldn't think of anything to say. Zane flipped the covers back and stood, and Eden nearly choked. Utterly naked. And magnificent. She knew she should look away, but she couldn't seem to do it. Zane's body was lean, hard, with muscles that rippled and made her mouth even drier. Her attention snagged on the plane of his abdomen and the happy trail that marched down it.

She'd always thought abs like that were only found in magazines. No real guy could look that way. Except this one did. Flat stomach, broad chest—but not too broad. His dick wasn't sad and limp, either. It was at least half-hard, which made her start to throb in places she didn't need to be throbbing right now. She remembered the feel of him on her tongue, and the way her body stretched when he'd slid inside her the first time. She hadn't been able to get enough of him.

Her skin burned as she dropped her gaze. Heat rolled from her like a sauna. A kernel of strange excitement shivered through her. Crazy to respond this way to a man she knew almost nothing about.

"You're shy now?" He sounded disbelieving, or maybe it was just amusement. Except he seemed too annoyed to be amused.

"I was drunk last night. That wasn't me. I, um, don't do one-night stands."

"No, but you'll marry a guy you just met."

Eden's gaze snapped to his. He looked irritated. Well, he wasn't the only one.

"You're the one who asked *me*. And I should have said no, but I was tipsy and you convinced me it was a great idea."

Surprise crossed his face. "I convinced *you*? Seems to me you wanted to get laid, plus you said something about how shocked everyone was gonna be when you showed up with me at your sister's wedding."

She remembered—but she darn sure wasn't the only one who'd wanted to rub it in someone's face. "Yeah, and you have an ex you want to get back at. So we're both at fault here, right? You probably shouldn't have asked me to marry you since you were going to get laid anyway, and I definitely shouldn't have said yes."

He looked even more annoyed than before. "Too late for that, huh? I did and you did. Now we gotta deal with it."

"I work for an attorney. I'll figure out how to fix this."

"I think it's called divorce, sugar." He looked at the ring on his finger and shook his head. "What the fuck was I thinking?"

Oddly, Eden felt as if he'd slapped her. After all his talk last night about how beautiful she was, how unique her freckles were, how sexy she looked, blah blah blah.

She told herself it wasn't personal, that he was as shocked by his behavior as she was hers, but it still hurt. Nobody ever chose her. She'd always been the last girl picked for the team, the girl that guys only talked to when they wanted to meet her sister, the girl whose friends were her sister's friends first. A lifetime of being overlooked hadn't magically changed last night when the handsome prince asked her to marry him. Zane Scott was no prince, and she was back to being uninteresting and maybe even a little repulsive. Cinderella's dress had turned to rags again.

"Clearly, you weren't thinking," she snapped, burying her hurt beneath an icy tone. "Neither of us were." She took her ID from her purse. "Here. I have a picture of yours, so you get one of mine. We can exchange numbers, and I'll be in touch when I have information about the divorce."

He still hadn't bothered to put on any pants. He went over to the bedside table while she admired his ass. Eden looked away as he grabbed his phone and stalked back to her. She definitely wanted to look at his front, but she wasn't about to do it.

He took her ID and snapped a picture before handing it back. Eden tucked it into her purse and slung the purse across her body like a shield.

"Number?" he growled.

She recited it, and her phone lit up with a text. She saved him to contacts and tried to think of something else to say, but what was there? Nothing. Eden tried to remove the wedding band so she could give it back to him, but her fingers were swollen and it wouldn't come off.

"Keep it," Zane said.

Her throat was tight as she headed for the door. The sooner she was out of there, the better.

"Hey," he called out, and she turned around.

"Yes?"

"You said last night you were on birth control. Is that true?"

Eden glared. "Yes. And you said you didn't usually have sex without a condom and promised you were safe. Is *that* true?"

"I wouldn't lie about something that serious."

"Neither would I."

He nodded. "It was nice knowing you, Eden."

"You too." Because what else could she say? He didn't say anything more as Eden grabbed the door handle and pushed it down. When it snicked shut behind her, she stood numbly for a long moment and wondered if she'd dreamed the whole thing.

But no, her body still had a residual tingle from the many orgasms she'd had in Zane Scott's bed. Of all the things she regretted about last night, that definitely wasn't one of them.

Chapter Six

"Damn, dude, you sure you got any relaxation out there in Vegas?" Muffin asked as Zane cleared his weapon and laid it on the table. He'd just popped nineteen rounds into a target, rapid fire, dead center.

"Of course. You think I'd lose my skills after one weekend?"

Muffin shrugged. "No, just kinda thought you might not be quite as intense as usual. If anything, you're more so."

Zane shrugged. "Vegas was fun, but I was mostly there for my sister, so I didn't consider it a vacation. Had to make sure no assholes thought they could take advantage of her or her friends."

And then there was Eden. Zane had been home for approximately seventy-two hours, and he hadn't stopped thinking about her since she'd fled his hotel room. He'd been pissed, yes. But he'd also been keenly aware of her. As she'd stood there in her little black dress and ogled him that morning, he'd wanted to throw her onto the bed and lose himself in her body again. But it wouldn't have helped the situation which was why he hadn't done it.

He'd already fucked up by going bare inside her. Hadn't needed to do that again, no matter how much he'd wanted to. *Still* wanted to if he were honest. Eden was sexier than she thought she was. There was something about a woman who didn't wield her beauty like a weapon. Eden was the exact opposite of Juliet in every respect, and she intrigued him more than she should.

Eden had accused him of wanting to get back at Juliet by marrying her. It'd stung, but he couldn't argue that she was wrong. It was true he'd been motivated in part by the thought of throwing a wife in Juliet's face. How fucking stupid could he be?

He'd considered calling Eden since he'd been home. More than once, but he hadn't done it. She was his wife, and that was weird as fuck. But if he separated out the fact he'd actually married her from the time they'd spent together, he'd had a great time with her.

She was interesting. Strong, though she didn't seem to think so. Her sister was marrying the man she'd fallen in love with, and she'd never once told her sister how much that hurt. Eden would smile and support Abby no matter what. He could understand that because he'd do the same for Mia. Whatever his sister needed, he'd do his damnedest to make it happen.

Then there was the guy who'd tried to assault Eden in the elevator. She'd been scared, but she'd gotten over it quicker than he'd expected. Someone else might have had a different reaction to what happened, but Eden had recovered enough to end up in his room, riding him reverse cowgirl style while she moaned and begged him to do dirty things to her. Which he happily had.

He could still feel her surrounding him, still see the perfect beauty of her back with all her freckles, the curve of her waist and flare of her hips. Still see his dick disappearing inside her glistening pink pussy, still hear the sounds they made together.

Damn, he wanted that again.

Zane broke down his weapons, put them in the range bag, and headed for the armory. He really fucking needed to call Eden. Find out what she knew about getting a divorce. How long it was going to take, what it was going to cost. Then he had to see Mendez and Ghost and tell them what he'd done. Or a version of it anyway. Getting married wasn't the kind of thing you kept from the CO and his second, not if you wanted to keep your position in the organization. Didn't matter if it was impulsive and temporary. It was a change in status, and he was required to inform them.

One thing he wasn't doing was telling his team, though. Other than Saint, his team leader. Last thing he needed was the ribbing that would come from having done something stupid in Vegas. Just like they'd told him not to do.

Yeah, he needed to call Eden. Or maybe he'd go over to her house. That way she couldn't ignore him or hang up on him, which he suspected she might do. He hadn't exactly been a ray of sunshine the morning after, had he?

"Hey, you wanna grab a pizza at Buddy's tonight?"

Mal asked when Zane walked into the armory. "Scar is studying for some kind of test at school. She likes it when I'm not bugging her."

Zane tried to think of a reason to say no, but nothing would come. Nothing he could use, anyway.

Sorry, man, gotta go see the wife and find out what she's learned about our divorce.

"Yeah, sure," he said because his brain utterly failed him in the moment.

"Great! I'ma see if some of the other guys can come, too. Be like old times, huh?"

"Yep."

Just last week Zane had missed the old times. Today, he was itching to see Eden. His soon-to-be ex-wife. Just to get a bead on where things were, of course. Not because his body craved more of hers. Not because he wanted to spread her wide and eat her up while she mewled like a kitten. And certainly not because he liked seeing the woman who'd declared herself to be boring, dependable, and plain, lose her absolute mind over the way he touched her. There was something seriously arousing about watching a woman who was convinced she had nothing to offer discover how wrong she was.

Probably not a good idea to do any of those things, no matter how much he wanted to. They needed to keep it business between them. Divorce. Move on from the mistake they'd made when they were both drunk and emotionally compromised.

Mal walked away and Zane took out his phone. There were no messages from Eden, and none from Juliet either. It surprised him how annoyed he was about the first. He was relieved about the second. Apparently, he'd sent Juliet a text at some point during the evening with Eden and told her he'd found the woman he was marrying. Juliet hadn't responded, but he knew she'd seen the message because there was a read receipt.

He'd wanted a response when he sent it, drunk and pissed off, but he hadn't gotten one. Now he was glad he hadn't. He had enough shit going on in his life. He had a wedding ring on his dresser at home and a wife wandering around Annapolis.

Fucking hell, what a mess.

By the time he went for pizza with Mal and a couple of the other guys, and shot a few rounds of pool, it was after eight o'clock. Zane got into his truck and the engine roared to life. He planned to go home and text Eden at some point, but instead he found himself driving east, across the Kent Narrows, heading for the town of Franklin where her driver's license said she lived.

He didn't know what he was going to say to her or why he was driving to her place after dark, but he was restless. Seeing her felt necessary. When he pulled up in front of the small house on a quiet street, the lights were on and there were two cars in the drive. One was a Honda CR-V and the other was a Porsche Carrera. A dark feeling twisted inside him. What if she had another man in there? What if her wild night with him made her realize she could have all the wild nights she wanted with as many partners as she wanted? What if *he'd* been the one who'd opened her mind to the idea of one-night stands?

Zane growled to himself as he punched the button to turn off the ignition. He picked up his key fob from the center console and shoved it in a pocket then exited the truck and strode toward the front door. There were flowerpots on the top step with yellow and orange flowers, several pumpkins, and a sign that said *Welcome* propped against one side of the door.

Zane hesitated as he watched the house from the sidewalk. He could text her. That would work. Unless she pretended not to get his texts. She could ignore him entirely if he didn't address this face to face. He wasn't sure why she'd want to, but he didn't need his whole life hanging on the edge of a precipice like this. He had to find out what came next and how to disentangle himself from the mess he'd made.

Zane was halfway up the sidewalk when the door opened. A man in a suit came out. He was about six-foot with short brown hair. He carried a briefcase in one hand and a cell phone in the other.

"Thanks, Eden. I appreciate the extra time you've been putting in lately. I don't know what I'd do without you."

Zane didn't hear her response before the man turned and started down the walkway. He pulled up short when he saw Zane. Eden had walked out onto the front step and now stood stiffly, watching Zane approach.

"You expecting anyone?" The man hadn't taken his eyes off Zane.

"It's okay, Mitchell. I know him."

So *that* was Mitchell Shaw, the man who'd been too

stupid to see what had been staring him in the face. The man who'd overlooked Eden for her sister and broke her heart in the process. Zane didn't like him on sight. And he wanted to make the man regret not seeing Eden for the beautiful, interesting woman she was.

"You more than know me, babe," Zane said, walking up to Mitchell and thrusting out a hand. "Zane Scott. Eden's hu—"

"Boyfriend!" Eden called out. "Zane is my boyfriend."

Mitchell shook hands with him. He seemed surprised at the news Eden had a boyfriend, which only pissed Zane off more. Not because she hadn't mentioned him, but because Mitchell seemed so genuinely shocked. Did he think she wasn't attractive enough? Zane told himself he had no clue that's what it was, but the idea was enough to ratchet up his irritation at her clueless boss.

"I didn't know you were seeing anyone," Mitchell said, turning toward Eden.

"I didn't want to jinx it," Eden said without missing a beat. "It's still new."

That's my girl.

Zane strolled up to her and wrapped his arms around her, picking her up off the step and swinging her around before he planted a big kiss on her pretty lips. She didn't fight, but she didn't melt either.

"Hey, baby. I know we said we'd keep this thing under wraps and all, but I want the world to know you're mine." Her eyes snapped fire at him. Her freckles stood out in stark relief against her skin, and he found himself fascinated all over again. Zane slipped an arm around her as he turned to face a surprised Mitchell. "You get it, right? This woman is a total babe. How she's been single all this time is a mystery. I'd have thought a smart man would have made a move on her before I came along. Lucky me, huh?"

"Uh, yes. Lucky you," Mitchell said, his gaze swinging between them.

"I asked Abby not to mention anything because this relationship is very new," Eden said, twisting her fingers in Zane's side just hard enough to make him wince. "She found out when we were in Vegas, but I begged her to keep it to herself. Please don't blame her for not telling you."

"Not my business, Eden. The only secrets I don't want Abby to keep are those that affect us as a couple. I wouldn't expect her to share her sister's secrets when they aren't relevant."

Zane felt Eden's flinch. He wanted to punch the idiot in his perfect teeth, but that wasn't an option. "Aw, that's mighty big of you, boss. Afraid it's my fault, really. The job kind of takes up a lot of time, and I didn't want to share Eden with anyone until we'd weathered some of the separation first."

"Don't let us keep you, Mitchell," Eden blurted. "And thanks for being understanding."

Mitchell Shaw revealed his perfect teeth in a megawatt smile. "Anything for my best employee."

"Soon to be sister-in-law," Zane added conversationally.

"Absolutely," Mr. Fancy Lawyer said. "Will we be seeing you this weekend?"

Zane didn't know what the man was talking about, but the way Eden's fingers twisted his skin tighter, he knew what his answer had to be. "Wouldn't miss it."

Eden twisted harder and Zane wanted to laugh. He could have told her he'd endured much worse during training sessions and real-life missions.

"Great," Mitchell said. "See you in the morning, Eden. Nice to meet you, Zane."

"You too."

Mitchell's Porsche chirped as he walked toward it. When he was inside and the engine roared to life, Eden stood stiffly next to Zane, waving as Mitchell backed out of the drive. As soon as he was gone, she shoved Zane as hard as she could. Zane took a step back to give her room to spin on her heel. Then he followed her inside.

She rounded on him, pretty green eyes glittering. "What the hell are you doing here?"

Zane spread his arms. "I can't come and visit my wife?"

"Wife?" she spat. "Since when are you comfortable with *that* term? You made it pretty clear before I left your room what you thought about our mistake, so don't you dare start being nice about it now."

She wasn't wrong, but he was more focused on the fact she was wasting her love on the asshat lawyer. "That guy doesn't appreciate you, Eden. Why the fuck do you think he's so awesome?"

Her face reddened before she spluttered, "He appreciates me! I'm his best employee."

"But you wanted more, and he was too stupid to see it."

She crossed her arms and glared. He took a moment to appreciate how appealing she was with her wild hair, flashing eyes, and those pretty freckles that were so unique. Her red hair was in a ponytail, but strands had escaped to curl around her face. She wore a pair of jeans and a loose-fitting top that hid her figure and made her look bigger than he knew she was. She looked frumpy and adorable at the same time.

"That's none of your business, okay?"

"You told me all about it, or don't you remember?"

"I told you because we were drunk. I didn't expect to ever see you again after that night."

"Until you married me."

"Right." She huffed and threw her arms open. "Why are you here? I was planning to text you in a day or two."

"Yeah, well I figured if I texted you, you'd ignore me. I was in the area."

She snorted. "In the area? You live in Annapolis."

"I'm aware of that. Hey, what did I agree to do this weekend anyway?"

"Mitchell and Abby are hosting a party for the firm on Saturday. It's basically an afternoon of lawn games and a cookout for employees and their families. There'll be a bouncy house for the kids and probably a magician, too."

"Sounds fun."

"You do *not* mean that."

"Why not? Some of my teammates have kids. I think

a bouncy house and a magician sounds like a great distraction so the parents can enjoy themselves."

It also sounded noisy and chaotic, but he wasn't admitting that.

"I'll make an excuse for you. You don't have to go."

"I'm going. Now are you going to make me beg for information or do you plan to tell me what I want to know?"

She dropped her gaze. "I don't know a lot. Mitchell has a big case right now, plus the wedding coming up, and I haven't had much time to research the steps to a divorce. I think we qualify for a mutual consent divorce, so long as we agree on the settlement, but that still takes time to go through the courts. And by settlement, I mean you keep your stuff and I keep mine, the end."

Zane frowned. Of course it wasn't going to be as simple as getting married had been. He knew that. *Fuck.* He was going to have to tell Mendez and Ghost tomorrow, before he knew how long a divorce would take.

But did he really want to tell them he'd impulsively married someone he didn't know and was now trying to get a divorce? How would that look for a guy with a top-secret clearance and access to one of the most secure facilities in the country?

Not good, really. Not good at all.

Fucking hell. Maybe all they needed to know was that he was married. Then, when he and Eden had the divorce figured out, he'd tell command it hadn't worked out. He closed his eyes and tried to think. He'd gotten himself into one hell of a mess, hadn't he? And he had no one to blame but himself.

Eden was still glaring at him like she wanted to murder him when he looked at her again. "I'm sorry for being an asshole that morning. I was kind of stunned."

"And you think I wasn't?"

"No, I know you were. But you were planning to skip out without waking me, so don't tell me you were handling it great either."

"I was going to leave a note."

He ran his fingers through his hair, frustration crackling inside. "Fine. You were going to leave a note, but I woke up and then I was a dick to you. Sound about right?"

She nodded, her color high.

"Okay then." He sucked in a breath. "I'm sorry for being a dick, and I think we need a change of plan."

The glare didn't improve. If anything, she looked suspicious. "What kind of change?"

He couldn't believe what he was about to say. But it was the only thing that made sense under the circumstances. "I think we need to embrace our marriage."

Chapter Seven

"You have got to be kidding me," Eden said, her heart beating faster at the implication.

"Not kidding."

She felt like she was in an episode of some kind of show where everyone was in on the joke except her. The too-sexy man standing in her living room, taking up all the oxygen, now wanted to be married to her? After the way he'd growled at her just a few days ago when she tiptoed out of his bathroom?

She was still annoyed with him for showing up unannounced, making an ass of himself in front of Mitchell, and, well, for being so damn good-looking and self-assured. He oozed confidence and masculinity. The kind of masculinity that said he could handle anything that came his way.

She didn't like the way he'd handled her, though. The way he'd strolled in and nearly blurted he was her husband to her boss. She'd convinced Abby that the whole thing had been a joke, that she hadn't really married the hot guy from the bar. Had a steamy night of sex, yes. But married him for real? Of course not! *Ha, ha, ha!*

She'd torn at the wedding ring in the elevator until she got it off her swollen finger and tucked it in her purse. Then she'd spun the picture as something crazy they'd done while drinking too much in Sin City. She'd been too mortified to confess to the truth. Abby hadn't pressed, probably because of the way Eden's face had been on fire when she'd admitted they'd had sex. Besides, she'd hoped to undo the marriage before anyone was the wiser. Because it wasn't real, and because Zane had been so pissed about it. His alcohol glasses had worn off the next morning, and he'd gotten a look at the real her. Of course he was angry!

Now, thanks to Zane's antics with Mitchell, she had to call Abby and explain that she and the hot guy from Vegas were dating. Except he wanted to skip past that and go straight to married for some reason. She could only imagine her sister's disappointment in her if she went along with his plan.

Then there was Mitchell. He relied on her, trusted her. What would happen when he found out she'd married a complete stranger and lied about it? Would it affect her application for one of the firm's scholarships? Johnston, Fife, & Shaw paid a portion of education expenses for all their employees. But they awarded two scholarships per year for employees who wanted to pursue the law. Eden had hoped to be one of those chosen next year. She'd wanted to make Mitchell proud of her.

But now this. One mistake and her whole life, all her plans, might come crashing down.

If she'd been going to do something crazy in Vegas, couldn't she have limited it to a hot, sweaty, dirty night with this man? Did she have to giggle her way to the marriage license bureau and then to the chapel, believing all his nonsense about how sexy she was? Because of course she'd double-checked, and they *had* gotten the license. You could get married without one, but it wasn't a legal marriage. Just a fun time at the chapel. *Why* hadn't they gone that route instead?

"You're giving me whiplash," she growled at him. Two could growl, after all. "Why the hell should I believe a word you're saying? *Why* do you want to embrace our marriage after the way you acted like I'd personally offended you with my entire existence the morning after? You couldn't wait for me to be gone."

"Because we *are* married, like it or not, and it takes time to undo." He blew out a frustrated breath and shook his head. "I wasn't at my best that morning, I admit it. But my job doesn't allow me to lie about something like this. If it was as quick to undo as it was to do in the first place, it wouldn't be a big deal. But I can't keep it a secret, Eden. I could lose my job."

And what about what she wanted? "First of all, what if *not* keeping it a secret is a problem for me? What about my job? And second, I thought you were in the Army. Last I heard, they didn't kick people out for getting married."

He frowned. "Look, I'm sorry if it's a problem for

you, but your sister's marrying your boss. I doubt he's going to fire you. Not if he wants to get married."

He had a point, but that didn't make it any easier for her.

"Not disclosing this marriage could literally cost me everything. I'm in the Army, but my job is… special. I work in a controlled facility, and I travel out of the country. A lot. I can't hide the fact that I'm married from my boss. I won't have access to a controlled environment for long if I don't disclose the truth and it comes to light. Which it will because this is a legal situation."

Eden stared. She was seriously annoyed with him, but also curious. And attracted to him, which made the annoyance worse. "What do you actually do in the Army? I think I have a right to know if we're going to be *married* now. Because contrary to what you seem to think, there are personal consequences for me, too. My integrity, my reputation, my boss's belief in my ability to make good decisions."

Potentially a scholarship, but she wasn't voicing that one aloud. Because saying it felt like willing it into existence, and she wasn't about to do that.

It took him a moment to answer. "Okay, yeah, you do. I'm a special operator. That means I get sent to war zones with my team. We take care of problems. Rescue people from shitty situations, deal with threats to our country, make sure the bad guys don't win. There's more, but that's as much as I can say."

Her irritation spiked. "So far as I can tell, you didn't say anything. What's a special operator? Is that a rank or something?"

"Fucking hell," he grumbled. "No, it's not a rank. It's a job. It means I strap on weapons and combat gear and go take care of business, preferably as discreetly as possible."

Eden could feel her eyes widening. She hadn't been sure what he meant before, but she thought she got it now.

"You're a SEAL," she said, feeling proud of herself for knowing what that was. She'd watched a few episodes of *SEAL Team* because Mitchell had said he liked the show and she'd wanted to be able to talk to him about it. But then he'd stopped watching because he didn't have time, which meant she had too.

Zane's frown deepened. "Similar, but no. SEALs are special operators, but they're in the Navy. I'm in the Army. Same concept, different branch. And no cute name."

Eden was still processing this information. "You go into dangerous situations and kill people? You could get killed doing it?"

His jaw flexed, and she realized maybe she shouldn't have stated it quite like that. It couldn't be easy to do what he did. She'd watched the Hollywood version, but what was it like in reality?

"I do what the job requires."

Maybe she should be horrified, but she wasn't. No, what she felt was an overwhelming wave of concern. "I'm sorry. It must be difficult, and I shouldn't have asked that way."

"It's okay. It *is* difficult sometimes, but it's necessary.

We do the messy work of keeping this nation free and safe. I can live with that."

She felt awkward as she clasped her hands in front of her body and stared at him. She'd been worried about a potential scholarship and her boss's opinion—still was—while this man had just confessed he risked his life for his country. It made her feel slightly ashamed of herself, even if she was frustrated with the situation.

Zane's gaze narrowed. It took her a moment to realize he was fixated on the fact she'd mashed her breasts together with her arms. Her heart skipped, but she told herself he wasn't really interested. He was just doing what men did. She unclasped her hands and folded her arms over her chest.

"Why did you do that?" he asked softly.

Heat suffused her. "I, um… Because."

He took a step toward her, and her pulse kicked up. "I didn't mean to make you uncomfortable. But you have to know you're a sexy woman, Eden. And I know what's under that sweatshirt. Makes it damn hard to concentrate on anything else."

Her face was beet red. She could feel it, but she couldn't find a damned word to say in response. Was he screwing with her, or was he serious? They weren't drunk now, but maybe he was softening her up so she'd cooperate.

She tilted her head back to meet his rainy gaze when he finished closing the space between them. *So close.*

"Are you uncomfortable?" he asked.

"A little," she replied past the tightness in her throat.

"With what part? The part where I stared at your breasts or the part where I said you're sexy?"

Her breathing was coming a little faster now. And she was hot. Too hot. Shouldn't have put on a sweatshirt in the first place.

Zane put a finger under her chin and tipped her head up gently. Her skin grew even hotter in the spot he touched. It was like all her nerve endings focused on that one spot. She couldn't feel anything but the place where he touched her.

"It's the sexy part, isn't it? You think I'm making it up. You don't believe you're sexy because Mitchell never noticed you."

Pain seared into her, but there was something else too. Excitement. Hope. Confusion. It was too much, and Eden took a step back, breaking the contact. Reminding herself he'd married her to get back at his ex. And then been angry about it. "You don't have to say things like that anymore."

"I don't have to," he admitted. "But I'm only telling the truth. You *are* sexy, Eden. Dicks don't lie, and mine wants you as much now as it did in Vegas."

She couldn't help it. Her gaze dropped to the bulge in his jeans, and she swallowed. Memories of what they'd done together seared into her. He hadn't faked it, because how could he, but she hadn't been herself that night either. She'd pretended to be more outgoing than she was, pretended to be confident and bold. She was none of those things. She was freckly, awkward Eden Hall, the girl who paled in comparison to her bold, outgoing, super confident sister. Zane was an incredibly handsome man. Even hotter and more appealing than Mitchell, and that was saying something in her book. So how could he possibly want *her*?

"I'm not who I pretended to be," she blurted, her thoughts crashing together. "I'm not sexy or confident, and some of what I did with you that night still makes me want to bury my head under a pillow and not come out for days. I was drunk and bold and it's not me. It's not really me at all. I'm sorry to disappoint you."

He stared at her with sympathy in those too-knowing eyes. "You done now?"

She nodded. But her heart still raced, and her skin burned. What was happening to her?

"Couple of things, babe." He ticked off fingers. "One, I get to decide what's sexy to me, not you. And I think you're gorgeous. I fucking love those freckles you hate. It's like a map of the stars on your skin. Constellations and universes and so many things to explore. We won't even talk about your tits and ass, which are fucking perfect."

Her mouth went dry.

"Two, so you drank too much and pretended to be bolder than you are? Pretty sure I could make you feel like doing all those things again without a drop of alcohol. And if you only wanted to bang missionary with the lights out, I'd take that deal in a heartbeat. Because sex is about more than what goes where or who does what. It's about how you *feel* during it—and I felt pretty fucking fantastic listening to the sounds you made when my face was between your legs."

Oh dear heaven…

"Three, the only thing that'll disappoint me is if I don't get to do it again. But that's your choice to make, so there's nothing I can do about that. You understand everything I just said?"

Eden needed to sit down before her knees gave out. She took two steps back and sank onto the couch. Was this man for real? Probably not. She had to be asleep and dreaming. It was the only thing that made sense. She closed her eyes and shook her head, but he was still there, still watching her. "I heard words. I'm not sure they make sense to me."

Zane shook his head. "Damn, sugar, who did such a number on you to make you so uncertain of your appeal? Because I'd like to sucker punch them in the face."

Eden laughed as she drew in a breath. "Experience did it, mostly. I've had an example of confidence and beauty every day since I was old enough to realize my sister and I are entirely different. My mother tended to point it out a lot, too. Usually when she was exasperated with me for wanting to hide from people. Abby's the one who shines in the spotlight. I don't, and I'm okay with that. I know my limitations. It is what it is."

"You realize that's bullshit, right? Phrases like 'it is what it is' are self-limiting. You're the one putting up limitations, not anyone else. If you'd really wanted your boss, you'd have gone after him with everything you've got, and your sister wouldn't have stood a chance."

Eden could only gape at him. He made her feel good, but there had to be more to it. "You're dying and need a kidney. Is that it? Because this is about way more than embracing our marriage."

His eyes widened. Then he laughed and shook his head. "Not dying. Not asking for a kidney. Just hate seeing you so shocked that a man could want to strip you naked and take you to bed for a few hours of heaven. But hey, you aren't going to get over a lifetime of programming in a few minutes, are you?"

Eden felt the sting of those words. "No, probably not. Why don't we return to this marriage thing instead? You can't hide it from your boss, or you'll be in trouble. So what's your plan to deal with that? And what about the ex? Did you at least get to rub it in her face?"

"I have to tell my commander I got married. I can't lie about how it happened, but I can gloss over the details. I can say it felt like love at first sight if I have to, and I can say I thought I couldn't live without you. It sounds so fucking bad otherwise. And I don't give a fuck about the ex."

She had to agree with how bad it sounded. There was just no good way to spin an impulsive marriage to a stranger. And she wasn't sure she believed him about the ex since she was pretty certain the name was still on his arm. But did it matter what she believed? They weren't really a couple, and they weren't going to be. They were married and had to figure out how to deal with it until the divorce. Maybe pretending it had happened because they were crazy for each other was a better way to go. Made them not look so stupid, anyway. And she'd get to enjoy the envious looks thrown her direction, though that was a pretty dumb reason to agree to do things his way.

Not that she really had a choice. More than that, she craved that feeling of everyone envying her for a change.

"You want people to believe we took one look at each other and had to get married even though we're strangers? Wouldn't it be easier to say we knew each other somehow?"

He shook his head. "I can embellish my feelings. I can't lie about the circumstances. I have to be able to pass a polygraph."

She certainly hadn't expected *that*. "They'll make you take a lie detector test about us?"

"No. It's just that having a security clearance at the level I have means it's a possibility. I don't lie about shit that could cost me my job."

"Ooookay. So you want to say it was love at first sight. But we're going to divorce, and we don't live together. How will that look?"

"We'll say we couldn't make it work. We were mistaken. Whatever you want to say. As for living together, we don't have to. That would take time to accomplish anyway, right? People will think we're working on combining households."

She nibbled her lip. "I feel like this is more complicated than I expected."

"Is for me, too. Look, I already know I'm attracted to you. And you're attracted to me. If we'd met under other circumstances, we'd go on a few dates, see how things went. No reason we can't do that while we're waiting for the divorce."

Eden blinked. The whole thing was surreal. "You want to date while we get divorced? Why?"

"Jesus, Eden. You haven't listened to a thing I've said, have you?"

"I heard you," she grumbled.

"Not sure you did."

She didn't know what she expected to happen, but him hooking his hands beneath her arms and pulling her up as if she weighed nothing wasn't it. Excitement bloomed beneath her skin as he dragged her against him, one hand on her hip and the other on the back of her head. A shiver of anticipation rolled through her.

"I've been telling you," he growled. "Looks like I need to show you."

Chapter Eight

He'd lost his mind. That was the only explanation for why he crushed his mouth down on hers. He half expected her to push him away, but she didn't. She kissed him back like she'd been hungry for exactly this.

Fucking woman was making him crazy. Zane couldn't figure out why he wanted her as much as he did, but her inability to accept that he did infuriated him. He was done with words. If she couldn't take it at face value that he found her sexy, he'd have to demonstrate. Provided she let him.

He slid his hands under her sweatshirt, around her back, traced the line of her bra. He thought about unsnapping it but decided that might spook her so he roved around and cupped her breasts in his palms instead.

Eden gasped as he brushed a thumb across one nipple. But she didn't pull away. Instead, she shocked him by sliding her hands beneath his long-sleeved shirt and pushing it up, exposing bare skin. A shiver of goosebumps slid down his spine as her fingers traced the waistband of his jeans.

He broke the kiss to rip her sweatshirt over her head. She gazed at him with big eyes, kiss-swollen lips—and doubt. It was the doubt that knifed into him hardest.

"I want you, but I'm not sure this is a good idea," she said, wrapping her arms around herself, hiding her breasts from his view.

"I think it's a fan-fucking-tastic idea," he said roughly. "But you're in charge here. Tell me you want to stop, and we stop."

"The right thing is to stop," she said, and disappointment twisted his gut. "But I have to confess I don't want to."

The last was said in little more than a whisper. Her gaze dropped. Shyness? Embarrassment? He didn't know.

"I don't want to stop either. Your move though."

It seemed an eternity while he waited. It was probably no more than a second before she launched herself at him. He caught her, lifting her until she wrapped her legs around his waist. She thought she wasn't bold? Holy shit, he'd hate to see her definition of the word. Because, for him, that move was fucking perfect. She wanted him, and she didn't spend a hell of a lot of time overthinking it.

He kissed her as her hair dropped around his face to curtain them both. He held her tightly, as if she might dissolve. But he wanted her to feel how hard he was for her. How desperate he was to be inside her again.

It defied logic, but he was. Been too long, maybe. In

general, not specifically. He hadn't been with anyone before Eden in a couple of months, not since Juliet had started messaging him again. He didn't know if he'd been waiting for Juliet to get her divorce or if he'd been punishing himself for responding to her in the first place. He'd always known it wouldn't work, that she'd never really be his, but he'd taken the bait anyway—and that pissed him off.

Too much history and feeling wrapped up in Juliet to ignore her messages when they'd started. Maybe there always would be, but he didn't miss her the way he once had. He never would again.

Eden wasn't his rebound lay. She was his palate cleanser, his first delicious meal in a long, long time. Eden was special. She wasn't going to change his mind about happily ever afters—nobody could—but they could have a good time together while they waited for their divorce. He could prove to her she was as desirable as her sister. More so in his opinion.

"Bedroom," he growled, breaking the kiss. Needing to get inside her as soon as possible.

"Upstairs." She started to put her legs down, but he held her and wouldn't let go. "You can't carry me up there. I'm too heavy."

"You aren't and I can. Where is it?"

"End of the hall," she whispered.

Zane took the stairs without effort and strode down the hall to toe open the half-closed door. He slid Eden down his body to her feet, making sure to drag her over his erection and let her know how much he wanted her.

A fat gray cat blinked at them from its spot dead center of the bed.

"Can we move the kitty?" he asked as he reached for the clasp of Eden's bra.

She stopped fumbling with his fly. "Oh! Of course." She scooped the cat into her arms, cuddling him. "Merlin, you have to move, sweetie. Mama's got things to do and she needs the bed."

Zane would have laughed at the way she talked to the cat, the things she said, but he liked it. She was sweet. Caring. He barely knew her, but he'd stake his life on the fact Eden cared about others. More than she should, probably, but that was what made her so sweet.

She carried the cat over and set him in the hall, then closed the door behind him. She didn't turn back to Zane, though, and he began to wonder if she was having second thoughts. He went over to her, put his mouth against the side of her throat, and licked the soft skin there.

"Stay with me, babe. Don't let the negative thoughts win."

"How did you know?" she whispered without turning around.

"How couldn't I?"

She turned with a shudder, and he took both her hands in his and walked backward to the bed, tugging her gently with him.

"I shouldn't be doing this," she said. "It's crazy. We made a mistake and now we're about to do it again."

"It's not a mistake to do something that feels good.

The mistake was the marriage, but we're gonna fix that, right?"

She nodded. Her bra was loose but still covering her breasts. Zane slipped the straps off and pulled it away. "Fucking perfect, Eden." He cupped her breasts, ran his palms up and over shoulders, then back down again. "I love your skin. You should be proud of how unique you are, how unforgettable."

Her mouth opened but nothing came out. Zane dropped to his knees, intent on worshipping her breasts with all the attention they deserved. He sucked one perfect nipple between his lips, and Eden curled her fingers into his shoulders, moaning.

He loved the sounds she made, the way she squirmed when he sucked a little harder or faster. He made sure to lavish equal attention on both nipples, working her jeans open as he did so. He needed to feel how wet she was, how ready. When he had them unzipped, he shoved them down her hips, guiding her feet from first one leg and then the other. He tossed the jeans free, skimming a finger between her legs because he couldn't wait.

Eden gasped as he skimmed back and forth. Then he sank a finger into her, feeling the flutter of her walls as she held him. She was so fucking wet for him he groaned. His cock literally hurt with the need to be inside her. But he needed to take it slow, needed to make sure he didn't overwhelm her. This thing between them was fragile, could evaporate at any second when she found her wits again. When she wasn't blinded by the need crashing through them both.

He fought to keep the beast of his need at bay. To do everything gently so she wouldn't want to stop. He took his time teasing, testing, making her quiver. Preparing her. He dropped kisses down her torso, slid his tongue into her slit and lapped at her clit.

"Zane," she moaned. "Oh God."

A moment later she broke the contact with a quick step back. Zane's heart sank to his knees. But it was her decision. Always her decision. He wasn't the kind of man to force his needs, no matter how much it physically hurt to stop.

"I don't want to be the only one naked," she blurted, and the disappointment in his stomach loosened. Zane rose and finished stripping off the shirt she'd opened. She'd unbuttoned his jeans and now she helped push them down while he toed off his boots.

When he was naked, his cock standing proudly between them, she stepped back again. Only this time she let her gaze roam his body. He wondered if she knew how greedy she looked in that moment. He fucking loved it.

She wrapped a hand around his cock and stroked him, and he closed his eyes and let his head fall back. His heart thumped insistently as shivers of delight chased down his spine and into his balls.

"I want to feel like I did Friday night," she whispered. "Wild and bold and happy. You said you could make it happen without a drop of alcohol. I want you to do that now. Make me be that woman again."

She broke his heart, and he barely knew her. But he knew she sold herself short. That she didn't believe in herself the way she should. She *was* that woman, all on her own. Still, he'd play the game if that's what it took to make her feel free enough to be herself.

Zane reached for her, turned her, pushed her forward and down until her elbows were on the mattress and her ass was in the air. He wanted to watch his cock disappear inside her. But first he dropped kisses on her spine, across the place where the freckles were thickest, then down to the divots of her ass cheeks, biting one before working his way back up her spine to her neck. He licked an ear lobe, sucked it between his teeth while she made those mewling sounds he loved.

"It's gotta be this way first, or I won't last," he said. "I can't watch you bite that luscious lower lip as I fuck you, knowing it's me making you feel that way. Next time I take you, I'm watching every expression on your face as I make you come. You understand me, Eden? I want to see your face, see your beautiful freckles. I just have to do it this way first."

"Yes, yes. Please. I can't wait anymore."

Zane lined his dick up with her opening and teased at her entrance, slipping the tip in and out, in and out. He pinched one of her nipples, tugging it just enough to make her suck in a breath.

"Do you want me to beg?" she gasped on the next tug, the next tiny tease of his cock.

"If you want to," he told her. "What would you say, Eden?"

She pushed her hips back against him as he withdrew again, demanding more. He put a hand on one hip and held her, preventing her from impaling herself on him.

"Please, Zane. Please stop teasing me. I want you inside me. I want to feel the way I felt before."

He slid his fingers over her clit, and she let out a soft moan. "I think the words you're looking for are *Fuck me, Zane. Please, fuck me.*"

"Fuck me, Zane," she choked as he strummed her clit again. "Please, fuck me."

"Magic words, Eden," he said, slamming home inside her.

———

EDEN WAS FULL OF HIM, so full it ought to hurt. But it didn't. Zane was big, she knew that from Friday and how sore she'd been the next morning. She felt the sting of him now, but it was a good sting. So, so good.

This might be insanity, but she desperately craved it. He'd said he had to take her from behind the first time, and though she couldn't say why, she felt the same way. She wanted it like this. Raw, hard, impersonal in a way. She wasn't worried about her face or what he thought. Wasn't worried about anything but how it felt.

Eden clutched handfuls of the quilt as Zane set a brutal pace, slamming into her, their bodies slapping together as he planted himself deep before withdrawing and doing it again. Her body was on fire with need so intense it hurt.

And with pleasure. So much pleasure.

Her skin tingled everywhere. Like champagne

bubbles popping and fizzing inside. Addictive. She'd never known sex could be this amazing. It never had been before, but maybe that's because she'd been too much inside her own head. Zane didn't let that happen. He dominated her body, kept her from diving too deep into her thoughts.

"Fuck, you feel good," Zane groaned, echoing her thoughts. "Your pussy is so wet for me. I love it."

It *was* all for him. She hadn't been aroused until he showed up and made her that way. Zane Scott with his muscles and black clothing—and his badass warrior status. Maybe she was wrong to be turned on by it, but she was. Not the part where he did dangerous things, but the part where he said somebody had to defend their nation and he was proud to do it. How many people would be willing to put themselves in harm's way for an ideal like he did?

And then there was the way he'd taken that guy down in Vegas. It made her shiver.

Eden pushed back against him with every stroke, her entire body reverberating with the power of him. He gripped her hips hard, his fingers digging in, but she didn't tell him to stop. Didn't tell him it was too much.

Because it wasn't. The tingles in her body intensified as they moved together. She was beginning to see stars exploding behind her eyelids and she hadn't even come yet.

"Zane," she cried out as he smoothed a hand up her spine and gripped the back of her neck. He let go of her hip and circled around to her clitoris, his fingers playing her body like an instrument. Eden rose up on her tiptoes, seeking more. The stars were swirling faster now.

Zane hooked her leg and lifted her knee to the bed so she was fully open to him. Then he stroked her clit again, faster than before. He didn't stop the pistoning of his hips, slamming deep and sure, and Eden lost any inhibitions she might have had, begging him for more.

She was floating, sailing among a billion stars, her body splintering, when the wave overtook her. Her back arched, her body trembled, and a hoarse scream broke from her throat.

Zane's fingers tightened in her hair as she flew apart, shoving herself back against him, driving him deeper with every stroke. She wasn't thinking about anything except how he made her feel. She wasn't shy or self-conscious. Wasn't thinking about freckles or jiggly body parts.

When she would have collapsed, Zane held her up and drove into her until she felt his muscles clenching and trembling. He came with a shout that made her feel extraordinarily pleased with herself. *She* had done that to him. Not anyone else. Not Kate or Hannah or even Abby. Eden Hall had fucked a god and made him lose control. It was her body he was buried in, her back he lay against, her skin plastered to his.

"That was perfect," he panted in her ear. "Your pussy is heaven. Any man that never told you that was a fucking idiot."

Eden sprawled on the mattress, the quilt bunched beneath her, her body drenched with sweat, her limbs still trembling from the workout, and she wanted to laugh. She didn't though.

"Thank you," she said. "Pretty sure you've been told about your perfect dick, so I won't bother inflating your ego about it."

He snorted a laugh that she felt inside her because he was still buried in her. "You just did."

He levered off her, his semen dripping down her leg as he withdrew. He went into the en suite bath and returned with a towel that he used to wipe it away. The gentleness of his touch was at odds with the roughness of his voice when he spoke.

"If we're going to do this, it's exclusive. I don't share."

Eden rolled over and stood when he was done, her legs feeling way wobblier than she'd expected. He was looking at her with a serious expression and she realized he meant it. The fact he believed she could go out tomorrow and find another man to have sex with —that she *would*—probably should have pissed her off. Instead, she found it flattering. Maybe that was fucked up, but there it was. This man—this sex god— believed that a woman like her could find another man to screw around with while she was having sex with him. And that made her feel amazing and powerful.

"I don't share either." She purposely didn't look at the tattoo sleeve on his arm. She didn't want to see Juliet's name there.

"Good." He backed her against the bed, caging her between arms made of hard muscle, and kissed her leisurely. When he cupped her mound in one big hand, she sighed into his mouth.

"My pussy, Eden. Remember that."

She didn't think she could forget if she tried. Though she wasn't going to accept such an autocratic statement without comment.

"Only while we work on this divorce thing. And only if you don't piss me off."

He laughed. "Who told you that you weren't bold? Because I'm thinking they didn't know you at all if they could say that."

He made her feel good. "Trust me, I'm not in most circumstances. But you have a way of making me forget that about myself."

"Then I'm a good influence. Who knew?"

She laughed, too. "To a point. It was your idea to get married, and that was not a good influence at all."

"True. Mmm," he said, letting his gaze roam down her naked body. "But the perks are pretty damned good. You can't deny that."

He made her blush. "So far, so good."

He kissed her swiftly, his tongue delving between her lips. Her body started to melt again. His hand was on her nipple, tweaking it, when she heard a voice that doused the flame.

"Eden! Where are you?"

"Oh my God, that's Abby," she squeaked, pushing him away.

Zane leisurely straightened to his full, extremely naked height, watching her with a bemused expression as she shoved past him and ran for the bedroom door.

Eden twisted the lock before grabbing her clothes and frantically trying to drag everything on.

Abby's steps sounded on the stairs. "Eden!"

"I'm up here! I'll be right down."

"Mitchell said you weren't alone—"

"I'm not, for heaven's sake," she yelled back. "Give me a damn minute, okay?"

There was silence in the hall. Then the footsteps retreated. Zane calmly dressed while she freaked out. When she couldn't get her bra hooked, he turned her around to hook it for her.

"You're an adult," he said in her ear before he let her go. "You don't have to explain."

She whipped on her sweatshirt and whirled. "I know. But this isn't how I wanted her to find out."

He looked amused. "What did you think was going to happen when Mitchell left here in his fancy Porsche?"

He had a point. "I thought she'd call. Oh, shit. I left my phone downstairs. She probably did call, but when I didn't answer…"

"It's a little overreactive to race over here, don't you think?"

Eden sucked in a breath and considered how best to answer. "Abby had a bad experience with a guy a few years ago. He was, uhm, a bit obsessive. She can be suspicious of men in general, so please don't take it personally." She squeezed his arm. "Which is another reason I don't want to tell her we're married just now, okay? I need to ease her into it."

He frowned but nodded. "Okay. Doesn't change the fact I have to tell my commander tomorrow morning."

"I know. And thank you." She ripped the elastic from her messy hair, gathered the strands up again, and quickly made another, neater ponytail.

Zane tugged her against him and kissed her thoroughly enough to make her start melting again. "Adult," he said when he let her go. "Our business. Nobody else's. You don't have to explain. Got it?"

"I'm trying."

"Breathe, Eden. You got this."

She gave him a wobbly smile before opening the door and going down to face her sister.

Chapter Nine

ZANE FOLLOWED EDEN DOWNSTAIRS, WATCHING HER cute ass sway. He didn't know what the hell he'd gotten himself into, but he was enjoying it at the moment. The past hour was seared into his memory banks for the rest of his life. It wasn't what he'd expected would happen when he parked his truck and headed for Eden's door, but he wasn't upset about it.

Mostly. It was definitely a complication, but if they had to stay married for a while anyway, why not enjoy it? And damn but he loved making her come apart with those sexy little cries of hers.

Abby perched on a chair at one end of the living room. She sat forward, legs crossed at the ankles, looking prim and, in his opinion, more judgmental than she had a right to.

Her eyes widened a little when they landed on him before skittering back to Eden.

"When Mitchell called and said he'd met your

boyfriend, I had to pretend I knew what the hell he was talking about since he seemed to think I did."

She sounded upset. It set Zane's teeth on edge. Like Eden was twelve and hadn't told her mother where she'd been going or who she'd been playing with. Though, in Abby's defense, it was more or less his fault Eden had to make up an excuse on the fly. It was also his fault she'd gotten distracted and hadn't called Abby to warn her.

"Crap," Eden said. "I'm sorry. I panicked and said you only found out about Zane in Vegas and that I'd asked you not to say anything. I meant to warn you as soon as he drove off, but um… I kind of forgot."

Abby's nostrils flared as she took them both in, clearly understanding what was unsaid. She was a pretty woman, but Zane didn't see why Eden thought her sister was so much more beautiful than she was. Sure, her skin was clear of freckles, but those were one of the things that made Eden so striking in his opinion. Abby's hair was more gold than red, and she didn't have the curves Eden had. Her eyes weren't the green of Eden's either. They were hazel, or maybe brown. He couldn't tell at this distance. Pretty, but not the amazing knockout Eden made her out to be.

"I wish you hadn't done that," Abby said.

"All I could think was that you'd seen Zane before so I couldn't say you hadn't. I'm sorry I said anything. Was he mad?" Eden sounded worried.

"No." Abby turned her head to spear him a look. "What's your game anyway? My sister isn't rich. You've got nothing to gain if that's your angle."

Zane could only imagine how it made Eden feel to

hear her sister dismiss the idea he could be interested in her for herself. He knew how it made him feel. It fucking pissed him off, which was why he took a moment to rein in his anger before he responded.

"You ever think maybe what I've got to gain is spending time with your sister? Because it sounds like you think the *only* reason I'd be interested in her is for money. It's no fucking wonder she thinks she's not as pretty or as perfect as you are. Which, I have to say, she *is*."

Abby's eyes widened, her mouth opening as she blinked at him. Then she darted her gaze to Eden, who was also staring at him. But Eden's eyes were warm rather than surprised. That hit him in the feels a little harder than he expected. What the fuck was happening to him?

He was here to work out the details of a divorce and trying to make the best of being married for the time they had to stay that way. This wasn't permanent. Getting twisted up inside over this woman was not part of the plan.

"Eden," Abby said, her face draining of color. "I'm sorry. That came out wrong. You know I worry."

Eden shot him a grateful smile before turning to her sister. "I know you're trying to protect me. But I'm an adult. I can make my own decisions and my own mistakes. Not every man is like Trevor, sissy. Not every relationship is a disaster waiting to happen. You know that as well as I do."

"I know. But everything about this situation is odd, so I can't help it. It's not like you to be so impulsive."

"It's not, but I'm learning to let go a bit more. Just like you're always telling me. And why's it odd? Because we met in Vegas over the weekend and now he's here? Zane lives close by. If he lived in Spokane or Cleveland, we wouldn't be having this conversation."

Abby's lips seemed to tighten. "You only just met him. I mean a one-night stand is one thing. But now he's your boyfriend just because he lives in the area?"

Zane didn't blame Abby for being concerned about her sister. That was a point in her favor, though the fact she hadn't known Eden was in love with Mitchell was a giant mark against her. Abby hadn't known, or maybe she hadn't cared when she'd wanted him for herself. If that last was true, then he didn't like her at all.

Eden shrugged like it was nothing. "We hit it off in Vegas. We've got chemistry." She cut her gaze toward him, and he wondered what she was thinking in that pretty head. "We're exploring this thing between us. It's what we both want."

Abby dropped her gaze to her clasped hands and swallowed. "I didn't mean to suggest it could only be about money. You know I think you're gorgeous. I've told you again and again." Her eyes darted to Zane with suspicion. "I don't want you getting in the kind of mess I did. That's all."

His curiosity was definitely aroused, but he didn't ask. He wondered, though. What kind of mess? How bad? What had happened?

Eden sank onto the couch next to the chair Abby was in. She leaned toward Abby, squeezing her hands. "You've found the man you love and you're getting married. I want that too. But I won't get it if I don't take a chance."

Abby's lip trembled. "I don't want you to make a mistake."

"I don't want that either. But Zane isn't Trevor, just like Mitchell isn't. Trevor was not the norm, and you know it."

Abby sucked in a breath, her nostrils flaring. Then she nodded. "Right. I'm sorry." She shot him a look. "Thank you for saving Eden from the guy who pushed her into the elevator, and thank you for looking out for her that night."

"I'd have done the same for anyone. But you're welcome."

Abby got to her feet, shouldering her handbag. "I guess I should get back home. Mitchell should be there by now."

"I thought he was going straight home after he dropped off case files earlier," Eden said with a frown.

Abby shook her glossy head. "He said he had to run by the office for an hour or so."

"He's got a lot going on with this case."

"I know. I'll be glad when it's over. He's always working late, taking phone calls at all hours, and canceling plans these days. Two months until the wedding, and I hope this one is over by then."

Eden looked troubled. "I'm trying to help, but there are certain things only he can do."

"I know, sissy. I appreciate it, too." Abby's phone rang, and she yanked it from her purse. "Hey, sweetie.

You home yet? Yes, I'm about to head that way. Want me to pick up anything? Okay, love you too."

"Everything okay?" Eden asked when Abby slipped her phone back into her purse.

"Yes. He's finishing up now and going home. Which means I need to get back." She and Eden hugged. They were similar, but not so alike you'd think they were twins if you didn't know.

Abby thrust out a hand to him. "It was nice meeting you in person, Zane. I'm sorry if I don't seem supportive, but Eden's my only family, and I would go nuclear on anyone who hurt her. Please don't make me do that."

Zane didn't laugh at her threat. She wouldn't have liked it. Instead, he shook her hand. "Not my plan, Abby. It's nice to meet you, too."

She nodded very seriously. "We'll see you at the party with Eden on Saturday then."

"I'll be there."

Eden went and stood on the front step to watch Abby get inside her car and back out of the drive. When Abby's taillights disappeared, Eden let out an audible sigh.

"That went better than I thought," she said. "But I'm sorry she was rude to you."

"She wasn't. If Mia brought home a man she'd just met, I'd be a much bigger pain in the ass than your sister. Trust me, she was downright friendly by comparison."

Eden laughed. "If you say so. And thank you for what you said about spending time with me. I know we're not really having a relationship beyond what it takes to get a divorce, but it was nice of you."

"Wasn't trying to be nice. I meant it. Spending time with you isn't a hardship, Eden. Any man who makes you feel that way doesn't deserve you."

A blush colored her skin. "You say the nicest things for a man who wants a divorce. And no, I'm not used to it. I don't date much. My last boyfriend dumped me for a woman he met at Starbucks. That was before I went to work for Mitchell. In fact, it's *why* I did. He was a junior attorney at another firm, and I didn't want to look at him anymore. Especially since he ended up marrying the Starbucks woman a few months later."

"Damn. Sorry to hear that, but he was an asshole."

"He definitely was."

"So you planning to tell me about this Trevor guy? What happened that was so bad?"

Eden hugged herself. "Oh boy. It's not a good story, but you should know. It explains a lot about Abby. Trevor Hagan. He was a tech guy, owned a company with offices in Chicago, New York, and LA. Abby was a marketing director at a publicity firm in Chicago at the time. They met at a fundraiser and Trevor pulled out all the stops to impress her. They dated for about six months, I think. But he was controlling and possessive. He did things. He tagged her with trackers, bugged her phone and apartment, and had her followed. He basically took control of her life. And when she tried to break it off, he took her to Montana and kept her there for three weeks. She lost her job, and I think she would have lost her sanity if he'd had his way. But Trevor got arrested for tax fraud, and the FBI raided his house. They found her locked inside a barred room, though of course he claimed it was sex play. It wasn't. He did five years for the tax fraud and nothing for what he did to Abby because his lawyers spun it like she was a willing participant."

"Holy shit," Zane breathed. Not at all what he'd been expecting. Poor Abby.

Eden shivered. "I know. She texted me while she was gone, but it was stuff he dictated so I didn't know she was in trouble. She told me they were traveling and she was having so much fun, but she never had a good enough signal to send a picture or do a video chat. And I believed it like an idiot. I felt guilty about that for a long time, but Abby finally convinced me it wasn't my fault. It happened almost six years ago. As you can imagine, it's taken time for her to trust any man enough to agree to marry him. Which is why I'm happy for her. Yes, I love Mitchell, too, but I don't need him the way Abby does. He's been good for her. There's one more thing you should know—Trevor was released a couple of months ago. He hasn't tried to contact Abby that I know of. I think she'd tell me. I hope she would. If not me, then I hope she'd tell Mitchell."

He hoped she was right. He didn't like the sound of this Trevor Hagan at all, but that didn't mean the guy hadn't moved on. Five years in prison could do that to a person. "You said I wasn't like Trevor. What makes you so certain?"

He didn't want to scare her, but shit. Her sister had been held captive by a man she'd dated for six months, and Eden had let Zane into her life after a couple of hours in a bar. What if her judgement sucked? *He* knew he wasn't a psycho, but what if the next guy she dated was? She needed to stop being so trusting, for fuck's sake.

Eden looked at him like he was a couple of sandwiches short of a picnic. "Trevor viewed Abby like a prize. You saw her. She's gorgeous, warm, witty, and people want to be around her. She draws others to her like a magnet. She glows. I do not, and I'm pretty sure if you were some kind of psycho looking to attach yourself to a woman, you'd find one with something you wanted but couldn't get on your own. Money, for instance. Or the kind of beauty my sister has."

He wanted to shake some sense into her. Eden was far more naïve—or deluded—than she knew. "Some guys only want a woman they can control. Someone to be their emotional slave, doing whatever they ask. What if that's what I want?"

She blinked. Then she shook her head emphatically. "You don't. I saw you with your sister, and I spent time with you that night before we plunged off the deep end into the marriage pool. There are easier ways to pick your prey than everything that happened with us."

That was certainly true. If he were a manipulative prick looking for a woman to control, then he was a stupid one for taking it as far as an impulsive wedding with the King officiating.

"For the record, you're beautiful too," Zane said, because he wasn't letting the implication she wasn't pass without comment. "Your sister may be more at ease with people, but that doesn't make you less desirable."

Eden's smile was bright. Her cat came wandering into the room then, meowing softly. He swiped his fur against Eden's leg and then made a bee line for Zane, who bent down to pet him. The cat sniffed his hand and purred, arching his back and rubbing Zane's legs.

"If Merlin likes you, that settles it. You aren't a psycho."

Zane couldn't help but grin as he scratched the cat's ears. "That's one way to be sure." He stood, albeit reluctantly. "I should get going. It's been a long day, and as much as I want to stay for another round with you, I have to get up early for a training exercise."

She nodded. "It's okay. It's been a long day for me too."

At the door he bent to kiss her cheek, but she turned her head and their mouths met. Desire flared hot and strong as he trapped her against the wall, devouring her mouth like it was the first time tonight. She leaned into him, her palms sliding up his chest and around his neck.

Any second, they'd go up in flames. Again. He didn't know what it was about this woman, but she was gasoline to his spark. He was still searching for the strength to walk away when she broke the kiss. It was strangely disappointing that she was the one to do it.

"I'll text you tomorrow and let you know how it goes with the CO," he said gruffly.

She blinked up at him. "CO?"

"Commanding officer."

"Oh." Her pink lips were shiny from his kiss, and his

groin tightened at the thought of seeing them wrapped around his dick again. Precisely how he'd gotten into trouble with her in the first place. "Good luck with that," she added.

"Thanks. See you soon, Eden."

She smiled tentatively. "Goodnight, Zane."

"'Night."

She was still standing on the front step when he got into his truck and started it. He picked up his phone and shot her a text.

Go inside, Eden. Not leaving until you do.

He saw her phone light up as she read it. She waved and went inside. Only when the door was closed was he able to drive away. But he didn't stop thinking about the woman he'd left behind.

Chapter Ten

IT WAS A LONG DAY AT THE OFFICE, WORKING ON PUTTING together files for Mitchell, taking notes during depositions, and preparing for the trial, which would start with jury selection next week.

Eden was tired and exhilarated at once. She kept thinking about the night before, about Zane striding up her walkway and claiming her mouth right there in front of a shocked Mitchell. She'd been annoyed and aroused at the same time.

How was that possible? How did Zane make her feel both those things?

She caught herself glancing at Mitchell as he poured over documents, one hand propping his head up, the other stretched out on the desk to turn the page. He'd rolled up his sleeves, which she usually adored, but now she kept thinking how his arms weren't as big as Zane's. How Zane had walked up the stairs to her bedroom with her legs wrapped around him and hadn't broken a sweat.

When Zane kissed her, all her reservations evaporated. She was simultaneously embarrassed and aroused by the memories of what they'd done in her bedroom before Abby showed up. The way Zane had made her beg for more. The way she'd felt when he slammed home and started to move deep inside her.

She'd thought Vegas had been an anomaly until that moment. Until she'd found herself bent over her mattress, clutching handfuls of her quilt, her entire body on fire with sensation.

Zane Scott was an addiction. And he was her husband. For now.

He'd texted earlier to tell her he had a meeting with the commander at three. She glanced at her phone. It was three-thirty. Eden chewed her lip, wondering what was happening. How Zane was explaining that he'd gone to Vegas single and came home hitched to a woman he'd taken one look at and fallen for.

It was too far-fetched. His commander would never believe it. Nobody would believe it. People did not fall in love at first sight. Mitchell claimed to have fallen for Abby that way, but everybody fell for Abby when they first found themselves in the warmth of her orbit. Didn't mean it'd been love so much as lust, though.

Eden didn't know how she was going to break it to Abby and Mitchell that she and Zane were married. Maybe she would never have to. Zane had to tell the truth to his commander, but unless the man knew her sister or her boss, there was no reason the information would get out. Maybe the divorce would happen quickly enough that she would never have to admit the truth.

She'd have to make sure not to use an attorney Mitchell knew, but that wouldn't be too hard. She could call one from the other side of the state if she had to.

She was feeling much better about the whole thing when her phone buzzed fifteen minutes later.

Zane: *Told the CO. You'll need to come in for a briefing.*

Eden blinked. *Excuse me? A briefing?*

Zane: *It's a thing. You're part of the family and you need to know what that means. There's sensitive information about our mission to impart.*

She frowned. She hadn't really expected she'd be involved in anything once he told his commander about the marriage. *And you can't just tell me?*

Zane: *No, I really can't. Please make time next week. It'll take a couple hours.*

Eden scraped her chair back and headed for the hall, hitting the call button as she did so.

"You're pissed, aren't you?" Zane said in answer.

"I'm not pissed, but this isn't convenient. We're preparing for a trial! I don't have that kind of time right now."

"I'm sorry, I know, but it's necessary. I'll see if I can get them to do it at a time you can be there. There are things you need to know about the mission that can only be said in a secure environment. That's why I can't tell you."

Frustration rolled through her as she put her hand on her forehead and told herself to breathe. "Okay, fine. What else aren't you telling me?"

"Nothing. Boss wasn't too happy with me. There are protocols, and I broke them all. But it's done, and you have to be briefed. You'll be investigated for a basic security clearance, too. They'll talk to your boss, your sister, your friends. It's SOP, before you say anything."

Eden gritted her teeth. Standard Operating Procedure. So much for keeping this marriage secret from the people she knew.

"You do know I'm having no say in this and I don't like it, right? First *you* have to say we're married, and now I have to tell everyone too. Not how I planned on doing things, Zane!"

She heard him sigh. "I'm sorry, I really am. But you went to the license bureau and the chapel same as I did. You took part. I'd hoped we could dissolve it as quickly as we did it, but we can't. We're married, Eden, and there are things that have to be done on my end for me to keep my security clearance and my job."

She closed her eyes. "Fine. You're right, but I still don't like it. Maybe you should have told me all these things *before* we got married."

"Yeah, well, that means I had to be thinking with more than my dick that night, which we've established wasn't happening. Just like you weren't thinking with anything above the waist either."

He had her there. It wasn't fair to be upset with him when she was just as guilty of not considering consequences.

"Trust me," he continued. "I just got my ass chewed by a general. Not an experience I want to repeat anytime soon. Which is why I need you to find time for this."

Eden grabbed the end of her ponytail and tugged.

"If you can make it after four one day next week, I'll be there."

He sighed. "Thank you."

"You're welcome."

She thought he was done talking to her, but then he asked, "What are you doing for dinner tonight?"

"Working, unfortunately. Jury selection begins next week."

"Is Mitchell there?"

"He's the lead attorney on the case. Of course he's here. Why?"

"Just wondering. What if I bring food over? Can you eat with me?"

Warmth spread through her like she'd swallowed a shot of tequila. "I can do that. We'll be here until eight, probably."

"I'll be there at six if that works."

"It does."

"Then it's a date. See you tonight, babe."

"See you tonight."

The call ended and Eden leaned back against one of the paneled walls of the law library that she'd walked into. What on earth was happening? Since when was she, Eden Hall, the center of attention for the most gorgeous man she'd ever laid eyes on?

Since Friday night in Vegas, apparently. Viva Las Vegas.

ZANE PULLED into the parking garage near Johnston, Fife, & Shaw a few minutes before six. He had a takeout bag with Greek food that smelled divine, and he was about to have dinner with Eden. He didn't know why he'd offered to bring it, but he was glad he had. She was working late with Mitchell Shaw, her sister's fiancé. The man she secretly loved. Not that it was any of his business whether or not she worked late with a man she thought she was in love with. Zane was married to her, but they weren't really a couple.

A hot, sharp feeling bloomed in his chest. He didn't know why it should. He liked Eden, but that shouldn't make his chest ache. He grabbed the bag and headed for the law office, taking note of the cars in the garage, the slots they were in and who they were reserved for. Mitchell's Porsche was there. Eden's CR-V. A Toyota 4Runner. A BMW M-6. A tall Mercedes passenger van. As he walked to the stairs that would take him down to the ground floor, he noted a few other cars that weren't in reserved spots. The garage served businesses in the area and some retail stores as well, which meant a variety of cars coming and going. Not ideal from a security standpoint. He'd have to ask Eden if she always entered the garage with another person because he didn't like the idea of her going to her car alone when she'd been working late.

That was basic OPSEC in his opinion. Operational security didn't just apply to military missions. You had to be aware of your surroundings at all times. In fact, he probably needed to give Eden some personal defense training. She'd frozen when she'd been assaulted by the man in the elevator in Vegas, which was understandable, but she could have neutralized him with a couple of moves if she'd known what to do.

Zane took his phone out to call her and let her know he was there when a text bubble popped up on the screen. He halted abruptly.

Juliet: *I can't do this anymore. I've tried. Daniel won't ever change. Can we talk?*

Zane ground his teeth together as he stood in place, torn between responding or ignoring the message for a few hours. But, fuck, it was irritating how seeing Juliet's name on his phone could trigger a mess of feelings in his gut. He did *not* love her anymore. So why did he feel this way when she texted?

Zane swiped to Eden's name and sent her a text as he headed down the sidewalk. A few seconds later, she was there behind the glass door with the gold lettering, looking for him. When she opened the door and smiled, his heart thumped.

"Hey," she said.

"Hey." He bent to kiss her cheek, inhaling the scent of her. He'd noticed that Eden smelled like peaches and vanilla most of the time. Her skin was soft, and her hair was pulled back in a thick, red ponytail. A few strands had escaped to halo her face. Her green eyes were bright as they gazed up at him. The constellation of freckles on her face changed when she smiled. He found it fascinating.

"What did you bring? It smells so good."

"A Greek feast. You said you had no food allergies and you'd eat anything."

She laughed, and his heart hitched again. "That's right. I like food. I mean I'm not a fan of liver and onions, but I doubted you'd bring that so I didn't say anything."

Zane put a hand on his chest in mock surprise. "Damn, Eden, I almost stopped at my favorite diner and bought two liver and onion dinners for us. Good thing I didn't."

She bumped his arm playfully. "You did not. Come in and we can eat in the break room."

His phone buzzed again, but Eden didn't seem to notice. Zane ignored it too, watching Eden's ass as she led the way. She wore gray trousers that hugged her luscious bottom and a cream turtleneck sweater that emphasized the fullness of her breasts. He'd clocked a thin gold chain with a pendant that hung between her breasts and small diamond earrings. She looked pretty and professional, and somehow sexy as fuck at the same time. Why this woman thought she wasn't a show-stopper was beyond him.

She flipped on the light switch. A room with a galley kitchen and a couple of big round tables came into view. She went over to the refrigerator and opened it.

"What would you like to drink? We have soda, beer, tea, water…"

"Water's good."

She grabbed two bottles of water and came back to the table where he'd set the bag and started pulling out containers. He took the lids off chicken souvlaki, chunks of juicy lamb, tzatziki sauce, stuffed grape leaves, rice, hummus, and warm slices of pita. Eden grabbed paper plates from a cabinet, and they sat down to dish out food and eat.

"You think your boss might want some?" Zane asked, hoping the answer was no but trying to be polite.

"He's eating a sandwich at his desk."

Zane was glad to hear it. "I'm sorry about the briefing, Eden. I know it's inconvenient."

Eden stabbed a grape leaf and put it on her plate to cut off a piece. "I'm not usually so disagreeable, I promise, but this trial has been stressful. A rich man is accused of having his wife killed, but some of the evidence doesn't add up. So we're working long hours as Mitchell prepares his defense and the investigators do their work."

"I saw that on the news. The William Allen trial." The man had business ties to Antonio Benedetto, who was known to associate with the mafia, and he'd allegedly hired a hitman to kill his wife when he was out of town. "You don't think he did it?"

She swallowed the bite of stuffed grape leaf. "It doesn't matter what I think. It's the evidence that's important. We all deserve a fair trial and the presumption of innocence."

"But do you have an opinion?" He genuinely wanted to know. In his job, he went after people already guilty of bad acts. He didn't have to decide. He did what he was sent to do and that was that.

"I think it looks bad for him. The man who allegedly pulled the trigger is a known mafia enforcer who's done time before. He disappeared when Mr. Allen was arrested, but there's a digital trail between them. That doesn't mean Mr. Allen hired the hit, though."

Zane thought about it while he ate a piece of lamb. "You like this kind of work, huh?"

"Yes. I, um, don't remember if I said so in Vegas, but I want to get my law degree and be a defense attorney like Mitchell. He's one of the best, really. I'm lucky to work for him."

Zane didn't like the little shard of jealousy that pricked him. Why should he be jealous? Didn't matter to him if she admired Mitchell Shaw. Hell, he already knew she was in love with the man. Wasn't like he didn't have emotional entanglements of his own. Not love, but something else. Impotent anger, probably.

"That's a good goal to have. When do you think you'll do it?"

"Next fall, I hope. I'm saving money and applying for a scholarship." She frowned. "It's a scholarship from the firm. One of two they award every year. I'm hoping this thing with us doesn't negatively impact my chances."

He frowned. "Why would it?"

She gaped at him. "Because it shows a lack of judgement on my part?"

"Oh, you mean good old Johnston, Fife, & Shaw never made a mistake in their lives? Never fallen head over heels for a handsome soldier and taken the plunge because they were crazy in love?"

Eden laughed. "Crazy in love, huh? That's what we're going with?"

He popped a slice of pita with tzatziki into his

mouth. "I told you it sounds better than the truth, right? My CO is of the opinion I rescued you then lost my head over you and couldn't help myself."

He didn't miss the pink staining her cheeks as she concentrated on her food. "He'll never believe that story when he meets me. I hope you realize that."

Zane dragged her chin up with a finger. "Hey, I thought we discussed this? No more negative talk about yourself. I don't like it."

She arched an eyebrow. "*You* don't like it? You mean I have to do what you want?"

He leaned in and gave her a swift kiss. "Unless you'd like me to spank your pretty ass, then yeah. At least in this." He felt her shudder. It turned him on instantly. "You like to be spanked?" he growled.

"I don't know," she whispered. "But I might give it a try. You wouldn't keep doing it if I didn't like it, would you?"

"I want everything we do to make you feel good. I would never do something you didn't like, Eden."

She swallowed. "Have you spanked anyone during sex before?"

Good Lord, he was hard. Just hearing those words come out of her pink lips was making him want to lay her back on this table and fuck her until she screamed his name. "A time or two," he admitted. "It brings the blood to the surface, stimulates sexual pleasure. At least according to the women who wanted it."

Eden squirmed in her seat, crossing and recrossing her legs, and then sat back and primly cut a piece of chicken. Her skin was pink and the pulse in her neck throbbed a bit faster than before.

"Maybe we should focus on dinner," she said.

"Probably should."

They ate in silence for a minute or two.

"It was nice of you to bring dinner. What do I owe you?"

"Nothing. I offered, I paid."

"Thank you. I hope you didn't go out of your way."

"I live two miles from here. I didn't go out of the way. What would you have done if I didn't bring food?"

"There's leftover pizza in the fridge. I'd have probably heated a slice or two."

"You don't have to do that. I'm close. I'll bring food if you want me to."

"That's sweet of you, but you don't have to. Some nights Mitchell orders dinner for us from GrubHub. Or Abby brings something. I promise I don't usually have to rely on leftover pizza."

"That's good. But seriously, call me if you want something. If I'm in town, I'll make it happen."

She sighed. "I don't want to learn to rely on you too much, Zane. We're getting a divorce, remember?"

"I haven't forgotten. But we can still be friends when it's over. That doesn't have to change."

She put her fork down. Her eyes didn't meet his. "I really don't know how to handle any of this. We seem to have skipped the friends phase and gone straight to married and having sex. And though I've enjoyed, uhm, that part, I'm not sure it's a good idea to keep doing it. It makes everything more complicated. If we'd started as friends, we might stay friends. But this is backward." She slanted a glance toward the wall and lowered her voice. "I'm in love with someone else, though I know I can never have him. And you've got Juliet."

Hearing that name from her lips sent ice down his spine, followed by heat. He could guess that Mitchell was on the other side of the wall. The man didn't deserve her. "I'm not in love with Juliet. That was a long time ago."

Her gaze dropped pointedly to his arm. His tattoo was hidden beneath his uniform sleeve, but he knew what she was looking at. The script he should have had erased long before now.

"For a man who claims to be over a relationship that ended eleven years ago, you sure don't seem to be in a hurry to cover her name."

Those words smarted. He got where she was coming from, though. "It's never been a priority. Plus it reminds me not to make the same mistake ever again."

"What mistake is that?"

"Believing in the permanency of love."

"Oh no," she said, her voice a raspy whisper, "you wouldn't want to do *that*."

Chapter Eleven

THE AIR BETWEEN THEM WAS CHARGED. EDEN BIT THE inside of her lip. But dammit, somebody had to say it. Why not her? He'd chosen her to marry after all. Just to get back at Juliet, but still. *Her.* So she got to call him on his bullshit.

She didn't know why she was pushing back on the friend thing, but it rubbed her the wrong way. After the way he'd made her feel when he'd been inside her, when he brought her a meal, when he told her she was beautiful and sexy, he could talk about them being friends like it was some kind of natural progression to their situation?

Not relationship. Oh, no. She couldn't call it that when they'd both been thrown into it without a thought for the consequences of their actions.

Thrown into it? More like you jumped with eyes wide open for a hot body and soulful eyes that contained more secrets than Pandora's Box.

Yeah, she had. Damn her for being stupid. The first

man to pay attention to her in ages and she'd basically thrown herself at him.

Zane closed his eyes and spread his hands on the table. He was either seeking calm or trying to justify himself in his head before he laid that crap on her.

She didn't want to hear it. The man had a damned tattoo of a woman's name. A woman who'd dumped him eleven years ago. The same woman who'd been texting him the night they'd gotten married.

He said he didn't love Juliet anymore, but there had to be something there or he wouldn't still have that tattoo. And if he did for some reason, like time or money, he damned sure wouldn't make excuses for it. He probably also wouldn't have wanted to marry a complete stranger if he didn't have feelings for Juliet. She'd been texting him, hurting him, and he'd wanted to hurt her back.

None of that made Eden feel very good about herself, no matter how many nice things he said to her. He might just be a really good liar.

Zane's eyes snapped open, the rain-gray depths piercing her to her soul. She'd poked the bear, and he was spoiling for a fight.

"You've got your own problems with love in case you weren't aware."

Her heart throbbed. He wasn't playing around, was he? "Oh, really? And what would those be?"

He leaned toward her, eyes flashing. "You claim to be in love with the man marrying your sister. And yeah, you knew him first, but you *never* did anything about it. And now you can't, which is pretty fucking convenient, isn't it? You ever think maybe you don't believe in happily ever afters either? Because if you did, you wouldn't pick someone so fucking unavailable, would you?"

Oh, the anger snapping to life inside her. She could obliterate him if fury was a lightning bolt she could shoot from her fingers. The nerve of the man!

"He wasn't unavailable *then*. And you don't choose who you love. It just happens."

"You sure he wasn't unavailable, Eden? I think he *always* was because *you've* convinced yourself you aren't worthy of him. You're plain and uninteresting and awkward, not the social dynamo your sister is. Abby is so much better than you, more competent, prettier, blah blah blah."

His words hurt. So much. Because they were *her* words thrown back at her. But she wouldn't let him see he'd scored a hit. She gritted her teeth and stared him down.

"That's bullshit," he spat, not done yet. "All bullshit. You're fucking *amazing*—and the only one who doesn't see it is *you*."

Tears flooded her eyes and clogged her throat, but she wouldn't let them fall. How dare he? How dare he say things that made her heart squeeze and panic flood her system? Because what if he was lying to her? Or what if he was wrong and she was right? She couldn't bear to start believing and then find out she'd been right all along.

"What's going on here?"

Eden swung her blurry gaze to the entry where

Mitchell stood. She swiped her eyes guiltily. Zane still looked furious.

"Nothing," Eden said.

"I heard raised voices." Mitchell closed the distance and stood above Zane, glaring down at him.

Zane didn't rise, for which she was grateful. He was bigger and definitely deadly. She'd seen him in action in Vegas. She knew what he could do even if Mitchell didn't. Not that she believed he would, but if Mitchell tried to get physical, Zane could turn the tables in a split second.

Mitchell's nostrils flared. "You'd better not even think of harming Eden, my man. I'll come down on you like a load of bricks if you do. You'll never see daylight again when I'm done with you."

Eden shot to her feet, putting a hand on Mitchell's arm. She didn't usually touch him, so it didn't even register she'd done so at first. Later, she would think about how there'd been no spark, no zing, but right now she was more focused on deescalating the situation. "Zane isn't that kind of man. We were both yelling, and I'm sorry. We're just having a disagreement."

Mitchell looked doubtful. "Eden, if you're afraid, you know I won't let this man get to you. Just say the word and I'll take care of everything."

Zane still hadn't moved. His hot gaze was on hers. Eden swallowed. She'd never had Mitchell show so much emotion on her behalf. Then again, it was because of Abby. She was his sister-in-law in all but name now. And Abby would expect him to protect her.

"I'm not afraid of him," Eden said. "Zane would

never, *ever* harm me." She might not really know him, but she knew that. Felt it all the way down in her bones. "You can't tell me you and Abby haven't had a shouting match before, right?"

She said the last part as a joke, but almost immediately regretted it. That was private information she didn't really want to know. Because she'd have to be mad at him on her sister's behalf if he said they had.

Mitchell took a deep breath, his entire body relaxing. "We might have disagreed about some things," he said diplomatically. Always the lawyer. Not saying anything that could be used against him in the court of public opinion, or in hers anyway. "If I've overstepped, I'm sorry. But I heard voices, and I was concerned."

Zane finally stood. He was at least three inches taller than Mitchell. And broader. "I apologize for interrupting your work. I'm not offended by what you thought. It was the right call to make, considering how heated we got. But I'd never lay a hand on Eden in anger. You can call my commanding officer if you ever think I've done so. I'll give you the number."

Zane snatched a pen and paper from one end of the table and wrote a name and number on it. Then he handed it to Mitchell, who stared disbelievingly at the paper and then at Zane before he accepted. He folded it and tucked it in a pocket.

"Thanks."

Zane jerked his chin in one of those nods that only men seemed to do.

"I'm going home," Mitchell said with a sigh as he turned to her. There were dark circles under his eyes, and she knew he hadn't been sleeping well. The Allen case was high profile, and the pressure was on. "You go home, and I'll see you tomorrow morning."

Eden was surprised he was quitting earlier than usual, but she thought she did an admirable job of not letting it show. "Okay. Night, Mitchell."

"G'night. Will you see her to her car?" he asked Zane.

"I will."

"Thanks."

The atmosphere cooled a few degrees after Mitchell left. Eden set her plate aside and started closing food containers. Zane grabbed the one closest to him and did the same. They worked in silence for several minutes.

"I'm sorry," she finally said. "Your tattoo is none of my business. We aren't really a couple, and you don't have to explain. If you don't want to keep up the pretense of seeing each other, I'll still go do this briefing thing for you. I can make an excuse for you on Saturday. You don't have to go to the party."

"I'm going to the party," he growled.

Eden didn't argue. She asked him if he wanted to take the leftovers, and he told her to keep them for herself. Since she hadn't had a chance to hit the grocery store yet this week, she happily accepted, tucking them into the work refrigerator for lunch tomorrow. Zane waited while she gathered her files and put them in the leather briefcase Mitchell had given her as a Christmas gift last year. Then he walked her out the door and into the parking garage.

They took the stairs up to the second floor where her

car was parked, not speaking the entire way. When they were almost to the door, tires suddenly squealed nearby, reverberating through the garage. Then there was a strange sound echoing against the concrete.

Pop, pop, pop!

Eden would have frozen in place if not for Zane. He shoved her behind him and barked at her to stay. It took her a second to realize he'd produced a weapon from somewhere on his body and he was currently pointing it at the stairwell door.

Eden's heart pumped hard as panic flooded her system. The scent of gas and rubber was overpowering. The tires still squealed, but they were farther away and growing fainter.

"What was that?"

Zane's expression was stark. "Gunfire."

"Oh God." She shivered.

"You stay here, Eden. I'm going to see what's out there."

She curled a fist into his shirt. "Don't leave me, Zane. Please. I'll call the police and—"

"Honey, I'm here, and that's kinda like the police, okay? This is my job. Let me clear the area, and I'll get you to your car."

She didn't know what that meant, but she nodded. She had to trust him. He'd taken care of her in Vegas when someone had scared her. He would do so now.

"Don't move," he said. "Stay here. I'll be back soon."

He slipped out the door on silent feet while Eden pressed her back to the wall and waited. It didn't take long before Zane was shouting her name. She launched into action, bursting through the door and running to where he perched on his knees, bending over someone on the ground. Zane's gun was on the pavement, and he had both hands on a man's chest as blood leaked over his fingers and spilled over the man's shirt and suit jacket.

Eden crashed to a halt. *Mitchell.*

"No," she whispered, her heart drumming in her ears. "No!"

"Eden," Zane snapped, yanking her from the horror in front of her. "I need you to call 911. Now!"

———

"I DON'T UNDERSTAND," Eden said numbly. "Who would want to shoot Mitchell? Why?"

Zane sat next to her in the surgical waiting room of the hospital, his elbows on his knees as he leaned forward and let his hands dangle. Hands that had been covered in Mitchell's blood not that long ago. Hands that had saved Mitchell's life by stopping the bleeding long enough for the ambulance to arrive.

Or maybe not since Mitchell was still in surgery and they didn't know if he'd make it or not. But Zane had given him a chance. The EMTs had said so.

Abby had arrived, hysterical. When she couldn't stop sobbing, Eden talked her into taking a Xanax to help calm her down. She was curled up on a small couch that sat against one wall, her tear-stained face relaxed in sleep.

"Could have been a random attack. Wrong time, wrong place. Or someone who doesn't want the William Allen case to proceed," Zane said. "Could also be someone with a vendetta over a previous case. Mitchell's probably made some enemies."

"He has, but to try and kill him?" She shook her head as tears welled. "I don't understand."

Zane wrapped her hand in his and held on. His was warm while hers was cold. She closed her other hand around the outside of his, grateful he'd been there to save Mitchell. Or at least give him a fighting chance.

They sat that way for a long while, until Eden needed to get up and move. She paced around the waiting room, wringing her hands, thinking of all the people who could potentially want Mitchell to pay for getting a defendant freed. Or for not getting them freed. The possibilities could be endless, really. Depended on how crazy someone was willing to be. How far they'd go for revenge.

Eden was determined to go back through his case files and narrow down the list of potential suspects. Surely she could eliminate a big part of his past client list simply by checking verdicts, sentences, and other facts of the cases he'd argued. It would take time, but what else could she do? She had to know. Had to help. Her sister was supposed to be getting married. This was supposed to be a happy time for her, and now it might not happen.

Eden swallowed the hard knot in her throat. *No. He'll live. He has to.*

The police had been there to ask questions, their

faces sympathetic but politely distant. They didn't have answers yet. Or, if they did, they weren't sharing them.

As the night wore on, exhaustion settled onto Eden's shoulders, weighting her down. She couldn't really sleep, but she napped in small stretches. Each time she woke, Zane was still there. Still sitting in one of the chairs, scrolling through his phone and reassuring her with his presence. He wasn't obligated to be there with her and Abby, but he stayed. She wanted him there, but she started to feel guilty. He had a job and a life of his own.

"You don't have to stay," she finally said. "It could be a long night."

"I'm staying."

"You have a job to go to—"

"I put in a leave request with my boss. He approved it."

Her heart swelled and tears pricked her eyes. "Thank you."

The double doors opened, and a doctor came through. Eden jumped to her feet and grabbed Zane's hand. He joined her, standing tall beside her. A rock that she needed.

"Shaw family?"

"I'm his fiancée." Abby had bolted up when Eden did. She'd only wakened a short while ago. She was calmer now, though Eden thought she was still in shock. The rest of the meltdown would come later. Eden reached for one of her sister's hands and held it tight. Abby squeezed back. "Mitchell's parents are on a cruise around Italy and Greece. I've sent a message, but I don't think they've gotten it yet. Is he…"

"He's still with us. Mr. Shaw is a fighter. We've got some challenges ahead, but I'm optimistic he'll make a full recovery in time."

Abby sank onto a chair. Eden's knees wobbled. Zane steadied her as the doctor told them the rest. Mitchell was weak and not out of the woods yet, but they'd removed the bullets and fragments from his chest and abdomen. He had a collapsed lung and his liver had been nicked. Recovery would take time, rest, and physical therapy, but the outlook was positive.

Abby broke down and cried while Eden put an arm around her and squeezed.

"When can I see him?"

"He's going to be in ICU for a while, but you can go sit with him. Only one visitor at a time, I'm afraid."

Abby turned to Eden, clasping both her hands. She was smiling, though her mouth shook at the corners. "I'm going to go be with him. After I see him for myself, see that he's breathing, I'll give you a chance to go in."

"Spend as much time as you need, sissy. I'll see him later."

"Are you sure? You've known him longer than I have, and I know you care about him, too."

Eden's chest tightened. But no, Abby had no idea what Eden's feelings were. If she had, she'd have never gone out with Mitchell in the first place. Eden examined that place inside, waiting for the pain, but it didn't come. Maybe she was just numb. A lot had happened in a short time.

"I'm sure. You stay with him. I'll go by your place

and get some things for you both. What do you need me to bring?"

A tear dropped down Abby's cheek. "A change of clothes would be nice. A toothbrush." She shrugged. "Whatever you can think of."

"Got it. I'll be back in a couple of hours or so."

"No, don't do that. Get some sleep first. It's been a long night, and I'm sure it'll be a long few days." Abby's eyes widened. "Oh my God, the party."

"I'm taking care of everything. I already sent an email to everyone at the office, and I'll cancel the bouncy house and magician. What else should I cancel?"

Abby looked relieved. "That's it, I think. Everyone was bringing a dish, and we were going to supply the meat for the grill. I was going to Costco tomorrow to get it. Thank you for thinking about the party. I'd completely forgotten."

"You've got enough on your mind," Eden said. "Now, go."

Abby gave her a quick hug before rushing through the doors the doctor held open. Eden let out a breath and turned. Zane was there, a hulking presence she was happy for. So much. If not for him, Mitchell might be dead. And Abby would be shattered. Eden couldn't stand that a second time.

Tears of exhaustion and relief filled her eyes. A quick frown marred Zane's face until Eden threw herself against him, wrapping her arms around his solid body, sobbing with all the pent-up emotion that'd been building inside her.

Zane squeezed her to him, holding her tight against his chest while she cried. He stroked her hair. "It's okay, Eden. Mitchell's gonna recover, and everything will go back to normal. Just takes time."

She held on tight. She didn't know what normal was for her anymore. But the aching sense of loss she usually felt whenever she thought about Mitchell didn't seem to be there now. Must be the shock. She *was* afraid of something going wrong and him dying, but that was different from the feelings she usually had.

When she was done crying, she sniffled and took a step back. Zane's uniform shirt was darker in one spot than elsewhere. How embarrassing. He didn't look irritated, though.

"Let's get you home for a while. You can sleep and shower, then we'll go to your sister's place and get her stuff."

"You don't have to do that," Eden said hoarsely. "You don't have to give up your time to ferry me around and hang out in hospitals."

"I don't have to," he told her. "But I'm going to."

Chapter Twelve

Zane had been going over the events of the evening in his mind, but he was no closer to figuring out who'd shot Mitchell or why. The man had enemies, though. Could be the Allen case, or it could be another one where he'd pissed someone off. He seemed to do that a lot, according to the things Zane had read while he waited with Eden and her sister.

It bothered him that Eden could have been hurt if she'd been walking to the car with Mitchell last night. If Zane hadn't taken dinner over and she'd left the building with Mitchell Shaw, like she'd probably done a thousand times before, she'd have been lying on that pavement too. Bleeding out. Dead.

Zane wouldn't have been there to save her. Anger coiled tight inside him. He'd fired off an email to Saint to ask for the next couple of days off. Saint approved, especially when Zane told him what'd happened. Saint knew he had a wife, same as Mendez and Ghost did, because he was Zane's team leader and had to be informed. The rest of the team didn't know yet, but Zane would tell them soon. Just had to rip off the Band-Aid and get it over with.

"You could drop me at my car," Eden said in little more than an exhausted whisper when they were pulling out of the hospital parking lot. "It's almost five in the morning, and I'm sure you'd like to get some sleep. I can drive myself home."

"There you go again, honey. Not hearing a thing I say." He tried to make a joke, but the truth was he was angry deep down. His protective instincts flared hot, and he wasn't leaving this woman's side. Someone had shot Mitchell Shaw, and until Zane knew if it was a professional hit or a random act of violence, he wasn't letting Eden out of his sight.

"Okay," she sighed. "I won't argue with you. I'm too tired."

"I know."

He glanced over at her, at the swollen eyes and the tracks of her tears, and something twisted inside. She'd sobbed her heart out, clinging to him earlier, but it was for another man. He told himself that was okay, that it didn't bother him, that he didn't want or need her to feel something for him. He was emotionally unavailable. It was better if she didn't develop feelings for him.

"How do you do it?" she asked.

"Do what?"

"You were awake every time I opened my eyes. How are you not as tired as I am?"

"I slept. Not a lot, but enough. It's part of the training."

"You can't train yourself to need less sleep. That's impossible."

"No, but when you do what I do, you figure some things out to compensate or you fail the selection process. Only the best of the best get chosen. I got chosen."

"I looked up Navy SEALs and their Army equivalent. I came up with Green Berets and Delta Force."

"Sounds right."

"Is that what the briefing is about?"

"Yes. There are things you need to know about what I do and what can happen."

She was silent for a minute. He noted that she was sliding her pendant back and forth on the chain. A nervous gesture, or maybe it helped her think. "You knew what to do when Mitchell was shot. You saved him, Zane. He would have died if you hadn't been there. I'm grateful, but I also can't get it out of my head. The blood. How you didn't hesitate. You've seen that kind of thing before."

"It's the job, babe. People get shot. You have to know what to do. We all have medical training. Not like a doctor, but enough to patch up wounds or stabilize someone long enough to get them out of the danger zone. I did what I've been trained to do."

"I don't know why, but it scares me to think of you having to do that in the course of doing your job. Most of us go to work, do what we do, and go home again. But yours… There's a chance you or someone on your team won't make it home. Yet you willingly go to work every day."

He flexed his hands on the wheel. "Some of us are wired differently. Maybe I'm an adrenaline junkie, or maybe I just believe it's worth the risk. Mostly, we get the job done and everybody comes home. But there's always a chance someone won't. A chance I won't."

She slid the pendant back and forth. "I-I think I understand why your Juliet couldn't handle your life. It's a lot to carry around in your heart."

His stomach dropped like he'd just tipped over the summit of a rollercoaster. "She bailed long before I joined SpecOps. I was a regular Army grunt back then. But you're right, it takes a special kind of person to be with someone like me. They're out there, though. All my teammates are married except me. Every one of them has found a woman who accepts the job and loves him fiercely."

Eden touched his arm. "I'm sorry she hurt you, Zane. But I have to believe she isn't worthy of your continued devotion if she couldn't be there for you before your job got dangerous. I know you said you don't love her anymore, but that tattoo tells me you're still hanging on to something about her. I hope you can find a way to let it go."

She'd touched a nerve. His first instinct was to lash out, to point out how she lived in a glass house built around impotent fantasies of Mitchell, but he buried the impulse. Instead, he went with the truth. Shocked him, but he wanted to tell her.

"My parents have always been loving and supportive of both me and my sister. But Mia is ten years younger than I am. My parents were focused on her when I was a teenager because she was still so young. They reasoned I wanted to be left alone more than she did. And I did to an extent, but when I say they were wrapped up in her life, I mean Mia got all the attention. My dad's business was doing well by then, and that meant they could afford more for her than they could when I was her age. Like trips to Disney. They didn't take me because I was sixteen and didn't want to go. I should have, but I thought I was too old for Disney shit. Juliet was my girlfriend then, and she was everything to me. She was the person who put me first when my parents didn't. That's how it felt anyway."

He frowned as he thought about that time in his life. His parents hadn't been neglectful. He'd had everything he needed. But he'd felt like he was less important, and that had touched a place deep inside that he'd needed to soothe. He'd soothed it with Juliet.

"I thought she was my ride or die for life. I thought she had my back and I had hers, that we were there for each other when nobody else was there for us. She had her own issues at home, and we clung to each other during that time. We planned to get married when we were old enough. I went into the Army thinking I was doing the best thing for us both, making money and being independent. But it didn't work out that way. She cheated on me when I was gone, and she broke up with me at Christmas when I was home on leave. I was halfway through my four year enlistment then. I'd gotten her name tattooed on my arm at my first duty station, like young soldiers do, then had the rest of the tattoo built up around it. I planned to cover it, but that takes money and time. I was resentful that I had to. And then I just... didn't."

Eden was silent. He glanced at her, shocked to see a tear slide down her cheek. She dashed it away and turned to look out the window. He waited. Finally, she spoke. "It's none of my business, and I don't know why I'm fixated on your tattoo. I'm just tired and sick at heart, and I don't understand what's going on or why someone shot Mitchell. Pushing you over a tattoo seems so much easier than thinking about those things. But I shouldn't make you explain. I'm sorry you felt you had to."

He turned into the first parking lot he found and stopped the truck. Eden's eyes were big, filled with fear. "What's wrong? What's happening?"

He swore as he shoved a hand through his hair. He was tired and not thinking as well as he should. "Nothing's wrong, Eden. I didn't mean to scare you. I wanted to look into your eyes when I said this."

She blinked.

"You listening?"

"Yes."

He took her chin gently in his thumb and forefinger. "You didn't make me do anything. I wanted to tell you. I want you to understand. Hell, maybe *I* want to understand. I've done things on autopilot for a long time, not explaining myself to anyone. I haven't had to talk about this before, so I just haven't. But, fuck, you make me want to justify myself. My reasons. You're the first person I've said any of that to, and saying it helps. I love my sister and my parents. They're all great people, and part of why Mia is so great is that she had love and opportunities along the way. I had them too, just not as many opportunities because my parents struggled more when I was little. But I know they'd have given me the moon if they could've. It's why they were so wrapped up in Mia. A chance to do everything right. You understand me?"

She nodded and dashed another tear away. It broke his heart, made him want to wrap her in his arms and not let go until the sunshine returned to her eyes.

"I shouldn't cry. You aren't upset. But I was imagining how you must have felt at Christmas when she broke up with you. How you'd put her name on your body and made plans for the two of you, thinking she was your ride or die. And then she wasn't. She let you go and married someone else, and that makes me angry and sad at the same time. You didn't deserve that, Zane."

Jesus, this woman. Zane leaned across the console and put a hand behind her head. Then he kissed her. She melted into it with a little moan, and he was suddenly rock hard. Wanting her. Aching for her. Needing to make the world disappear for a while and knowing the way to do it was tangled up with her, thrusting deep inside her, feeling every inch of his body sizzle and burn from the heat.

He thought about taking her to the backseat, getting her naked, and making her shake apart as he fucked her. It was still early morning, but the sun was coming up and the parking lot would be illuminated in the next few minutes. Besides, she'd been through enough in the past several hours. He needed to get her home and into bed, but not so he could fuck her. She needed sleep.

Zane broke the kiss with reluctance. Eden stared up at him, her lips parted, her eyes soft.

"What was that for?" she asked.

He skimmed his fingers along her jawline, into her thick red mane. "For being who you are."

He straightened, his dick throbbing with disappointment, and put the truck in gear again, pointing them toward the Chesapeake Bay Bridge. The miles faded behind them as they headed for the small town of Franklin. Eventually, the rhythmic sound of Eden's breathing told him she'd fallen asleep. Maybe when they got to her place, she'd be rested enough for an orgasm or two before he let her sleep again.

By the time he turned into her driveway, a soft rain was falling. The sun had never come out, though it was full daylight now, and the temperature had dropped a few degrees with the rainfall and cloud cover.

Eden's eyes blinked open. He could see the confusion on her face, and the moment it cleared. "I slept all the way home."

"You needed it. Come on, let's get inside. You can go back to sleep for a few hours before we return to the hospital."

She shook her head and yawned, a jaw-cracking yawn that told him she needed more rest than she'd had. As if he hadn't already known it. He got out of the truck, went around and helped her out, took her keys from her hand, and led her up the stairs to her front door. Eden swayed against him, her eyelids drooping. He inserted the key in the lock just as a small projectile *thunked* into the wood beside his head.

The sound followed, cracking in the air. Eden startled.

Fuck!

Zane twisted the lock and shoved the door open, grabbing Eden and pushing her inside. He slammed the door behind them just as another *thunk* hit. When the glass shattered, he was more than pissed that someone was shooting at them.

"Do you have a basement?"

"No."

"An interior room with no windows? Pantry, hall closet, anything?"

"Hall bath under the stairs."

"Get in it. Get down as small as you can and don't come out unless I tell you to."

She caught his sleeve as he moved away. "What's happening, Zane?"

"We're under attack. I don't know why, and I don't know who, but I intend to stop them. Get in the hall bath and dial 911, Eden. Tell them someone's shooting at your house and give them the address."

"Please, Zane—I don't want you getting hurt."

He caressed her cheek. "I'm not getting hurt, babe. This is what I do."

He slipped his Glock 19 from the Kydex holster at his back. Extended mag, of course. Plenty of ammo to fuck a motherfucker up.

"Don't move until I come for you."

Chapter Thirteen

EDEN HAD BEEN EXHAUSTED, READY TO DROP, NOT AT ALL certain she could make it upstairs to bed while she stood on the front step and waited for Zane to open the door. Between one moment and the next, she'd snapped fully awake, her body going into alert mode. Her heart pounded as adrenaline flooded her system, her hands shaking as she dug her phone from her purse and dialed 911 for the second time in several hours.

When the dispatcher answered, Eden blurted out that someone was shooting at her and she needed help.

"Ma'am, I need you to be calm. Are you in a safe place?"

"Y-yes, I think so. For now. B-but my husband. He's out there." She recited the address. "Please, I need you to hurry. I don't want him to get hurt."

"Units are on the way, ma'am. Can you stay on the phone with me?"

She didn't want to. She wanted to strain her ears to listen for gunfire, to listen for Zane's footsteps returning for her. But she didn't say any of that. She stayed on the phone, answering questions, trying to hear sirens. After what seemed like an eternity, she did. Relief melted through her like candle wax.

There was a knock on the door, followed by Zane's voice telling her it was okay. Eden dropped the phone and fumbled with the lock. Then she yanked the door open and launched herself at Zane. Vaguely, she thought that she was always doing that.

He caught her and squeezed her tight. "It's okay," he said, his breath against her ear. "He's gone."

She didn't tell him that while she was happy the gunman was gone, she was happier he was safe. It was what she cared most about right now. After seeing Mitchell's bleeding body on the parking garage floor earlier, she was more attuned to how fragile a human body was. Even badass Army dudes who weren't Navy SEALs but did the same sort of job. Zane wasn't invincible. Nobody was.

The police arrived, sirens screaming. After piling out of their cars and searching for the shooter, they returned to ask questions she didn't have answers to. She told them what she could recall about the incident and what she knew about her boss being targeted.

A cop removed the bullet from her door jamb and dropped it in an evidence bag. Soon after, Zane strode just out of earshot to talk to the sergeant who seemed to be in charge before returning to her side.

"They're going to be here a little while longer. Go grab some clothes and whatever else you need for a few days. We're going to my place."

Eden thought she should protest, but the truth was she didn't want to. She wanted to go where he went. Wanted to be near him. Zane could protect her. Not that she thought she was in any danger, not really. Whoever had taken a shot at her door could have been aiming for him. It might not have had a thing to do with Mitchell, but of course that's what everyone thought.

"Why would someone shoot at me?"

He looked angry. "I don't know. I'd hoped to catch up to the shooter, but he disappeared when he heard the sirens."

"Should I have waited to call 911?"

"No. You did what I wanted you to do. I knew there was a possibility I'd lose him, but your safety's more important. This gives us a chance to get you away from here before anyone can try again."

Eden shivered. "I've been thinking about it. All I've done lately is research on the Allen case. I don't think there's anything explosive in it, but I could be wrong. I don't know what it has to do with me, though."

Mitchell was the public face while she was a researcher. She didn't have a law degree or argue cases. She knew some of the law, but she had a lot left to learn. Nothing she'd seen about the Allen case was worth killing for. It made no sense.

"It could be another case you both worked on. Unfortunately, it doesn't need to make sense to us. Just to the person unhinged enough to target you both." He tugged her toward the stairs. "Let's get your stuff. I want you out of here ASAP."

Merlin zipped out from beneath her bed when she

went upstairs and entered her room, meowing a touch angrily. "Oh my poor baby," she cried, picking him up and cuddling him. "Did you miss Mama? Did the noisy guns scare you?"

Merlin purred and rubbed his face against her cheek. She closed her eyes and told herself not to fall apart over what might have happened. She was well. Zane was well. Merlin was incensed.

"Do you have a carrier for him?" Zane asked.

Her heart squeezed because he'd thought of it. "Yes. It's in the mudroom downstairs. I have to get his food and litter. I'll need to dump the box and wash it so we can take it."

"We'll stop and buy a new one. Litter too. Where's the food?"

"Pantry. It's in a clear plastic container with his name on it. There's some in a bag, too. I can get it when I come down."

"I'll get it and put it in the truck. We need to be out of here in about ten minutes. Can you do that?"

His urgency made a little spark of panic flare to life inside her. "Yes, I can do it." She sucked in a breath. "Zane," she said when he turned away.

"Yes?"

"You don't have to get involved if you don't want to. I can go to a hotel."

His frown was glacial. "Eden, for fuck's sake, you aren't going to a hotel. Someone shot Mitchell at your work location. Then they waited here, at your home, to do the same to you. They aren't going to stop trying. If they found you here, they'll find you at a hotel. Until this person is caught and stopped, you're not going anywhere alone. Thought I made that clear earlier."

"I… You did. I just thought maybe you wanted a way out. A week ago, I wasn't your responsibility. If you'd known what you were getting into, there's no way you'd have done it. I just wanted you to know I don't expect you to give up the life you normally lead for me."

"I'm not giving anything up. I'm doing exactly what I want to do. What I've been trained to do. So get your stuff together and let's go. Understood?"

She nodded, her eyes prickling with tears. "Yes."

"Good. Get moving, babe. I'll be back in a couple minutes."

She kissed Merlin and put him on the bed, then dragged out a suitcase and started tossing clothes inside.

ZANE PILED EDEN, her suitcase, her cat, the cat's food and toys, and himself into his truck and drove them back across the bridge. Yeah, he was tired, but like on any mission, the adrenaline and training had kicked in. He could go for a while yet before he crashed. He'd slept at the hospital in snatches. Twenty minutes here, an hour there, another thirty minutes after that. Hospitals were notoriously not great places to catch some shut eye, but he'd had his share of time spent inside them waiting for news on teammates over the years. He understood how to make the most of it.

Eden sat in the passenger seat, glassy-eyed, while the cat meowed in his carrier. Zane had never had a cat before. He'd never had a dog either, but he'd always thought of himself as more of a dog person. Pets and his lifestyle didn't go together, though.

"I'm sorry about the noise," Eden said after a particularly demanding meow. "He doesn't like riding in the carrier. He thinks he's going to the vet."

"Won't he be surprised," Zane said with a chuckle.

"He sure will. Thank you for bringing him."

"You couldn't have left him. I don't mind."

"You say that now. He's going to get the zoomies at some point, probably in the middle of the night, and you're going to ask yourself how you ended up with a cat disrupting your life."

Zane glanced at the cat in the back seat, staring forlornly ahead. "I've had worse things wake me in the middle of the night. How long have you had him?"

"Five years. He was a tiny kitten cowering in my backyard. There was no sign of a mama cat or any other kittens. I took him to the vet, researched rescue organizations to take him to, and never called any of them. He was so sweet, and I'd never had a pet before." She shrugged. "So he stayed."

"You never had a pet growing up?"

"No." She played with the pendant again. "Our mother was a bit of a germaphobe. She thought animals were dirty and carried disease. Abby and I never had any pets."

It was only the second time she'd mentioned her mother. He hadn't liked the woman the first time Eden had talked about her, and he liked her less now. He also hadn't forgotten that Abby had said Eden was her only family. He wanted to know more about that, but now didn't seem like the time to ask.

"I didn't have any pets either," he said. "My parents didn't have the money when I was a little kid, and then they didn't have the time. My sister talked them into a dog when she was nine. I was gone by then, though. They also got a couple of cats because Mia talked them into that, too. She loves animals."

"I want to get another cat, but I don't think Merlin would like it. He enjoys being the center of attention."

Merlin chose that moment to yowl his displeasure. It was loud enough and startling enough that they both laughed. Then Eden turned and started talking a stream of baby talk to the cat, assuring him he would be out soon, that he could have food, and she would hold him and pet him as long as he wanted.

Zane thought that last part sounded pretty good to him. He wouldn't mind being held and petted by Eden for as long as he wanted.

He checked his rearview as they drove, taking alternate routes, doubling back on himself a few times. A drive that should have taken forty-five minutes was going to take double that, but it was what he had to do to protect her.

The conversation eventually died, and Eden dozed off. The cat settled enough to emit a meow every so often instead of continuously. Thank God. Little fur-bag was loud as shit.

When Zane was sure nobody had followed him across the bay, he eased his way toward home. He could bug out a different direction if he spotted a tail, but there was no one. When he reached home, he circled the block a couple of times before pulling in the drive. The truck was too big to fit in the garage, so he backed it in to make escape easier if they needed it. He hoped they wouldn't, but training and experience dictated he be prepared.

He needed to call his team and apprise them of the situation. He'd informed Saint about the hit on Mitchell, but targeting Eden had taken it to a whole new level. He needed his brothers to help. Which meant telling them he'd gotten married a few days ago in Vegas. *That* was going to be fun. He'd never live it down that he'd done something so, well, *zany*.

His phone buzzed. He looked at the screen, frowning.

Juliet: *Is everything okay? You never replied last night.*

Wasn't going to now, either.

Zane pocketed the phone and woke Eden with a soft shake on her shoulder. She blinked awake, her eyes bloodshot, confusion clouding their green depths. But then she focused on him, and the confusion cleared. She gave him a soft smile that pinched his heart a little tighter than before.

"Zane."

"We're home," he told her, his throat tightening on the last word. What the hell was that about?

"Oh, good. I'd really like a shower. Maybe a snack. And a few hours' sleep." She frowned. "I have to call and make sure the bouncy house and magician got the emails, though."

"Give me the info, and I'll do it for you while you

shower." She reached for the door, but he stopped her. "I'll come around and get you. Safety protocol," he added at her puzzled look.

She waited while he got out and went around the truck. He kept an eye on their surroundings, but nothing was out of place on his quiet little street. No strange cars or delivery vans. One neighbor he recognized a few houses down with her barky little dog.

Zane opened the door. The electronic running boards dropped, and Eden stepped down. She put her hand in his when he offered. But when she stepped to the ground, she didn't quite make it. Eden yelped as she fell forward. Zane held on tight to keep her from sinking to her knees. She wrapped her free arm around his neck and swayed against him. Her body molded to his, all her soft curves pressing into him. Damn, he liked the way that felt.

"Sorry," she whispered, big green eyes staring up at him.

He didn't let go, instead letting his free hand roam from her waist to her hip, holding her firmly. "You okay?"

"Yes, fine. My knees gave out. I'm just tired is all."

Tired, probably a bit shocked, and running on empty. Zane hooked an arm behind her knees and swung her against his chest.

She squeaked as she wrapped both arms around his neck. "What are you doing?"

He carried her toward the front door. "What's it look like?"

She swiveled her head to the door and back. He

shifted her and dug out his keys, then inserted one in the lock.

"You realize what this is, right?" she asked.

"What?"

"Zane, you're about to carry me across the threshold. Maybe you should put me down and let me walk in."

He cocked his head. "Why?"

"In case you want to carry your real wife across the threshold someday." She said it like it was a thing.

Zane snorted as he unlocked the door and pushed it open with his foot. "Babe, that's some 1950s bullshit right there. I'm carrying you inside because you're dead on your feet. Then I'm getting your cat and all your stuff." He carried her inside as she held on tight. "See, no big deal," he said as he sat her down near the couch.

"You say that now, but someday when you have a big romantic wedding to a gorgeous woman who knocks your socks off, she's gonna be disappointed she wasn't the first you carried inside."

"She also wouldn't be the first wife, would she?"

Eden shook her head. The look on her face made him laugh.

"Don't worry. Not happening, babe. After this marriage, I'm never getting hitched again. I'm gonna get the cat, then you're gonna take a shower if you still want to, eat something, and fall in bed for at least six hours. We'll figure out what happens next after you wake up."

He recognized the willful look that crossed her

features. "I have to go over to Mitchell and Abby's and get some clothes for her—"

"Not happening, Eden."

Her eyes widened at the command in his voice. But he wasn't arguing with her. It was his job to take care of her, and she was going to do what she was told. Even if he had to put her in restraints to make her do it.

Oh, Jesus. There was an image he didn't need in his head. Zane shook it off and continued to stare her down until she stuck out her bottom lip in a pout.

"I promised. I can't just leave her there without support. She needs me."

"She'll understand. Abby doesn't want you in danger any more than she wants Mitchell in danger. I'll get someone else to take her some clothes."

She gave him a pleading look. "It's about more than clothes, Zane. It's having someone there for you."

"I know what it is, babe. Someone nearly killed Mitchell last night. Today, they came for you. Until I know what and who and why, you don't go anywhere near Mitchell Shaw."

Her hand went to her throat. "Oh my God—he's in a hospital bed, unconscious. What if they try again?"

Zane put his hands on her shoulders, steadying her. "The police already put an armed guard on him."

"What about Abby?"

"She's there, so she's safe. I'm gonna get in touch with my team, see what we can do. I'll make sure Abby has someone watching her back at all times."

Eden nodded, unshed tears shimmering like diamonds on her lower lashes. "Thank you."

"It's what I do, honey. Now let me go get that vicious animal of yours before he has a shit fit out there all alone."

"Oh no, we didn't stop for a box and litter!"

"We did. I ordered it for pickup while you were packing. Swung by and got it while you napped."

The relief on her face made him feel like a million bucks. "You really are too good to be true."

He walked backwards toward the door, throwing his arms wide. "That's me, hon. Just call me Mr. Perfect."

She laughed, which was what he wanted. The situation was serious, but he didn't want her in a constant state of fear and panic. That kind of thing wasn't good for anyone's mental state.

"Sit down, sugar. I'll show you where everything is when I get all your stuff inside."

"Thank you, Zane."

"Think you mean Mr. Perfect, honey."

She laughed again. "Fine. Thank you, Mr. Perfect."

He grinned and saluted. "At your service, ma'am. Don't worry about a thing. I'm gonna make sure the people you care about are safe. Promise."

"I know," she said simply.

Chapter Fourteen

Eden thought she would wilt in the shower, but the hot water worked its magic on her body, loosening tension and giving her a burst of strength that she knew wouldn't last. Long enough to make sure Merlin was settling in and to get a bit of something on her stomach, she hoped. She hadn't eaten much in the waiting room last night. Zane had gone to get sandwiches for them, but Abby's had remained untouched, and Eden had only taken a couple of bites of hers. Now her hunger was roaring back. It'd been hours since the dinner she'd shared with Zane in the break room.

That seemed a lifetime ago, but it was only sixteen hours. She knew because she'd checked her phone before getting in the shower. Sixteen hours ago, she'd been sitting with Zane and talking about spanking, her temperature skyrocketing as blood rushed to her erogenous zones.

It'd scared her, that giddy, needy, high feeling. Like sitting at the apex of a rollercoaster and waiting for the thrills when you tipped over the top. But then he'd said they could still be friends after the divorce, and she'd felt the pain of those words deep inside in a way that made her afraid her feelings were heading in directions she didn't want or need. That's when she'd opened her big mouth and said maybe they didn't need to keep seeing each other while they waited for the divorce. Then she'd accused him of still caring about Juliet.

It didn't make a lot of sense, even now. A man she'd known for less than a week, and she'd been overcome with jealousy and fear about his feelings for another woman. If that wasn't a red flag moment then she didn't know what was.

The tension had been thick enough that Mitchell noticed and came looking for the source.

Eden closed her eyes. The last time she'd spoken to Mitchell, it was to defend Zane and say goodnight. The next time she saw him, he'd been lying in a pool of blood and she'd been convinced he was dead. And now someone was taking shots at her too?

It didn't make sense.

Eden scrubbed her hair and body clean, rinsed, and turned off the shower. Then she stood for a long moment with the towel to her face, breathing deep and trying to ward off tears. She was emotional with good reason, but that didn't mean she liked it.

She dried off, studying Zane's bathroom as she did so. It was small, with white subway tiled walls and a black-and-white tiled floor. The vanity was a single sink with white cabinetry, and the shower was just a shower. No tub. Zane's towels were white, but the rug was black.

It was a very masculine room with just a few toiletries. Nothing like what Mitchell used. She knew because she'd had to order things for him a few times when he'd been slammed with a case and had no time. Since he and Abby had gotten serious, he'd never asked her again. Presumably Abby did it when he couldn't.

Eden put on a pair of lacy panties and a sports bra before tugging on yoga pants, a tank top, and zipping a fitted athletic jacket over top. She looked at herself in the mirror and frowned.

"Ridiculous," she muttered. She'd purposely picked her nicest underwear. Purposely packed fitted workout clothing—as if she worked out with any regularity—and left the baggy sweats at home. And why?

Because Zane Scott was a sexy beast, and he *might* want to get her naked again. And though she told herself it was really best if she didn't let that happen, her nether regions had other ideas. Her core ached at the mere thought. Excitement zipped along nerve pathways like a lightning strike on a power line.

She'd had fantasies about Mitchell, *before* he started dating her sister, and none had ever made her feel like a Roman candle on the verge of exploding. Zane did. She didn't want to examine that too closely, but she suspected it was everything to do with the circumstances of their meeting and impulsive marriage. She'd pretended to be someone she wasn't, and it had felt good. Zane told her she was all those things she wanted to be, but she wasn't sure she believed him. He didn't know her like she knew herself.

Eden plugged in her hair dryer and grabbed the

round brush from her bag. She studied her face in the mirror while she worked on drying her hair. Her freckles were as thick as always, marring her face with their unevenness. Zane had called them constellations. Nobody had ever said that to her before. She turned her face this way and that, studying them. They still weren't pretty, but maybe they were interesting. In a way.

When she was reasonably sure her hair was dry enough it wouldn't turn into a curly mess, she turned off the dryer and put it on the sink. She emerged from the bathroom feeling tired but refreshed. A quick text to Abby resulted in a short message that Mitchell was still unconscious but stable. Thank God. Eden didn't tell her sister about the attempt on her own life. Abby had enough to worry about.

She went downstairs, following the smell of cooking food. She found Merlin perched on a table by a window, chattering at the birds in the trees outside. She stopped to pet her kitty before continuing to the kitchen. Zane's house wasn't big, and it wasn't decorated, but it was clean and comfortable. The kitchen was a small square, but there was room for a two-person table in one corner. There were also two bar stools at the counter that faced the living room.

Zane looked up. He must have taken a quick shower in another bathroom because his hair was slicked back from his head and his chest was bare. *Bare.*

Dear God, his muscles had muscles. Not that he was huge. He wasn't. His muscles were well-defined, but not overly pumped like a bodybuilder on steroids. His skin was golden and sported a round puckered scar on his torso as well as a long, narrow scar on his left arm. The right arm was covered from shoulder to elbow in that damned tattoo.

She focused on the name. *Juliet.* The script was flowery but very readable. Too readable in her opinion.

Zane's gaze followed the direction of hers. She dragged her eyes up to his and pasted on a smile. "What's for breakfast? And aren't you worried about splatter?"

He glanced at the pan. "Nah. It's just some eggs scrambled with mushrooms, tomatoes, and cheese. No grease. Gonna make toast, too."

"Smells good. Can I get the toast?"

"Sure." He nodded toward a cabinet. "Toaster's down there. Bread's in the pantry."

She bent to get the toaster. Zane's kitchen was neat. Sparse. His pantry was ordered with military precision. Not that there was much in it. Bread, a few spices, packets of taco and chili seasoning, cereal, oatmeal, and a couple bags of chips. There was bottled water and some sports drinks on the floor.

She grabbed the bread and opened it. "Don't eat at home much, huh?"

"Not a whole lot, no. I can cook the basics. I usually pick up takeout on the way home. Might order a pizza if football's on and I'm home to watch it."

She dropped two slices in the toaster and pushed the lever. "You aren't always?"

"No. The job means I can be called away on short notice. I never get through football season without being gone for a portion of it."

She didn't like the sound of that. "Do you have a team?"

"Do you?"

"Not really. I've never understood football. What are all those first down things anyway? And then you think they have it but they don't, so they have to try again. Nope, not for me."

He laughed. "I could teach you. My team is the Arizona Cardinals."

"You're from Arizona?"

"Yeah."

"I've never been there. Never been out west until I went to Vegas."

"Look how that turned out," he drawled.

"Lost my head out there. Married some guy who promised me great sex."

"We both lost our heads," he agreed. "But the sex has been great. You can't deny that."

She really couldn't. Even now, her girl parts were thinking about what it was like to be filled by him. Pinned to the bed and taking him deep. *Oh wow...*

"I won't deny it, but we've only done it a couple of times. I'd say you got the raw end of the deal, though."

"Why do you say that?"

"Because it's been more trouble than not. Being with me, I mean."

"Honey, trouble is my middle name."

"No, it's not. Your middle name is Alastair."

"Don't remind me."

"You don't like it?"

"It's a family name. Sounds stuffy, like a guy with a tweed jacket and a pipe."

She laughed.

"And your middle name is Leigh," he said.

She didn't know why the fact he remembered her middle name made her feel warm inside. "I guess we know that much about each other then."

The toast popped up and she grabbed the slices, putting two more inside. She found the butter in his fridge—imported Irish butter, no less—and started to slather it on.

"I know a few things about you," he told her, stirring the eggs in the pan. "But not as much as I'd like."

"What do you want to know?"

"Abby said you were her only family. You mentioned your mother today, and it made me wonder if she's gone."

Eden felt that tight squeeze inside that she always got at the thought of her mother. "In a manner of speaking, yes." She dragged in a breath. "Our mother's in an institution. Her obsession with germs only scratches the surface, really. She has Lewy Body Dementia. She's been in a home for the past three years. She doesn't know who we are anymore. Or who she is."

He'd turned off the burner under the pan and came over to wrap her in his arms. She pressed her palms to his warm chest and closed her eyes. She liked the way he felt. Too much. She was really going to have to stop letting him touch her like this.

But not right now.

"I'm sorry, Eden."

"It's okay. There's nothing that can be done. Abby and I have had genetic testing, though it's not strictly a genetic disease. We don't appear to be at risk, though." That was something she'd have had to tell a potential life partner at some point if children were a consideration. She'd always been ambivalent about kids, but maybe with someone like Zane. A protector. A man who took care of those under his charge and kept them safe. She'd consider it then. Maybe.

"That's good. It must be hard, though."

She sniffed and pushed back enough to look up at him. "Maybe it should be harder, but the truth is I'm relieved I don't have to go see her. Maybe Abby is, too. I don't know. Our father left when we were five, and our mother raised us. She wasn't… motherly. She was cold. Distant. Resentful of the fact she had to give up her life for us. Her words, not mine."

He stroked her cheek as if she were precious. Why did he have to be so sympathetic? "I'm sorry."

"It's okay. I've had years to come to terms with it. Our mother was angry our father left her, and she took it out on us. Not directly, but she developed a martyr complex and let us know how much of a sacrifice she'd made every single day. She didn't like mess or chaos, and she made us suffer for any we created. She definitely preferred Abby to me, though that's not saying much. Mostly she told me I needed to be more like Abby, but she was hard on Abby too. We left home the moment we turned eighteen and we didn't look back. I worked to put myself through school, and Abby did the same. That's why I'm thirty and not a lawyer yet. Took me eight years to get through an undergraduate degree."

"But you did it."

"I went to community college classes, and I took tests for college credit. I applied for small scholarships everywhere I could find one I qualified for. Wrote a lot of essays and won some of them. Night school, online courses. I did what I had to do. It was a lot of work, but it beat spending even a minute under Loretta Hall's roof."

"Where did you grow up?"

"You mean you don't know?"

His eyes made her heart skip when they focused on her like now. Soulful. Filled with secrets she could only guess at. He'd seen a lot, this man.

"No, I don't."

"We grew up in Easton."

"Not far from where you live now."

"I never intended to go back, but Loretta got sick and I felt like I owed her. She'd spent years telling us we did, and I believed it. Abby refused to come back. To be fair, she had her own trauma she was dealing with. So I went for us both, taking care of things for Loretta, working, and going to school. I didn't live with her, because I wouldn't have survived that, but I lived near enough to check on her and make sure she had what she needed. When she couldn't be left alone anymore, she raged at me." Eden's eyes filled with hot liquid as she remembered. "Her dementia wasn't completely debilitating then, but close. She still knew who I was, and part of the particular dementia she has is strong hallucinations. She accused me of wanting her dead. Of actively trying to kill her. She told everyone who'd listen that I was poisoning her so I could get her house and sell it. The irony of course is that we did sell the house, but only so we could pay for her care."

Eden shuddered. Those were dark days she didn't like thinking about, especially since she'd been alone for most of them. She didn't resent Abby for not getting involved back then. She understood it. But that didn't change the fact she'd been the one to endure the insults and anger.

Zane tucked a lock of her hair behind her ear. His touch was gentle, and somehow exciting too. "You're the strong one, Eden. Whether or not you believe it, it's you who's got the guts, the will, the strength to see it through. You were there for your mother when she needed help, even if you'd have rather not been. You made the hard choice. You always will."

Eden blinked as emotion welled in her throat. How was it that he made her feel like a warrior woman instead of a doormat?

Before she could ask, Zane guided her until the backs of her knees collided with a chair. "Sit, honey. Let me feed you before these eggs get cold."

"The toast," she said. She hadn't finished it.

"I've got it. You want coffee?"

She nodded. There was no way in hell it'd keep her awake at this point, so she'd might as well have it. Zane fixed her a plate with steaming eggs, tomatoes, and mushrooms with two slices of buttered toast. Then he poured her a cup of coffee and set it down.

"Cream and sugar?"

"Cream."

He pulled a container of half-and-half from the fridge. "This is what I've got. If you like that flavored shit, we can get some."

"This is fine. Thank you."

He returned to the table with his own plate, piled high, and a cup of coffee. Once she put her cream in, he poured a generous amount in his cup and stirred until it was something between caramel and white.

"I like cream when I can get it," he said with a shrug. "Which I can't downrange, so I make up for it when I'm home."

Eden took a bite of eggs. "Mmm, these are good."

"Anything would be by now. It's been hours since you ate."

"Don't be modest. It's delicious. I can taste the butter and salt. I like it."

His smile was warm. "Good."

He wasn't wrong that she was starving, though. She shoveled in eggs and toast, drank coffee, and felt like a new person again. Almost as soon as she started to relax, the events of the past few hours reared in her mind and her body coiled with new tension. She had to *do* something.

"I need to go through Mitchell's past case files. I have to go to the office."

Zane's expression didn't change. "No can do, babe. Anything Mitchell is off limits for now. It's not safe."

Frustration built inside her, frothing and churning.

"If I don't go through the files, how will I find out which case is the problem?"

"Do you really think Johnston and Fife are going to let you remove Mitchell's case files from their office?"

"I don't need to remove them. I need to comb through them. I can do that there. You'll protect me."

"Not how it works, Eden. If I have to risk my neck for you, I dictate the terms. Those terms are that you stay here."

"For how long? I have a life, Zane." She felt ridiculous saying these things when he was only concerned about protecting her, but her emotions were getting the best of her. Her frustration was erupting, and she couldn't seem to stop it.

"You do now. But you won't if you don't trust me."

"I do trust you." Her throat ached. She hated that he was right, but he was. It wasn't fair to ask him to take unnecessary risks. Yet she felt so helpless sitting in his house and doing nothing. Like she was going to explode if she didn't do *something*.

"You aren't in this alone, Eden. I'm not letting whoever did this get away with it. But it's gonna take time to make it happen."

"Okay." She clasped her hands together, squeezed. "But I need to be involved. Please, Zane. I can't sit back and let you do everything. I have to have something to focus on."

"I know, honey. I'll do my best."

———

"ZANY, ZANY, ZANY," Mal said, shaking his head. "You went to Vegas and did something *incredibly* zany, didn't you?"

Zane stood with arms crossed and legs spread apart, glaring at his teammate. Yeah, he'd done the zaniest thing of his life in Vegas. He wasn't ever living it down with these guys, either. Didn't mean he had to take the ribbing, though.

Easy elbowed Mal in the ribs. "Like you aren't predisposed to zaniness yourself."

Mal snorted. "Who, me? Puh-leeze."

"Yeah, you. Wasn't it you and Corey Vance from the SEAL Team who got into that vendetta situation with Victoria Brandon? Wouldn't have happened if you weren't pranking people all the time."

"Dude, I was innocent! That was all Shade's doing. If it wasn't for him, I wouldn't have been throwing a bowl of gloppy muffin mix in the first place. Wasn't my fault Victoria got in the way."

"Sure, buddy," Jax "Gem" Stone said.

The rest of the team chimed in, ribbing Mal for a practical joke blowing up in his face. Zane had to admit he'd rather enjoyed Victoria's revenge. Especially since he hadn't gotten caught up in it. Never piss off a contract sniper, especially one with a reputation for cold, calculated decision-making and incredible patience in carrying out those decisions. She'd taken over the locker room and pelted Mal and Shade with muffin mix and paintballs. They'd then had to clean it up with toothbrushes because Mendez had had enough.

Zane's teammates perched around his living room.

He'd called Saint earlier and asked for help. The guys were due some comp time, so they'd taken off work early and arrived in a fleet of vehicles about fifteen minutes ago. He'd met them at the door and asked them to keep it down. They were doing a good job of it, too.

Eden was still asleep, and he hoped she'd stay that way for a while longer. He'd mentioned earlier he may have some teammates over because he hadn't wanted her to be surprised. If she emerged, it would be because she wanted to.

"Sometimes you gotta do the crazy thing," Zane said by way of explanation. He'd told the CO and deputy CO that he'd lost his head over Eden Hall, and that was the story he was sticking with. Nobody needed to know he'd been drunk and pissed off at his ex for jerking his chain, or that Eden was in love with the man currently fighting for his life in the ICU. To everyone else, they were a couple. She'd agreed it was best, though she was still apprehensive about having to tell her sister they'd gotten married.

Best to rip off the Band-Aid and get it done, though. He knew it for a fact because he was living it now. The wedding ring on his finger was proof. Didn't feel as odd as it had the morning after the wedding.

"You certainly did," Dean "Wolf" Garner said. Merlin the cat was currently ensconced on Wolf's lap, purring up a storm while Wolf rubbed his ears.

"What can I say? I took one look at Eden and the earth moved."

"Something moved all right," Muffin said, *sotto voce*.

The guys snorted. Zane rolled his eyes. "Fine, have a

laugh. But that's my wife you're talking about. Be careful what you say."

"Copy that," Muffin said. "When can we meet her?"

"When she wants to meet you," Zane replied. "She's been through a lot the past twenty-four hours."

"Man, you gotta let her out of bed sometime," Mal said.

Saint got to his feet and put a hand up. All attention turned to him. "All right, you've had your fun. Our boy Zany here went to Vegas for his little sister's party and came home with a souvenir none of us could have predicted. They're married, and Eden gets the same courtesy and protection that all our families get. She hasn't had the official briefing at HQ, but it seems as if circumstances have taken a turn. She's one of us now, and we're going to do what we can to keep her safe and find the motherfucker who gunned down her boss. Any questions?"

Nobody spoke. All of them knew they weren't officially sanctioned for such an operation, but that'd never stopped them before. Eden's safety was at stake, and she was one of them. Not a chance on earth they were letting her swing in the wind. HOT was a family, and Eden was its newest member.

"Okay then," Saint continued. "Let's get to work."

Chapter Fifteen

EDEN HEARD VOICES COMING FROM ZANE'S LIVING ROOM. She was upstairs in the master because he'd insisted she use it. She'd asked him to lie down with her, because she hadn't wanted to be alone, and he had. They hadn't done anything other than sleep. Not that she'd been capable of it anyway. He'd put an arm around her, and she'd turned into him, throwing a leg over his and snuggling close. She'd needed that contact so badly. It was the last thing she remembered.

She fumbled for her phone on the bedside table, goggling at the time. It was after two in the afternoon. She hadn't thought she was so exhausted, but apparently she had been. She checked for messages from Abby. There was one.

Abby: *Are you okay, sissy? Zane called to tell me what happened. OMG! Mitchell is stable, btw. Don't worry about coming back. Kate is going by the house to get clothes for me. Still haven't gotten his parents yet, but they weren't going to have good* *connectivity while traveling. Stay safe! PS: There's a cop outside Mitchell's hospital room at all times, and I'm not leaving his side.*

Eden hadn't wanted to worry Abby, but Zane had convinced her that Abby needed to know what was going on so she could be vigilant. Eden had reluctantly agreed.

Eden typed out a reply. *I'm fine. Zane won't let anything happen. He's a soldier, Ab. A good one. He saved Mitchell, and he saved me.* She hesitated as she stared at the phone. Then she figured, what did it matter? Like Zane said, you had to rip off the bandage sometime. *The picture in Vegas wasn't a lie. We really did get married. Yes, it was crazy, and no I didn't know what I was doing and neither did he. I should have told you the truth, but it's embarrassing. Anyway, I'm married, but we're working on a divorce. Still, I'm VERY glad Zane was there last night and today at my house. Must be fate that sent him my way.*

She added a shrugging emoji and sent the message, her heart thundering. She had no idea how Abby was going to take that news, but at least it was out in the open now. Her gaze landed on the wedding ring on her finger. She'd put it back on before falling asleep because Zane had said they should. It was a narrow gold band, polished to a high shine, and it looked odd on her. Like somebody else's life, really.

Eden yawned, her jaw cracking. She was groggy as hell, but she needed to force herself awake. If she fell into another sleep cycle, it'd be two more hours before she woke again, and she'd never feel right for the rest of the day. Not to mention her sleep would be jacked for days.

Eden sat up and blinked the sand out of her eyes. Then she went into the bathroom to pee, brush her teeth, and comb her hair. It was a losing proposition, so she pulled the long strands back in a ponytail and secured them. She opened the bedroom door and hesitated.

Male voices, several of them, spoke in a low hum. She couldn't tell what they said, and she couldn't find Zane's voice among them. Her heart thumped. Did she dare go down there and walk into the middle of their gathering? Or did she stay upstairs for as long as it took and wait for them to go away?

Her introverted soul wanted to stay put, but her stomach growled. And she couldn't put off meeting these men forever. Except what would they think of her? Would they stare? Oh God.

Her phone buzzed with a text.

Zane: *I hear you up there. Coming down? Or waiting for the guys to disappear?*

She sighed. *I was hoping they were leaving.*

Zane: *No chance now. They heard you moving too. I couldn't blast them out of here with a block of C4 before they get to meet you. But if you don't want to, I'll figure out a way.*

Eden: *They're here to help me, aren't they?*

Zane: *Yes.*

Eden: *Then as much as I want you to make them go away, I think I owe them more than hiding away and waiting for them to leave.*

Zane: *Do you want me to come get you?*

Eden sniffed. She thought of Zane saying that she

did the hard things when necessary, that she was strong. She wasn't going to prove him wrong now.

No, I'm coming down.

It wasn't easy to traverse those stairs, knowing that only a few steps more and she'd be in view like a debutante making a dramatic entrance. She hesitated, then dragged in a breath and went the rest of the way down.

Zane's small living room was filled with men like him. Big, muscular, tall. All of them with piercing eyes that saw more than the average man.

Eden froze. They watched her, assessing her. Her freckles, her frame that could lose a few pounds. They would find her lacking. They would know the whole thing was a sham. No way would a woman like her end up with a guy like Zane.

As if he knew the direction of her thoughts, Zane came forward and looped an arm around her waist. He put his fingers under her chin and tipped her head up, dropping a kiss on her mouth. "Breathe, honey," he whispered. Then he turned to the men and squeezed her against him. "This is my wife, Eden."

They were polite. They stood as Zane eased her forward. Each man shook her hand and introduced himself while her heart pounded and she searched for some sign they didn't approve. She committed the names to memory—both their actual name and the code name Zane said they were also called by. She was good with things like that. She wouldn't forget.

"Welcome to the family, Eden," Cade, aka Saint, said. "I know this isn't how you wanted to meet us, but we're here to help."

"Thank you," she said, her throat tight. She'd been doing the hard stuff alone for so long that she had trouble believing what he said. She hadn't leaned on Abby when she'd needed her sister most, during the worst of the ordeal with Loretta, because Abby had been dealing with the aftermath of Trevor Hagan. And then she'd found happiness with Mitchell, and Eden still hadn't told her how bad it had been trying to help their mother. Plus, Eden was carrying the burden of unrequited feelings for the man she'd loved first and could never have. She hadn't shared that with anyone except Zane.

Hot tears pricked her eyes as the lump in her throat grew. She wanted to be part of their family, even if it didn't last for long.

Zane wrapped an arm around her and hugged her close. "It's okay, Eden."

"I know. I'm just tired and emotional." She sniffed back her tears and faced the men watching her. "I'm sorry. It's been a long and difficult couple of days, and I'm at a loss as to why this is happening."

"We're going to do our best to find whoever targeted you and Mitchell Shaw," Dean, aka Wolf, said. Merlin was sitting at his feet, looking up at him with adoring eyes. The cat picked up a paw and tapped Wolf's leg. Wolf scooped Merlin up and held him in one big hand. Merlin rubbed his cheek against Wolf's chest. Eden was so surprised she forgot her tears.

"Um, how can you do that?" she asked. "You aren't the police."

The men exchanged a look. Zane chuckled. "Told

you, babe, we've got our ways." He pointed a finger at one of the men. "That right there is one of the best computer experts in the land. He can get into records, believe me."

"And the ones I can't, for practical or ethical reasons, my wife can," Sky, aka Hacker, said with a smirk. "Are Mitchell's case files digitized?"

Eden swallowed. "Um, yes. But they're restricted. You can't get in."

"I'm sure I can," he said as if it was something he did every day. "But first I can check the public case files and verdicts for the past couple of years. See if anything stands out."

That sounded reasonable. She'd been so focused on accessing the files from the inside that it hadn't occurred to her to look at the public records. There wasn't as much information there, but maybe that was a good thing. Defendants, plaintiffs. Guilty, not guilty. Sentences. It might be enough to pinpoint a case that warranted further investigation.

"If you narrow it down, I can probably get the files," she said. "So long as Zane will take me to the office."

"Might be easier," Hacker said. "We'll also dig into William Allen's background and criminal ties."

"We'll go to the office if we have to," Zane replied. "But first things first. The rest of the guys here are going to split up, check out the parking garage and your place, see if they can find anything."

"Like what?" she asked.

"Tire tracks, camera feeds, bullet casings," Saint said. "The cops are probably thorough, but this is just another crime in a list of crimes. They've already got a lot to deal with, and maybe it'll take them more time than it will us. So we'll go see what we can find. Might be nothing, but maybe we'll get lucky."

"Have to turn over a lot of stones to get the worm," Mal said.

The rest of the men looked at him. Nobody said anything.

"It's a fishing metaphor!" Mal said. "For crying out loud."

Muffin slung an arm around Mal's neck. "Dude, your metaphors don't always make sense, you know?"

"Scarlett thinks they do. Man, you guys are dense. You turn over stones to dig for worms. Jeez."

Eden sensed that his frustration was mostly playful. These men really were a family. Not actual brothers, but brothers all the same. And they were there for Zane. She benefitted from it, but it was for him.

"Or you could stop at the bait shop," Gem said with a grin. "Saves time."

"Or fish with a lure," Muffin added.

"If you people are finished?" Zane said.

"Yeah, we're finished," Mal said. "Asshats. Oops, sorry, ma'am."

He was apologizing for saying asshat? Was that adorable or what? He seemed like a goofball if the way these guys were treating him was any indication.

"I'm familiar with asshats," she said. "Run into them all the time in the criminal justice system. No need to apologize."

Mal grinned at Zane. "Way to go, Zany. I like her."

Zany? She'd missed that somehow. It made sense though. Only because of his name. He certainly wasn't zany in any sense of the word.

"All right, kids," Saint said. "I think we've got our marching orders. Let's get moving so we can get home to our families."

Zane kept an arm around her as they went to the door. They said good afternoon to the men who piled out the door and into various SUVs, sports cars, and trucks. Merlin sat in the window and meowed for his new love, and Eden had the strangest sense of belonging as she waved at the men driving away.

"That wasn't so bad, was it?" Zane asked, his mouth to her ear as they watched the cars recede down the street.

"No. I like them."

Zane tugged her back and pushed the door closed. "They liked you."

"How can you tell?"

"They made jokes in front of you. And Mal said he did. Trust me, Mal isn't known for subtlety. If he didn't like you, he wouldn't have said anything."

Eden glowed inside. "If you say so, I'll take your word for it."

They walked toward the small kitchen. Merlin had ceased his meowing and hopped up on the couch to curl up in the spot where Wolf had been sitting. Fickle cat.

"You hungry?"

She thought about it. She'd been so nervous she hadn't paid attention, but now her stomach emitted a tiny growl. "Yes."

"I don't have much here. We got back from a mission just before I went to Vegas, and I haven't had time to shop. But I know I have canned soup, some frozen dinners. Or I could order something from UberEats."

Her heart pinched at the idea he'd been on a mission right before they met. But he'd clearly survived it, so why was she anxious? "How long were you gone?"

A line appeared between his brows for a second. "Only a few days. Why?"

"Um, I don't know." She shrugged. "I just wondered. Soup is fine."

He studied her. Then he shook his head. "No, it's not. You need something better than that. I'll order from the diner down the road. They're about as close to home-cooked as you get. You have any preferences?"

"No liver and onions. Do they have meatloaf and mashed potatoes?"

He made an *are you kidding me* face. "Of course they do. This is America, isn't it?"

She couldn't help but grin. "Then I'll take that. But let me pay for it, Zane. You've already done too much."

"Nope, you're my wife, and it's my job to take care of you."

"Zane. It's the twenty-first century. Women have jobs and everything."

"Says the woman who got all worked up about the threshold and being carried over it."

He had her there. The heat of embarrassment prickled her skin. And yet it was somehow fun bantering with him about stuff that didn't really matter. Took her mind off the serious things for a little bit. "Some women care about traditions like that. I was trying to save you from a sticky situation with your next wife."

"You're sweet, honey, but there won't be a next wife. So don't worry your pretty little head about it."

She frowned, and then she laughed. "You just said that part about my pretty little head to wind me up, didn't you?"

He grinned. "You're easy to wind up."

"About some things. Thank you, Zane. For taking care of me, for distracting me, and for being willing to help. None of this is your problem, but you're getting involved anyway, and I'm more grateful than I can ever express in words."

"You don't have to thank me, Eden. But if you insist on it, all you gotta do is let me strip you naked later and lick your pussy until you scream my name."

Her stomach tightened as wetness flooded her core. He could lick her now and she'd come in two seconds flat. But she needed to show a little restraint here. Eat dinner. Call Abby. Find out more about Mitchell's condition.

Her jaw opened to reply, but nothing came out. Excitement sizzled and popped inside her. Fear followed. It would be so easy to lose herself with this man.

"I'm sorry if that was out of line," he said, frowning. "You don't owe me for helping you. You said yesterday that you didn't think sex was a good idea anymore. If you still feel that way, I won't push you. It's always your choice, Eden. But if you change your mind, I'm down for it."

She wanted to tell him to take her to bed right now and make her forget her own name. But it wasn't smart, and she needed to be smart. She had goals and plans, and she didn't have time to get distracted from any of them. She feared Zane could become a huge distraction if she wasn't careful.

"Honestly, I don't know what I want when it comes to you," she admitted. "Nothing about meeting you, marrying you or sleeping with you, has been what I thought would happen to me. I like the way you make me feel, but I fear liking it too much. I hope that makes sense."

He nodded. "Understood." He took his phone from his pocket, switching gears faster than she seemed able to do. "What else you want with that meatloaf and mashed potatoes? They've got fantastic mac and cheese, green beans, collards, creamed corn. You can choose two more. Here," he said, handing her the phone. "Take a look at the menu and pick your sides."

Eden scrolled through the options and made her choices. Once she gave the phone back, she couldn't have said what she'd picked. Compared to the emotional turmoil inside, what she ate for dinner didn't seem to matter much.

She wandered over to the couch to sit next to Merlin and pet him while Zane ordered. She was still exhausted somewhere deep in her soul, though her body felt awake enough. She lay her head back on the cushion and stared at the place where the opposite wall met the ceiling.

Her phone buzzed, startling her. Dread pooled in

her belly as she picked it up. Abby was going to chew her out for lying about being married.

"Hey," she said, submitting to the inevitable.

"S-sissy?"

Eden sat up, her stomach twisting. "What's wrong, Abby? Is Mitchell…"

Abby sniffed. "N-no. He's still in ICU. B-but Kate went to get my clothes earlier. She…"

Alarm lifted the hairs on Eden's arms. "What is it? What happened?"

"S-she's dead. Somebody shot her."

Chapter Sixteen

"I can't believe it," Eden whispered, her face pale beneath the freckles when he glanced at her. "We were together in Vegas just a few days ago."

"I'm sorry." Zane squeezed her hand. They were in his truck, speeding to the hospital. He didn't like leaving the house, but Eden needed to see her sister. He could protect her for a visit, so that's what they were doing. With a little help from his team.

She turned glassy eyes on him. "She's the one who ordered a drink at the bar so she could talk to you. Hannah dared her to do it, and she did. But then your sister came along, and Kate told us you were taken."

"I remember her. Brunette."

She'd been a little too polished for his liking. She'd looked expensive and high maintenance. Reminded him of what Juliet had become in the last couple of years he'd been with her. When he'd ceased to know her anymore. When she'd decided to leave him for a man with family connections and money. Now, she drove around their hometown in a Maserati convertible and lunched at the country club.

"She's Abby's friend more than mine, but she's nice. *Was* nice." Eden put a hand over her face. "My God, what's happening? Why would somebody target Mitchell and me, and then go after Kate? She doesn't work with us. She's a marketing manager, like Abby. It makes no sense."

Zane had been thinking about that. "She was at Mitchell's place. She might have startled someone looking for something. Maybe they came to your place looking for it, too. It might not be you they're after, but something Mitchell has. Did he give you anything to hold onto?"

Eden's eyes were wide as she met his. "No. He dropped files for the Allen case the other night when you met him, but they were all routine. He just needed me to go through them and do a comparison of information. I did that and returned them to the office. There was nothing explosive inside. Nothing worth killing for."

"Can you make note of everything you remember?"

She frowned. "To a point. Anything that's privileged information can't be shared. I'm not an attorney, but I'm bound by Mitchell's confidentiality agreement."

He didn't like it, but he understood. "Okay. Just write down what you remember. It might help us find who's doing this."

"William Allen can't be behind it, Zane. Mitchell believes in his innocence. He has a defense prepared—oh shit, we were going to jury selection on Monday. One of the other attorneys will take over the case and try to get a stay, but it probably won't be for long. Certainly not until Mitchell returns." Her brow scrunched. "Maybe that's the point. Maybe someone wants the case to proceed without him. That way Mr. Allen stands a greater chance of being found guilty."

"Who would want that?"

"His wife's family, probably. She comes from money, and he inherits her estate. So they'd benefit if he couldn't inherit. Not that I think they need the money, but maybe it's the principle of the thing."

"Why come after you though?" It was a good theory, but incapacitating or killing Mitchell should be enough. Going after Eden, killing Kate—neither of those things made sense.

Eden shook her head. "I don't know."

Zane tapped the steering wheel as he drove. He checked the rearview for a tail. He'd also been taking detours. It was habit when in protection mode. "It doesn't add up. This can't be about the Allen case. Or at least not solely about the case. Someone wants something. It's not just a matter of getting Mitchell off the case and throwing it into disarray. It's more than that."

"I fear you're right. But I have no idea what it could be. Mitchell trusts me more than anyone else at the office, but there are always things he keeps to himself."

Zane pulled into the hospital garage and found a spot where he expected he would. He'd made contact with his team before leaving the house. Saint was home with his pregnant wife, and Wolf had to take care of the baby while Haylee and her mom went early Christmas shopping.

Hacker was supposed to call as soon as he'd accessed the police report on the situation. Mal and Gem had offered to reconnoiter the parking garage in the meantime. The report had come back all clear. Still, Zane had access to his weapons if he needed them. His Glock was in a hidden holster at his side, and he had a KBAR in his boot. Wasn't supposed to go into the hospital armed, but what they didn't know wouldn't hurt them.

Mal strode across the parking deck, swiveling his head to look for anything out of the ordinary. When he reached them, Zane lowered the window.

"We've been here for twenty minutes. A bit of traffic coming and going, but nothing suspicious. Nobody hanging out in a car. We did a spot check of all the vehicles on this deck. It's about as safe as it can be," he finished.

"Thanks, man. 'Preciate it."

"No problem. You doing okay, Eden?"

She smiled, but Zane knew it was forced. She didn't like to look weak in front of anyone. "As much as can be expected. Thanks for asking."

"Sure thing. I'm sorry about your friend."

"Thank you."

"We'll do our best to get the bastard, I promise." He leaned forward and sniffed the air. "Did you bring dinner?" he directed at Zane.

"Sorry, bud, only got food for me, Eden, and her sister." He'd already ordered the food when Eden got the call, so they stopped by the diner to pick it up. He'd bought another meal for Abby when he got there. Didn't know if she'd eat it or not, but at least she'd have the choice. Cafeteria food was all right, but it didn't compare to the Eagle Diner.

Mal sighed. "That's okay. You can buy me dinner next week."

"Whatever you want, bro. You staying here to watch the vehicle while we're inside?"

"Yeah. We picked up some MickeyD's, so we're good. Text when you're exiting."

"Copy," Zane said. "Thanks, Mal. Tell Gem thanks too. I owe you both."

"Damn right. You owe me dinner from wherever you got that food from." Mal threw his hand up in a casual salute and strolled back toward the car he shared with Gem.

Zane grabbed the plastic bag with the takeout and went to help Eden out of the truck. When they reached the ICU waiting room, Abby slumped inside, looking wilted and shell-shocked. As soon as she spotted Eden, she yelped and jumped to her feet. Then she flung herself into Eden's embrace and started sobbing.

Eden held her close, stroking her hair and whispering. Zane didn't know what she said, but eventually Abby quieted and stepped back. She wiped a hand under her nose. "I'm sorry. I'm emotional and tired and, God, confused. I don't understand. Why is this happening, Eden? What has Mitchell got himself into?"

Eden pulled her sister over to a table that sat at one end of the waiting room. Then she motioned to Zane to bring the food.

"I don't know why it's happening, Ab, but Mitchell

isn't into anything except helping his clients. He didn't cause this."

Abby raked a hand through her limp hair. "I know. I'm sorry. It's just that my life—our lives—were going so well, and now this. It's like I'm cursed. Just when I think everything is perfect and I've found happiness, something goes wrong."

Eden took the Styrofoam container that Zane handed her and set it in front of Abby. She also placed a plastic bag with a fork, knife, spoon, and salt and pepper beside the container. "You need to eat, sissy. You aren't cursed. You're just tired and heartsick and bewildered. Believe me, I get it. I feel much the same, but we won't do Mitchell any good if we make ourselves sick, right? So you have to eat. Zane and I will eat with you."

Abby's eyes strayed to him, almost as if she finally realized he was there. "You two really are married. Did you know each other before last weekend?"

It was a natural question to ask but he feared it was headed in the usual direction of somehow dismissing Eden's natural appeal. "I never saw your sister before last Friday night. When I did, I knew I had to make her mine."

Eden smiled at him, and his groin tightened. Damn, she was pretty. He'd singled out one freckle in particular at the corner of her mouth. It was shaped like a tiny flower, and he wanted to kiss it.

"It's okay, Zane. I told her the truth." She swiveled back to her sister. "We were both drunk and attracted to each other, and we took it a little too far. It was meant to be a joke, I think, but it's hard to make rational decisions when you're drunk."

Abby's gaze darted between them. "And now you're getting a divorce. Why not an annulment? Wouldn't it be easier?"

Eden sighed. "It's a lot harder to get an annulment than a divorce. And though I suppose we could lie, we technically don't qualify. We've, uh, slept together. More than once."

Such a mild term for what they'd actually done. He wasn't correcting her, though. Abby got the hint. "If you're divorcing, why is he here?"

"Because I protect what's mine," Zane said before he could stop himself.

Abby's brows lifted. Eden shot him a look. "Zane is an expert in personal security. I want him here. He makes me feel safe."

Abby sighed and nodded. Then she took a bite of her food. Eden ate too, and that simple fact alone made him happy. She'd eaten well at breakfast, but that was before she'd gotten the news about Kate.

"I don't know why anyone would hurt Kate," Abby said after she'd wolfed down half the contents of the Styrofoam. Tears brimmed in her eyes, spilling over to slide down her already puffy cheeks. "She was doing me a favor. I feel like it's my fault."

"It's not your fault," Zane gritted out. "You couldn't know someone was waiting there. The fault lies squarely on the person who did this."

Abby swallowed and nodded. She looked miserable, though, and Eden put an arm around her shoulders and squeezed. "He's right, Ab. Someone wants something. Revenge, or something they think Mitchell has. That person is the one doing this. You didn't cause it."

Abby dashed a hand across her cheeks. "What you say makes sense, and yet I still feel like if I hadn't asked her to pick up my clothes, it wouldn't have happened. Why didn't I just ask her to go to Target and buy some things? I could have given her my credit card, and it's a lot closer than our house."

"I know, honey," Eden said softly. "It doesn't make sense and it never will. But it's not your fault."

Zane's phone buzzed. He could see it was Hacker, so he got up and walked into the hall to answer. "You have anything?"

"Kate was shot with a nine mil round at long range. Same bullet the police dug out of the wood at Eden's place. Mitchell was also shot with a 9 mil round, but at closer range."

"Two different weapons then."

"Looks like it. Police don't have the complete ballistics report yet."

"I'm guessing a carbine rifle for the longer range." Carbines were shorter-barreled than standard rifles and lighter. They were deadly accurate and packed the punch of a nine-millimeter round.

"Could be an AR-15 conversion. That's a popular mod, and the conversion kits are easy to get."

"Yeah. Fuck. Anything else?"

"Not really. The police have no suspects yet. There are cameras at Mitchell's place. I'm working on accessing them. The parking garage as well. And Bliss is helping with the case files."

"Thanks, man. I appreciate it." More than he could express. He'd been there for his brothers when they needed him, and he knew they were always there for him. But he'd never expected to call on them for something personal. That they stepped up without hesitation threatened to choke him up if he let it.

"I wish I had more, but that's it for the moment. If I find anything on the video, I'll give you a shout."

"Roger that. Say hi to Bliss for me."

"Will do. Over and out."

Zane stood in the hallway, breathing in the sterile scent of the hospital and thinking about the shooter. If somebody shot Kate with a long-range carbine, then they'd been lying in wait. They hadn't been looking for anything. Same thing at Eden's place. That could have been a one-off, but it was a pattern instead. Somebody wanted Mitchell dead. They'd wanted Eden dead. And Abby? Was that why they'd waited at Mitchell's?

Made the whole thing more personal. Who was so angry with Mitchell Shaw that they wanted to kill him and anyone connected to him? That was what Zane needed to find out.

His phone buzzed again, only this time it was a text from Juliet.

Are you on a mission again? Is that why you're ignoring me? I know if you are that means you won't answer. But I need to talk to you, Zane. I miss you. I've never stopped loving you. I know that now. Please call me when you get back.

Zane's teeth ground together as he stared at the

words she'd typed out. *I've never stopped loving you.* He wanted to call her and fling those words in her face. And he wanted to soak them in like a vindication. *See. See how wrong you were for leaving me?*

Except she didn't mean them. Not really. Juliet was selfish and hurting. Her marriage was breaking down and she was grasping for anything that made her feel good again. He didn't know who was at fault in the breakdown, and he realized with a jolt that he didn't care.

He couldn't tell her right now, though. He had more important stuff to worry about, and Juliet was a low priority. She thought he was unable to answer, so he planned to let her keep thinking it until he had the space and time to reply.

Then he'd tell her it was over for good. No second chances, no going back.

She'd taught him that love didn't last. It was a lesson he wasn't forgetting.

EDEN STUDIED Zane as he returned to the waiting room. She couldn't tell what was in his face, but he seemed to be contemplating something pretty intensely. He met the question in her gaze with a blank look. She didn't like it when he shut her out.

That was a shocking realization, considering they hadn't been married a week yet. Almost, though. Tomorrow, in fact. Her life had taken the strangest turn that night, and it was getting stranger still. A man had tried to assault her, might have raped or murdered her, until Zane stepped in. Now they were married, her boss had been shot, she'd been shot at, and one of Abby's friends was dead.

Nobody knew who'd done it or why, and whether or not Eden was still in danger. But Zane was her official protector now. His team was also on her side, and that gave her more comfort than she could say. If she'd had to go this alone, she'd probably be dead. Because she would have frozen at her front door with the first shot and the shooter would have found his target on the next one.

That thought made her shiver. She hugged herself and rubbed her upper arms absently. Zane lasered in on the action and shrugged out of his flannel shirt to reveal the tee beneath. Black, of course. He draped the shirt over her shoulders, and she took it with a murmured thanks, hugging it to her. She could smell him on the soft fabric, and she loved that.

Her gaze lingered on him as he picked up their trash and bagged it so he could throw it away. She loved watching the play of muscles beneath the fabric and the way his ass looked in his jeans.

"Why get a divorce?" Abby asked, pitching her voice low when Zane opened the waiting room door and went to toss the containers into the trash outside it.

Eden jerked her thoughts back from where they'd been. "Because we don't know each other? Because what we did was impulsive and crazy and not real?"

Abby looked tired and heartsick, but she also looked doubtful. "Eden, you fell into bed with a man you didn't know, married him, and fell into bed again that night when I came to your house. This isn't like you, which tells me there's something to it. Yes, I thought he was a con artist at first, but I can see he isn't now. He's attracted to you. Possessive, even, but in a good way. I don't get stalker vibes from him, and he's done so much to help since this happened. Why wouldn't you want to make a go of it? If it doesn't work, then end it. But my God, when the universe hands you a man who oozes sex appeal and seems to care about you, you say, 'Thank you, universe. I accept this gift.' Anything less is sacrilege."

Eden blinked at her practical sister. "Since when do you believe in the universe sending gifts? Coincidences, you always say."

Abby fluttered a hand. "I've been reading about the power of positivity. And I choose to believe that my thoughts create my reality. Mitchell *will* get better, and we'll stand together in the church in December and get married like we planned. If I can believe that, I can also believe you and Zane were meant to find each other in Vegas and do something completely out of character for you both. Which means there's something to it, sissy."

Eden's heart squeezed as Zane returned. "Not everything is divinely inspired," she whispered. "But yes, Mitchell will get better, and you will have the December wedding of your dreams. I believe it, too."

Abby lay back on the couch where they'd retreated after eating. Her eyes closed and she shook her head, rolling it on the cushion behind her. "Grab this chance with both hands, Eden. You may never get it again. Life is fragile. Unpredictable."

"We'll see," she said, because she knew Abby didn't want to hear anything negative. But even if Eden believed the universe had sent her a gift in Zane, he wasn't onboard with it. He was damaged, thanks to the mysterious Juliet, and he wasn't looking for a relationship ever again. He was fine with sex, and fine with being her protector, but being her ride or die for life? Nope, not happening. Which meant she had to be careful. Embrace her marriage? Hell, she'd be lucky to get out unscathed. Though she told herself she was in love with Mitchell and she'd be fine, that Zane couldn't touch her heart, there were cracks forming in the walls of that theory with every passing hour.

Abby smiled. "Good."

The door opened and a nurse came in. "Abigail Hall?"

Abby bolted to her feet, catching Eden's hand and squeezing. "Yes? Is Mitchell okay? What's wrong?"

Eden stood beside her sister, ready to support her if needed, her own heart pounding with fear and hope.

The nurse smiled. "Mr. Shaw is awake. And he's asking for you."

Chapter Seventeen

ONE WEEK AGO TODAY, ZANE HAD BEEN BOARDING A plane for Las Vegas and his little sister's twenty-first birthday celebration. He'd had absolutely no idea his life was about to change in a massive way, thanks to too much tequila and a sweet, sexy woman who didn't believe in herself as much as she should.

Now he stood in his kitchen, waiting for the coffee to brew, while his wife of a week was still in bed, sound asleep. It was six a.m., and he couldn't sleep any longer. When they'd returned from the hospital last night, she'd seemed quieter than usual, which was saying something since she was already the kind of person who didn't chatter unnecessarily. He hadn't pressed her because a lot had happened. Kate Vann was dead, Mitchell Shaw was awake but not out of the woods, and the person who'd shot them both was still out there, still dangerous. And potentially still gunning for Eden and her sister.

Until Hacker found something in the files or on the cameras from Mitchell's house or the parking garage,

Zane was keeping Eden close. She had the rest of the week off because of what'd happened, but she had to return to the office Monday and help a different attorney with the Allen case. He wasn't sure how he was going to watch over her then, because he had to go back to HOT HQ, but he'd come up with a plan that he expected her to follow for her safety.

Though, if they were lucky, the bastard would be in custody by then.

The coffee pot beeped to let him know it was ready. Zane poured a cup, added a generous amount of cream, and took the first bracing sip. Merlin sauntered into the kitchen and meowed up at him.

"What, buddy? You want food?"

The cat meowed again, so Zane went over to the pantry and took out the bag of kibble. There was still food in the bowl, but he'd learned from Eden last night that, to Merlin, seeing the bottom of the bowl in any spot, no matter how small, meant it was empty. Had to cover up that little bit of stainless steel showing at the bottom at all costs or he'd never stop bugging you.

Zane poured some food on top, jiggled the bowl to spread it evenly, and accepted Merlin's leg rub of thanks. He patted the cat's head and then Merlin dived into his breakfast, ignoring Zane from that moment on.

He'd never had a pet, as he'd told Eden, but it was kind of nice to have one around. He was discovering the benefits of cats. They didn't need to be taken outside, and they didn't need a lot of attention. This one didn't, anyway. He was affectionate, but when he had his love, he was happy to go to sleep.

Zane chuckled. The cat was kinda like most men.

There were also downsides. The litter box could be a challenge when Merlin took a dump and stank up the laundry room, but otherwise it was out of sight, out of mind. Eden had some kind of powder she sprinkled, plus she scooped it out regularly, so it wasn't that bad.

At least they always knew when the cat had done the deed because he raced out of the laundry room and down the hall like his ass was on fire. Eden said he always did it when he took a crap. It was funny as hell in Zane's opinion.

He thought about taking coffee to her, but until he heard her moving around, he wasn't going to wake her. They'd slept in the same bed last night, though they hadn't done anything but sleep. Second night they'd done that. He'd told himself he needed to go to the guest room and let her have the master, start putting that barrier between them because she already had too many things happening in her life and didn't need more, but she'd been so rattled over what'd happened to Kate that when she'd said she wanted to climb under the covers, he'd gone with her. She'd put on a pair of cream silk pajamas that clung to her ample breasts in delightful ways, but he'd managed to keep his dick from getting worked up over it.

He'd slipped under the covers beside her, and she'd snuggled into his arms like it was something they'd done every night for years instead of only a couple of days. He'd dropped his nose to her hair, inhaling the vanilla and peach scent of her.

He loved the color of her hair. It made him think

of this time of year when the trees were turning colors and pumpkins were everywhere. Growing up in Arizona, he hadn't experienced the changing of the seasons. It was something he loved about living in Maryland. Fall was his favorite season, probably because it was football season, Halloween, and Thanksgiving rolled into one.

Zane yawned and scrubbed a hand through his hair, then went into the living room and turned on the TV at a low volume so he could watch the news. There was a report about Mitchell's shooting followed by speculation on how it would affect the William Allen case. Zane listened intently for any details he didn't already know, but there was nothing. Allen was accused of hiring a hit on his wife, there was a digital trail between his cell phone and the killer's, and he was business partners with Antonio Benedetto, who had mob connections. It looked bad for Allen, and yet Eden said Mitchell believed in the man's innocence.

And Mitchell Shaw had a staggering record of convincing juries that his clients weren't guilty.

Zane thumbed his phone open and sent a text to Hacker. The reply was swift. Zane didn't think the dude ever slept.

Hacker: *Nothing stands out in the case files thus far. There's always someone unhappy with a verdict, and anybody can snap given enough pressure, but there's nothing to focus on here. Parking garage footage was tampered with. Same for Mitchell's house.*

A chill crept down his spine like a finger of dread. What the fuck?

Zane: *This is bigger than somebody snapping. It was planned.*

Hacker: *Yep. Takes effort. Somebody jammed the cameras before they committed the crime. Professional level stuff, there. I've got Bliss helping to look for connections, but nothing so far.*

Zane frowned. Professional level tampering didn't mean professional level shooting, though. Mitchell had been shot in the chest and arm. The bullet had missed his heart but done damage. A pro with military training would have double-tapped him and been done. One to the heart and one to the brain. Nobody was getting up from that.

Then there was the attempt on Eden. A wide miss to the door jamb when a pro would have tapped them both before finishing the job. He guessed mafia enforcers weren't necessarily precision shooters, though he imagined some of them were. Assuming it was the mafia who'd shot Mitchell. Maybe Benedetto didn't want his partner going free. Maybe he'd been the one to set up the hit on the wife, for whatever reason, and now he wanted William Allen to swing for it.

Zane: *Appreciate it. Need me to do anything?*

Hacker: *Yeah. Bring the ol' ball and chain over tomorrow. Impromptu team get together at my place to welcome her to the family.*

Zane's heart thumped. Not quite what he'd expected, but he was touched. He couldn't refuse on the grounds of wanting to protect Eden, either. She couldn't possibly be anywhere safer than surrounded by his team, which meant there was nothing he could do but accept. And then break it to Eden that she had to meet everyone's wives while pretending to be in love with him. No biggie.

Zane: *What time?*

Hacker: *3 p.m. Don't bring anything. We've got it covered.*

Zane: *Will do. Thanks.*

Hacker: *NP. I'll keep going through the info. If I find anything, I'll let you know. If Eden thinks of anything that might help, call or text. I'm here.*

Zane: *Thanks, man. You got it.*

Zane put the phone down with a sigh of frustration. He wasn't liking any of this, but short of using Eden as bait, how the hell were they supposed to find who was behind the shootings? Because he damned sure wasn't signing on to that proposition.

A creak upstairs told him that Eden had gotten out of bed. He listened to her walk into the bathroom. She might go back to bed and sleep some more, but he decided to take coffee up anyway. If she didn't want it, no big deal. If she did, then she could climb back in bed and drink it beneath the covers. No sense coming downstairs when it was chilly and she'd be warmer there.

He went into the kitchen to get the coffee, fixing it the way he remembered she liked. Merlin sat beside his bowl, licking his paws and wiping his face.

"Come on, bud. Let's go see your mama," he said to the cat. Amazingly enough, Merlin trotted after him soon after, then bounded up the stairs, beating him to the top. He sat and waited for Zane to hit the top step, then turned and ran through the door Zane had left ajar.

"Baby!" Eden cried. "How's Mama's kitty?"

Zane couldn't help but grin at the way she talked to that cat. Made him warm inside for some reason. He strode over and pushed the door open.

"Knock, knock," he said. "Brought you something."

Eden was holding Merlin to her chest, petting him and accepting chin butts as he rammed his head against her. It was silly to be envious of a cat, yet he was. He wanted to lay his head against her chest. Preferably when she was naked.

Eden smiled. "Coffee? Bless you."

"Get in bed and drink it there."

"Are you staying?" she asked, one eyebrow lifted in question.

The warmth in his chest was growing. "Yeah, I'm staying. You mind if I climb in there beside you?"

"Not at all." She sat Merlin on the bed and got under the covers after propping the pillows against the headboard. Zane handed her the cup, and she took it with both hands, lifting it to her nose to inhale with a sigh.

Merlin plopped himself down beside her, effectively putting his plump body between Eden and where Zane would be, but he didn't care. It was domestic as shit to get in bed with a woman and a purring cat. He set his cup on the bedside table, pushed his pillows against the headboard, and climbed in to join them.

Cozy. I could get used to this.

Zane tapped the mental brakes. Big whoa to that. It was nice and cozy now, but every day for years? Nope. And it wasn't like he'd never spent the night with a woman. He rarely did, but it wasn't completely out of character for him.

Two nights in a row without sex?

Yeah, now that was out of character for sure. He didn't spend entire nights holding someone close without some action.

Until Eden. For some reason, holding her was satisfying. He wanted more, because of course he did, but he was also content to just be with her.

"You feeling okay this morning?" he asked.

She shrugged. "Okay enough. I still can't believe Kate's gone. It's so senseless."

He'd told her last night about the ballistics. She'd taken it well enough, but he'd seen the fear in her eyes. She'd been thinking about how close she'd come to being a victim, too.

He leaned over to press a kiss to her temple. He didn't know why he felt compelled to do it. "I know, honey. I'm sorry."

"I didn't know her well. She worked with my sister, which is how I met her. She never made me feel like I didn't belong." She nibbled her bottom lip. That gesture, without fail, made his balls tighten. "I can't help but think how she'll never fall in love or get married now. Never have kids or go on bucket list trips. It's not right."

"It's not right, Eden." He sighed. "I've seen a lot in this job, and one thing you never really get used to is seeing a life cut short. All that potential, gone. All that life experience that never gets to happen. It's okay to get pissed about it. You *should* get pissed. But don't dwell on it too much. You can't fix it and you can't make it right. All you can do is live every day the best you can."

She nodded and sipped her coffee. "Thank you."

He didn't know if she was thanking him for coffee or advice, but it didn't matter. "You're welcome."

"When did you wake up? I didn't hear you leave."

"About an hour ago. Been downstairs watching the news." He didn't tell her that he was trained for stealth and she wouldn't hear him unless he wanted her to.

"Anything interesting?"

"Not really. They talked about Mitchell and the Allen case... Do you think it's possible Antonio Benedetto could want Allen convicted?"

A shadow appeared between her eyes as she frowned. "It's possible, I guess. Benedetto is supposed to be a silent partner in Mr. Allen's business, but he wanted more control over the past year. He was actively demanding it according to Mr. Allen. The business has been losing money, and Mr. Benedetto wanted to take it in a different direction."

"Is that Mitchell's defense? That William Allen's partner committed the crime in order to get him out of the way so he could take over?"

Eden shrugged. "Nothing is off the table with Mitchell. He'll use what he can to sow doubt in the jury's mind. Because a verdict is supposed to be *beyond* a reasonable doubt. Mitchell plants doubts and makes them grow."

"But if Mr. Allen is found innocent, he retains control and he inherits his wife's estate. He could shore up the business and do what he wants with it."

"I think that's about right. You think Benedetto ordered the hit on Lisa Allen? And now he wants Mitchell out of the way, and possibly me too?"

"Who knows more about Mitchell's strategy than you?"

"Nobody." Her eyes widened. "Oh wow, you mean the mafia is trying to kill me? Holy cow. I've watched *The Sopranos* and *Tulsa King*. That's bad, bad stuff."

"First of all, honey, that's Hollywood. Second, yeah, it's not good. But if that's what's going on, it's a crime with a countdown timer. It won't be necessary after the trial's over. If they want you out of the way now, it's because of what you know. You can assist another attorney with Mitchell's notes and defense. After the trial, it doesn't matter."

"Right. But I have to go to work Monday and do just that. Mr. Fife emailed this morning."

He didn't like the idea of her going anywhere near Johnston, Fife, & Shaw until this was over. "It'd be better if you didn't."

"I can't do that, Zane. We don't know for sure that's what's happening. It could still be one of Mitchell's past clients, or a victim's family who thought the client should have been found guilty. He's gotten accused murderers set free before. If someone believes that person killed their loved one and got away with it, they might concoct a revenge scheme."

Zane nodded, though his gut was telling him that scenario was too random. Benedetto was the strongest possibility yet. "That's true. It might not be Benedetto at all. But we have to act like it is because it's the best theory we have at the moment."

She stared at him over the rim of her cup. "What aren't you telling me?"

He thought about it. Should he tell her about the cameras or not? Would it worry her to the point of distraction? Or would she take it in stride?

"Spill, Zane."

Her voice was diamond edged. That did it for him. Shy, reserved woman his ass. Eden Hall knew her mind and didn't seem to have any trouble speaking it to him. She could handle what he threw at her.

"The camera footage in the parking garage and at Mitchell's place has been tampered with. That means we aren't dealing with a rando shooter here. This is someone with access and ability."

"Oh, Jesus," she breathed.

"Yeah. It's serious, Eden. Somebody planned to take Mitchell out, and probably you too. They did legwork to figure out your schedules and where you'd be, not to mention where you live. I fucked the plan by being there so that you didn't walk out with Mitchell that day. Meant they had to find you at home."

Her face had paled. "In the two years I've worked for Mitchell, I've never seen him scared of anything. He made me believe that being a defense attorney was a calling, and that so many of the people he defends are innocent and deserve a fair trial. He instilled that desire to help people into me, Zane. To think someone wants to stop him—and *me*—from doing that..."

She put a hand over her heart, her speech dying as

she crumpled her silk pajamas in her fist. Tears glistened in her eyes. Zane took her hand, brought it to his mouth, and kissed her palm.

"You're safe, Eden. You're going to get that law degree, and you're going to do whatever you want with it. You aren't letting some asshole stop you from following your dreams. I believe in you."

A tear spilled over, slipping down her cheek. He thumbed it away as she gave him a wobbly smile. "The only person who ever tells me she believes in me is my sister. Mitchell encourages me, but he never says he *believes*."

He was glad she had her sister, but he hated that she didn't have more people who believed in her ability to succeed at whatever she set her mind to. "Well, now you've got me. I'm gonna tell you, too."

"Thank you." She sucked in a breath, let it out again. "I never do impulsive things. I'm always taking the safe path. The boring path. But I'm glad I was impulsive with you. Though maybe *you* aren't glad because you didn't have all this drama happening before you met me, but I think without you, Mitchell would have died. And so would I because we'd have both been in the garage together."

The thought she might have died before he'd ever met her made his guts twist into a knot. "I don't mind the drama, Eden. I thrive on it. And being impulsive with you has been more fun than not."

"I don't know how you can say that, but I accept."

He liked seeing her smile. "Hey, do you know what today is?"

"Uh, Friday, right?"

"That's right. It's also our one-week wedding anniversary."

She arched an eyebrow. "Technically, I think it was after midnight when we tied the knot."

"Sure, but that was there, and this is here. It was *technically* Friday here."

"I don't think that's how anniversaries work, Zane."

He liked that he'd distracted her enough to banter with him. "They work however we want them to work."

She took another sip of coffee and leaned back against the headboard. "It's sweet of you to distract me, but you and I both know we aren't celebrating any anniversaries. Thanks for trying, though."

"I can think of other ways to distract you," he said, waggling his eyebrows to tease her.

She giggled, but then her teeth caught her bottom lip and her lashes dropped, shielding her eyes, and he *knew* she was thinking about it. A low-level ache started in his groin. He wanted to suck that lip. Kiss the flower-shaped freckle at the corner of her mouth. Dip his tongue inside and listen to her sighs.

"I know you can," she said softly.

"You ready for a refill?" he asked, needing to do something before he grabbed her and stripped her naked.

She smiled at him again, and his heart skipped a beat. Damn, he must have some kind of arrhythmia situation going on. He was going to have to report it and undergo medical evaluation to make sure it was nothing.

"A refill would be great. But I can go downstairs with you. You don't have to bring it up."

"Nah, you stay here. I'll bring up something to eat, too."

Her eyes widened. "Breakfast in bed? You're setting the bar really high for the next man in my life, you know," she finished with a wink.

Something dark twisted inside him at the thought of Eden with someone else. It made no sense, but it was there, nonetheless.

"Good. Never settle for half-assed, bare-minimum bullshit from a man who says he loves you. You deserve the best, Eden. Never forget it."

Chapter Eighteen

After breakfast and a shower, Eden dressed and went downstairs. Zane was cleaning up the kitchen when she found him. He looked up, frowning at whatever he saw on her face.

"What's wrong? Is it Mitchell?"

She shook her head, her heart pounding. "He's fine. It's not that." Her gaze skittered around the room as she tried to collect her thoughts. "I just... I keep thinking about what you said about the cameras, and the fact I'd have been dead if you hadn't been there to s-save me. The fact somebody *still* wants to kill me—"

She put a hand to her mouth and pressed, trying to hold the tears in. Why was she on the verge of tears anyway? It made her feel weak, and the last thing she wanted was to be weak. Especially in front of Zane.

He walked over and tugged her into his arms, pressing her face to his chest with a palm on the back of her head. His other hand settled on her hip, holding her in a way that felt dominant, possessive.

Eden closed her eyes and breathed in the scent of him. It gave her a chance to find her center again. To tell herself she was overreacting and everything would work out. His team would find the person responsible. Mitchell would recover. Kate was gone, her life cut short, but somebody *would* pay for her death.

Eden repeated it until she started to believe. Her senses focused on Zane, on how solid he was, how real. She loved the way he held her. How safe she felt in his arms. Sure, it might be a false sense of security. There were ways to get past a man like him, but she thought it unlikely someone would. She hoped she was right.

She skimmed her palms over his abs, the firmness of his pecs, loving the feel of him. She had to get out of her head. Had to stop thinking and start feeling.

She wanted to feel the heat of him. How strong he was. How perfectly honed his body was. When he eventually made a strangled sound, she snapped her gaze to his, the fog of her thoughts clearing for a moment.

"I'll hold you as long as you need me to," he said, his voice rough, "but if you don't stop touching me like that, I'm going to want a lot more."

Her heart throbbed, excitement prickling to life inside her. Her brain tried to tell her she needed to ease back on the throttle with this man, but her body wanted no part of braking. Today was what they had. Tomorrow was never promised.

She skimmed a hand over his thick cock where it lay in his jeans, molding the shape of it. So big and hard. "You mean like that?" she asked.

His forehead dropped to hers, his breathing a little

shallower than before. "Like that, yes. But more than that, too."

She swallowed. "Then show me. Please show me."

Part of her felt guilty for wanting him after everything that'd happened to the people in her life. But another part of her needed this physical connection with another human being to feel like she was still alive. He'd said he could distract her, and she desperately needed distracting.

He walked her backward into the counter, then fused his mouth to hers, thrusting his tongue between her lips. Eden threw her arms around his neck and moaned as he framed her rib cage between his big hands and pressed the ridge of his cock against her mound. He rode her there, trapped between him and the counter, until the sparks behind her eyes were a fireworks show and she was ready to explode with the final masterpiece.

Before she could, he stepped back and dragged her shirt over her head. Then he pushed her jeans and panties down until she was naked in his kitchen. The blinds were open, but his backyard was surrounded by trees. Nobody could watch from there.

Eden squeaked as he picked her up and set her on the counter. Then he dropped to his knees and spread her legs apart. Eden's heart thrummed a hard beat as she gazed down at his dark head between her legs. He inhaled her, which she thought she should find embarrassing but somehow found erotic instead.

"Beautiful," he murmured before he licked into the heart of her. Eden arched her back and thrust her pelvis toward his mouth, her eyes closing as she bit back a moan. She wanted the moment to last, but she didn't think it was going to. Zane lapped at her clit until she was making animal noises, begging him to finish. Instead, he thrust two fingers inside her and moved them in and out in a way designed to make her beg.

"Zane," she breathed. "More."

"More what, beautiful?" he asked, his breath hot against her slick flesh. "More of this?"

He spread her folds with his thumb and forefinger, then ran the flat of his tongue up and down over her clit faster than before. She was ready to blow when he backed away and moved those lazy fingers in and out again.

Her eyes snapped open, and she glared at him. He was driving her mad on purpose. "You're a terrible person," she told him as he gazed up at her with hot eyes. "Terrible."

"Terribly good," he said, sucking her clit into his mouth and tugging just enough to make her see stars.

"Oh my God," she gasped, her legs beginning to quake. "Don't stop. Please don't stop."

He stopped.

"Zane!" She was going to come unglued, and not in the way she most wanted. "What the hell are you doing?"

"Building excitement."

"Any more excitement and I'll have a heart attack."

"You can take it, Eden. All of it." The way he said that last bit had her insides turning liquid again. Any wetter and she'd need another shower.

What was happening to her? How had she gone from an awkward, self-doubting woman who thought she wasn't attractive enough to someone who sat on man's kitchen counter in broad daylight, naked as the day she was born, ready to beg him to fuck her?

"I can take it. I want it, Zane. Give it to me."

He bent to her pussy again, swiped his tongue from bottom to top, then crawled his way up her body. She hooked her fingers into the hem of his shirt and dragged it off so she could touch his torso.

He kept his jeans on, but she unbuttoned the top button to reveal more of his flat abdomen. His dick strained against the zipper, the crown peeking over the top of his underwear. She wanted to wrap her lips around it and suck him, but he wasn't about to give her a chance. He unhooked her bra and dropped it somewhere, then dragged his tongue over her aching nipple, sucking it into his mouth until hot, sweet pleasure spiked deep in her core.

"What do you want, Eden?" he whispered against her skin as he worked his way up her neck to her earlobe. "You want my cock inside you? Or would you rather come on my tongue? Maybe you want me to spank you first…"

Eden's nipples tightened. Her pussy ached. The idea of being spanked… could she do it? Did she really want to? Mousy Eden wouldn't dare. But brave, bold Eden? She thought of Abby in the hospital last night, telling her to grab her chance with both hands. That she may never get another opportunity. She hadn't been talking about *this*, but it was the same thing, really.

"Spank me," she whispered.

He lifted his head. "You sure about that, babe?"

She skimmed her palms up his flat abdomen, over his chest. "Mmm, yes. I want to try. If I don't like it, you'll stop."

He nodded. "Always."

Excitement crested inside her as he helped her down and turned her so her arms were on the counter while he freed his cock from his jeans. When he licked her pussy from behind, she gasped. Then he was there, his dick sliding between her wet folds until she groaned at the fullness of it.

"This ass is fucking perfect," he said, caressing the roundness of her cheeks.

"It's a little too big." More than a little in her opinion, but she wasn't saying—

A sharp slap stung her skin. She gasped in surprise. Her first instinct was to tell him no fucking way was she doing this. But then he slapped her again, another short, sharp sting across her other cheek.

"No disparaging this ass, Eden. It's mine. Another word and I'll spank you again."

She felt the heat, the blooming of it across her skin—and the corresponding arousal as her sex grew more sensitive. Zane started to move deep inside her, and everything felt sharper than before.

"It's not yours," she said. "It's mine."

Smack, smack.

Eden yelped, but again the heat and sensation blooming through her body was arousing.

"Mine," she said just to taunt him. To make him do it again.

Smack, smack, smack, smack.

"Oh my God," she groaned as her skin flamed. He moved inside her, driving her toward the summit, her entire body on fire with a mixture of pleasure and heat. She'd never had sex like this before. It wasn't just her body involved.

It was her emotions, her mind. Every atom of her felt alive. It was like finding out you'd been sleepwalking and then waking up to discover nothing was the way you'd thought it was during your dream. Colors were brighter. Sounds sharper. Scents a thousand times more potent.

She was close to implosion when he withdrew. Her strangled cry became something else when he lifted her onto the counter, sliding so deep inside she felt him to her soul. "I have to see your face when you come," he growled.

The burning of her cheeks was cooled instantly by the cold countertop, but the arousal was still there. She wrapped her legs around him as their mouths met again. His kiss was ravenous, but he moved inside her with a tenderness that hadn't been there moments ago. "Are you okay? Did I spank you too hard?"

She loved that he was concerned. "No, I liked it."

He ran a hand down her side, over her breasts, caressing her so softly she wanted to weep. His touch raised goosebumps, and she shivered.

"Mmm," he said, dropping his mouth to her neck, moving his hips in a slower, more sensual rhythm than before. "So fucking sexy. I love the way you feel wrapped around me. Like my own personal Eden."

Her heart squeezed painfully. For a moment, she'd thought he said something else. Something, it shocked her to realize, that she wanted to hear.

But he loved the way she *felt*. He did not love *her*. And he never would. She'd been telling herself she didn't care, but it hit her suddenly that she did.

In that moment, Eden hated the mysterious Juliet more than she'd ever hated anyone in her life. Because of her, Zane was damaged and unwilling to risk his heart ever again. Which was a shame because he was a good man. A decent man. He deserved more than a life without love.

She closed her eyes tight, trying to stop the flood of emotions she didn't want or need. *No, she was fine! She loved Mitchell. Mitchell!*

Not Zane. Never him. He was temporary. Only temporary.

"I need you to fuck me hard and fast," she blurted because she needed him to lose control, to stop being tender with her. She needed his animal side to make her stop feeling everything but the physical connection between them. She didn't want to feel emotion. She couldn't handle it.

Raw, physical attraction. That's what she wanted.

He frowned at her for a moment as if confused. But then he lifted her off the counter and took her to the living room, never breaking the connection between them. He dropped them onto the couch and did as she asked until she flew apart, wave after wave of ecstasy crashing through her, splintering her into pieces that couldn't think about anything. Certainly not about love.

That was what she wanted. What she understood. *Fucking.* It was great sex, but it was still only sex. Eden closed her eyes and floated back to earth, pushing her chaotic feelings into a box, squashing them. She was satisfied, happy.

It still didn't feel right, though.

When she opened her eyes, Zane was on the other end of the couch, leaning back against a cushion. He had an arm flung across his eyes and his breathing was as steady as if he'd been on a leisurely stroll through a park. She let herself admire the perfection of his body, the sheen of perspiration glistening on honed muscles. And then, because she couldn't stop herself, she looked at the tattoo, at Juliet's name, and a fresh wave of despair filled her.

He moved his arm and met her gaze. There was something in the depths of his rain-gray eyes she couldn't quite decipher. Disappointment maybe. Or maybe she was imagining it. What did he have to be disappointed about? He'd come inside her only moments ago, his body clenching and trembling, her name a groan on his lips.

"What was that about?" he asked, cutting straight to the chase.

Eden tried to hide the quaking deep inside. It was getting stronger. She wanted to run, hide, but that was ridiculous. "I-I wanted it that way. It felt right."

He studied her. "Seemed like you were with me and

then you weren't. Was it the spanking? I told you to say something if you didn't like it."

Remorse flooded her as she sat up and hugged her knees. She couldn't let him think he'd hurt her, or that she was afraid. "I did like it, Zane. I really did. I just…"

She dropped her chin until her hair fell across her cheek, curtaining her face so she could say the next part. Hiding from him? Not very brave, and yet she couldn't look at him as she spoke. "It was intense. Everything, I mean. I-I needed to get out of my head. Needed to remember that this isn't a relationship, that I love someone else. It's meaningless sex, that's all."

He was so quiet that she finally had to look at him and see if he'd heard her. He was frowning. "Got it. Thanks for telling me."

That was it? Just like that?

He got to his feet and headed into the kitchen. When he returned, he'd tugged his jeans on and he had her clothes, too. He handed her a kitchen towel for cleanup.

"I'm gonna go to the downstairs bath and take a quick shower. You can have the master if you want."

"Um, sure, that'd be great."

"Cool." He frowned again and she thought he might say something else. But he didn't. He strode down the hall. A door shut behind him.

Tears flared in Eden's eyes, her throat knotting up. She'd just had the most exciting sexual experience of her life. Instead of feeling exhilarated, she felt terrible. She'd messed up, and Zane was angry. Or was he hurt?

A chilled shuddered through her. Surely he wasn't

hurt by what she'd said. Zane didn't have feelings for her. But he *did* have feelings, and she'd quite possibly trampled them when she'd told him that sex with him was meaningless.

She dropped her head in her hands, groaning. She'd implied he was just a body, a means to an end. Reminded him she loved someone else. If he'd said any of those things to her after earth-shaking sex, she'd have felt worthless and used.

She'd screwed up. Big time. She hadn't wanted to feel emotion, but her emotions were in chaos. It was worse, not better. Because she realized with all the clarity of a thunderclap that she didn't love Mitchell. Maybe she never had. Maybe it was just an infatuation that had gone nowhere. Or maybe Zane was right, and it'd always been about Mitchell's unavailability.

Love was based on more than infatuation. Love happened when you found someone who believed in you and saw all the good parts of you that others didn't see. Someone who defended you when they didn't have to and got pissed when other people disparaged you in any way.

Someone who made you breakfast in bed, took care of your cat, and made you see stars when you were naked together.

Someone like Zane.

Eden squeezed her eyes shut. She was in so much trouble.

MEANINGLESS SEX.

It's what he wanted, so why did those words coming out of Eden's mouth bother him so much? That's what he couldn't figure out. Zane stood beneath the spray in the shower with the water turned up as hot as he could stand it and thought about everything that'd happened since the first moment he'd seen her sitting across the club in Vegas.

She'd intrigued him, with her mass of russet curls and constellation of freckles, her sparkling jade green eyes, and that lush body he'd watched moving on the dance floor. He hadn't known then that he'd end the night married to her, or that he'd be standing here a week later, wondering how she'd gotten under his skin.

There was no doubt she had. From the beginning, he'd known she was in love with Mitchell Shaw, but to hear her say it after he'd made her come apart so spectacularly—*fuck*.

It'd jabbed that wound deep inside that Juliet had left. He didn't love Juliet, and he didn't love Eden, but *something* was happening. Something that pissed him off and made him want to head to the gym and hit the punching bag until he couldn't hit it a single time more.

He was starting to feel things he shouldn't. That much was clear. Not love. He was too scarred for that. But he liked Eden, liked being with her. He liked that damn cat of hers, and he liked climbing into bed with her and drinking coffee. Hell, he even liked sleeping beside her all night, her occasional snores, the way she threw her leg over him and burrowed into his side.

Merlin slept on her pillow sometimes. Once, Zane

had awakened with the cat between his knees. Damn them both for making him *enjoy* their company.

He stuck his head beneath the spray and let it rain down on him until he had to take a breath. He twisted the taps and grabbed a towel. When he caught sight of his reflection in the glass, he looked pissed. Haunted? Maybe. Juliet's influence, no doubt.

He wrapped the towel around his waist and grabbed his phone from the counter.

Zane: *I don't love you anymore, Juliet. Sorry. You fucked me up, you know that? Fucked up my belief in love and my desire to have any relationships based on anything but meaningless sex. Because I never believe they'll last.*

He blew out a breath. There was that fucking word again. Meaningless. Then he kept typing.

Sorry your marriage is a disaster, but trying to rewind the past isn't going to work. You chose Daniel. You chose to give up on everything we'd ever had for a shot at the country club set. I can't buy you fucking Hermes purses, and the only thing about it that pisses me off is that I even know what the fuck a Hermes purse is. Thanks to Mia, who said you sure seemed proud of yours when you were flashing it around town after you married Daniel. Stay with him. Or divorce him. I don't fucking care. What you do doesn't affect me. I want a good life for you. I want one for me too. But it's not together. Not anymore. Take care, J. I loved you a long time ago, but that's done. I'm blocking your number. Don't text me again.

Zane's thumb hovered over the send arrow. It was a huge fucking block of text. The kind his mother sent because she wanted to tell him everything in one go. He always laughed and groaned when one of those suckers came in, but he read the whole thing. His dad was all about the phone calls. Mia texted in the kind of Gen-Z emoji-laden shorthand that made him roll his eyes sometimes.

But thinking about his family wasn't getting this done. Texting Juliet the truth was the right thing to do. He had to cut the cord between them. Had to put her back in the past and leave her there. He pressed send and then went to his settings to block her number.

He looked at his reflection again. He didn't look any different. Didn't look relieved or like a weight had been lifted. He looked weary. But inside, where it counted, there was a spark of something that felt very much like relief.

Chapter Nineteen

Eden was a ball of nerves. Zane had just pulled up on the street outside of a gorgeous house in Georgetown, which meant they were about to go inside. Her heart hammered and her armpits were damp. He'd told her this morning they were expected at his teammate's house today. He'd also told her she had no choice. She hadn't argued.

Since yesterday morning, they'd been polite to each other, but they hadn't talked the way they usually did. After Zane had showered, he'd gone outside into the yard to blow leaves into piles. He'd stuffed them into yard waste bags and carried them to the street. He'd also trimmed bushes and carried the cut limbs to the street, too. In short, he'd spent most of the day outside, working in the yard. When she'd asked if she could help, he'd said he was good.

So she'd hung out inside, working on email and texting with Abby. She'd hoped she could use Abby as an excuse to get out of going today, but Abby thought it was a fantastic idea and told her to have fun. Mitchell was improving, the cops were sticking close, and Abby was basically living in a hotel near the hospital with a police guard when she wasn't with Mitchell.

When Eden had finished her email, she watched some videos on YouTube where people had moved to France and renovated chateaus. Not that she wanted a chateau or to move to France, but it was fascinating how people could risk their entire savings on a crumbling old ruin and turn it into something amazing.

Something she wasn't good at was picking up broken pieces and making them better than new. Her life was an example of that. Especially now.

After dinner, Zane had fallen asleep on the couch watching a movie. She hadn't known what to do so she'd stayed until she fell asleep, too. When she woke this morning, she'd been in his bed. Alone. He'd carried her up there, but had he stayed? She didn't know and she couldn't ask.

"They think we're in love," he said now, slicing through her thoughts. His hands rested on the steering wheel. He didn't look at her. "I think if we hold hands and don't act awkward, nobody will think twice about that. Can you manage it?"

Her stomach was a knot. "I can. Can you?"

He nodded. "No problem. You ready?"

"No, but I'll never be ready."

His gaze softened as he finally looked at her. "You'll be fine, Eden. You're every bit as interesting and dynamic as your sister. Don't forget that. You charmed the fuck out of me in Vegas. And you charmed my team. Their women like you already. You can't fuck this up. Trust me."

She swallowed and nodded. He came around to open the door for her, which she'd learned to let him do. Then they walked to the house holding hands, and her skin felt like it was on fire. It was agony to be touched by him and not be alone together.

She wanted to tell him she was sorry, to explain, but the words wouldn't come. She was tongue-tied in a way she'd never been with him. She'd been trying since yesterday.

She knew what it was. The moment she'd realized she had feelings—real feelings—she'd lost the ability to be at ease with him. It was like all those times when she'd sat across a table from Mitchell and wondered what to say, how to make him interested in her.

Except it was a hundred times worse because this was Zane. She'd already been as intimate with him as it was possible to be. She knew him, knew how he felt about relationships, and she didn't know how to talk to him anymore.

Worse, her heart throbbed with feelings that she hadn't been prepared to deal with. When Mitchell had met Abby, he'd fallen hard. Abby said it was mutual, but she'd been the one who was reserved. Damaged. Still, it hadn't taken long for her to open herself to Mitchell.

Eden didn't know if she knew what love was, but the thought of Zane not being in her life physically hurt. She was going to have to get used to it, though. They were getting a divorce. Even if they were together right now, it wasn't going to last. Whoever'd shot Mitchell and killed Kate would be caught and life would go back to normal.

She had to believe that. Because if they weren't caught, would she ever feel safe again?

The door opened before Zane could ring the bell. Sky Kelley stood in the entry looking tall and handsome. At his side was a gorgeous woman in black leather leggings, booties, and a rust-colored oversized sweater. Her dark hair fell down her back in waves, and her face was striking.

Eden felt huge and awkward compared to her. She'd worn a soft green V-neck sweater and a pair of flared-leg jeans with black booties that helped even out her proportions. She thought she looked nice—until now.

"Hi!" the woman said, offering her a hand to shake. "I'm Bliss, Sky's wife. It's so nice to meet you, Eden."

Eden murmured her hello, her throat constricting. She was going to have to get over this crap if she ever hoped to be a defense attorney. She cleared her throat and tried again. "Thank you for having me in your home."

Bliss smiled and nodded as Sky said, "Welcome, guys. Come on in. Everyone's here."

Zane squeezed her hand, grounding her. She was grateful to him for it. They walked into a big kitchen that opened onto a living room with wooden beams overhead. The men she'd met a couple of days ago were all there, but now there were women and children too. The kids were playing a board game in the living room, except for the baby that Wolf held, and didn't look up at their entrance. But everyone else smiled, introducing themselves as they welcomed her and Zane.

There were dishes of food on the kitchen island and a cake. A white cake with a couple on top. *Oh no....*

"Said it before, but welcome to the HOT family, Eden," Cade Rodgers said. "We know you don't know what that is yet, but you'll learn soon enough. What it means, though, is we have your back." He glanced at the people standing around the kitchen. "Things are scary for you right now, but we wanted to have this gathering to show you we're happy you've joined us, maybe help you relax a little. We know you didn't have a wedding reception in Vegas, so we thought we'd throw you a small one here."

Zane looped an arm casually around her shoulders. Her skin prickled with awareness. She wondered what he was thinking, but he seemed cool about the fact his team was throwing him a wedding reception.

"Thanks for this," he said. "Eden and I both appreciate it." He dropped a kiss to her temple, and she found herself wishing he would linger, kiss her again. "Eden's a little shy, but once she gets comfortable, she'll talk your ear off."

Eden blinked up at him. Then she pushed him playfully. It felt right to do so. "I *am* a little overwhelmed with meeting you all," she said, turning her gaze to the watching eyes. "But thank you so much. It's very thoughtful, and I'm honored. I also promise I won't talk your ear off."

"You gotta tell us," Mal said. "Why did you marry this guy anyway? You could do so much better."

Eden felt her eyes bugging out. The woman with Mal—Scarlett—rolled her eyes and hip-checked him. "You have to excuse Mal. He has no filter."

Everyone else laughed and chimed in to agree about Mal. Zane still had his arm looped around her. It felt nice. Comforting. She could almost pretend they really were a couple celebrating their recent wedding.

"She could do better," Zane said. "But she chose me. Now she's stuck."

Eden glanced up at him. Nobody was going to believe that statement, but it was a sweet thing to say. Even if it wasn't real.

"Still don't get how you got her to marry you so fast," Mal said, swiping a chip from a bowl. "I mean you're not nearly as charming as I am, and it took me a few weeks to get Scarlett to fall for me."

Zane snorted. "Dude, maybe you aren't as charming as you think you are." He glanced down at her. "Not sure how it happened, but I saw her across the room and I just knew."

Eden's heart hammered. "It was the same for me," she said, backing him up. "I just knew. Maybe getting married was crazy, maybe we should have waited, but we didn't. It felt right."

His eyes were intense on hers. She felt the heat of that gaze in her bones, her core. Her body softened with the beginnings of arousal. If they were alone, that look of his would have her on her knees, unzipping his pants and freeing his cock so she could take him in her mouth.

"Who's getting hungry?" Sky said. "Need to get these steaks and shrimps on the grill."

There was a chorus of people claiming they were starving. Zane took a deep breath before they broke apart. Then he went to help with the grill. In fact, all the guys paraded outside into the cool afternoon air together, carrying their drinks.

Brooke, the petite blonde with the baby bump, shook her head and laughed. "How many men does it take to operate a grill?"

Haylee, a gorgeous golden-skinned woman with long black hair, deadpanned, "All of them. One to actually cook and the rest to discuss their own grills and point out how they'd be flipping those steaks when the time comes."

The women laughed. Eden joined in, though she still felt awkward with this group. They were clearly friends, and they knew each other well. They were at ease together. She was used to being the outsider in gatherings like this. Abby had a lot of friends. When she hosted girl's nights, Eden was always invited, same as Vegas. She went along sometimes, and though the women were nice to her, she didn't feel like she was really a part of whatever it was that brought them together.

She wasn't a part of this group either, no matter how much she might want to be. Because there was a timeline on her relationship with Zane Scott, and the clock was ticking down. She didn't need to get invested in these people or let them be invested in her when she'd be gone again in a couple of months.

Alaina came over and stood beside her as the other women worked at putting dishes in the oven, taking others out of the refrigerator, and arranging them on the island.

"I know how you feel," she said, offering Eden a glass of white wine.

Eden accepted. "Thank you."

"You're overwhelmed and thinking you don't fit in, that everyone's just being nice to you." She took a sip of her drink. "I was you just a few months ago. I was new and didn't feel like I really belonged. I had a kid." She nodded to the little boy who'd left the game and gone outside to be with the men. He was standing in clear view, his stance mimicking that of the man he stood next to. His stepdad, Eden assumed. "But they welcomed us both with open arms. I married Ryder this summer, and he's been the best dad to Everett. Slowly, I started to feel like I was part of this family. I sometimes still get that jolt of not belonging, because it's part of who I was for so long, but then I tell myself I'm wrong and I get on with it."

Eden was clutching her wine glass, her pulse skipping along. She took a sip to help steady her nerves. "Thank you for telling me. I-I'm a bit of an introvert. I never know what to say when I meet new people, beyond the usual platitudes about being happy to meet everyone. I get anxious about saying the wrong thing or looking awkward. Which probably makes me *more* awkward."

"You're with friends here. Really. We're a pretty exclusive club, married to the men we're married to, and though we aren't the ones strapping on guns and going into danger, we know the special hell of waiting at home for our husbands to come back safe." She stopped talking, then frowned and shook her head. "I'm sorry, I shouldn't have said that. You've only just married Zane and he hasn't had to go on a mission yet. It's like a business trip, only you don't hear from him every day. Then you do, and you're happy."

Fear sat heavy in her belly. She knew what Zane did was dangerous, but she hadn't expected to be a part of his life the next time he had to go away. They'd have still been married, but beyond communicating when there were updates about the divorce, she hadn't thought they'd be in contact at all.

Then he'd turned up and told her he wanted to embrace their fake marriage, at least until they got that divorce, and here she was. Entangled in something she hadn't intended, lying to these good people, and pretending to be one of them. Well, she wasn't one of them, and she wasn't going to be, no matter how sweet Alaina was to her or how welcoming they all were.

Still, she could pretend. She had to pretend for Zane's sake since his job depended on truth.

The other women started to include her and Alaina in the conversation, asking questions and sharing stories of their own. Before Eden knew it she was chatting freely about her job and her dream to go to law school. Everly was a lawyer who worked on Capitol Hill for a group that advocated for laws affecting the elderly. She had also worked for her mother, a Congresswoman who'd resigned her seat not long ago, and Eden was fascinated by all the things she'd been involved in.

Jenna was planning to go to law school next fall. She,

Everly, and Eden spent time talking about the challenges and benefits. They discussed schools, how much work there'd be, and the timeline for getting through school and taking the bar.

It was going to be hard work, but Eden loved an intellectual challenge above all others. She was most comfortable when she was researching case law and learning new things. She sometimes worried how she would handle arguing cases before a jury, but she loved the research enough that she knew she'd be prepared when the time came.

After an afternoon surrounded by the men Zane worked with and their spouses, eating too much good food and enduring a wedding toast with champagne and cake, the party broke up and Zane drove them back to his place.

"I'm sorry about the toast and cake," he said. "I didn't know they were gonna do that."

Eden had drunk three glasses of wine over the course of the afternoon and evening, then a glass and a half of champagne, and she was feeling relaxed. "It's okay. They were trying to be sweet. You're lucky to have friends like that in your life. And at least there weren't any presents. That would have been really awkward."

He scratched his chin. "Yeah. Not saying there won't be, but for now they just wanted to meet you and welcome you into the fold. Wait another month and we'll be getting a jelly of the month or something."

Eden laughed. "No way. Those people are classier than that."

"Mal isn't."

Eden thought of the big goofy guy who was constantly making cracks—and being ribbed for his practical jokes gone wrong—and groaned. "Oh no. He'll send it to your house at least. You can deal with it."

"Come to think of it, jelly of the month is too tame. If he can get away with it before Scarlett can stop him, it'll be a sex toy of the month club."

Eden's cheeks flamed, but she laughed anyway. "Lord."

"Yep."

If they hadn't had that awkward moment yesterday, she'd say they could try them out. Or he would. But neither of them said a thing. The tension grew until Eden couldn't stand it a moment longer.

"I'm sorry," she blurted. "For saying sex with you was meaningless."

He shot her a look, then fastened his eyes on the road again. "It's fine. You reminded us both where the goalposts are. This is temporary, and while the sex might be good, it *is* meaningless. Like a continual one-night stand. That's the way it needs to be."

Eden's heart felt like he'd stabbed it. The perils of letting herself feel too much, apparently. "You're right," she said, because what else could she say? "But if you don't mind, I think I'd rather not have any one-night stands for a while."

Because sex with him was anything but meaningless, and she didn't want to be so overcome that she blurted out words she couldn't take back. Words he wouldn't return.

Eden rubbed her forehead, feeling the beginnings of a headache. How had she gone from *best sex of her life* to *couldn't handle it anymore* because she thought she was falling for him?

No idea, but nothing about meeting and marrying Zane had been normal. She'd felt a pull from the beginning. She'd trusted him. And then she'd married him and fallen into bed with him when he might have been a very convincing serial killer instead of a hero.

"If that's what you want," he said. "Not a problem for me."

Not a problem for me. Those words echoed through her head, hurting in ways she hadn't expected.

They fell silent, staying that way for the rest of the drive. When Zane pulled to a stop in front of his house, there was someone sitting on the porch. Eden watched curiously as the woman stood and brushed her hands over her jacket. She was blond, with skinny jeans tucked into tall boots and a black jacket belted at her waist.

She was stunning, in fact, and Eden felt hopelessness seep into her. No way would she ever look like that.

"Fucking hell," Zane growled.

Eden dragged her gaze from the woman. His jaw was thrust out, his brows drawn low. He muttered under his breath. He did not look happy.

"Ex-girlfriend?" She tried to keep her voice light.

He shot her a look that she thought might be filled with dread. And quite possibly remorse. What could have wound him up so tight?

Then came the death blow to her heart. "That's Juliet."

Chapter Twenty

Fury and dread rolled in Zane's stomach as he helped Eden from the truck and started up the sidewalk. She tried to pull away, but he tucked her arm into his and wouldn't let her go. She made a noise that he thought might be a growl, but she stopped trying to fight him.

"Zane," Juliet said in that breathy voice that used to make him want to throw her onto any horizontal surface and fuck her senseless.

"What the fuck are you doing here, Juliet?"

Her gaze strayed to Eden. Hardened. When it landed on him again, her blue eyes were liquid. Pleading. "I, um, needed to see you. I wanted to talk in person."

"There's literally nothing to talk about. I told you how I feel."

Beside him, he felt Eden's curiosity spike. He hadn't told her, because it didn't matter why he'd done it, but she was part of the reason he'd found the balls to do what he should have done the first time Juliet texted him. For himself. For his future. He didn't think he could risk his heart with anyone ever again, but at least he could cut the weights of the past that still held him down.

Juliet was still beautiful. He hadn't seen her in eleven years, other than at a distance when he was in town. She still had the same willowy figure, the same golden blond hair. The same expressive blue eyes. She had that fresh-faced look that'd drawn him at one time. But her power to affect him was gone now. He no longer cared. No longer found her Barbie doll looks as appealing as he once had.

Juliet thrust her lip out. It started to quiver. She bit it to stop the quivering, but she also did it for attention. He didn't give a shit.

"How did you get here?" he pressed.

She folded her arms and sniffed, shooting another glare at Eden. "Obviously, I took a plane. And an Uber Black."

Uber Black. Not just an Uber. She had to throw the fact it was an Uber Black in there. His gaze dropped to the luggage she'd stacked by the door. Louis Vuitton. He assumed the purse sitting on top of the luggage was one of those Hermes things Mia had told him about.

"What I meant was how did you get my address? I never gave it to you."

"I, um. I asked your mom." He must have looked furious because she hastened to add, "I told her I had something of yours I wanted to mail back to you. She didn't know I planned to surprise you."

Surprise him. Like they were still friends who'd never lost touch.

Zane sighed and pinched the bridge of his nose. It wasn't his mom's fault. She was kind, and she would have thought Zane would want whatever bullshit thing Juliet wanted to send him. The breakup was a long time ago, and Zane hadn't told his parents about Juliet's marital trouble or the fact they'd been texting. He also hadn't told them he'd gotten married in Vegas when they were all together last weekend.

Fuck.

"Okay, well this is how it's going to be. You're going to call another Uber *Black*, get your fancy ass in it, and go to a hotel."

Her lip quivered harder now. There was a time when he hadn't been able to resist her tears. When the first hint of one would have had him apologizing for the sky being blue and promising to make it whatever color she wanted.

"I-I'm sorry. I didn't mean to just show up—but you cut me off with no warning. You're my oldest friend, Zane. I can't stand for you to hate me."

He felt her words in his gut. They *had* been each other's oldest friends. Best friends. Lovers planning a future. Until she'd betrayed him and trampled all the plans they'd ever had.

"*Now* you're worried about me hating you? What do you think I felt when I found out you were fucking Daniel when you were supposed to be mine? When you left me for him? Mild dislike?" He shook his head. "We aren't friends anymore, Juliet. We haven't been friends since you made the choice to cheat on me with someone else. I bought a fucking engagement ring, Jules. And you broke up with me in your parents' living room my first day home on leave. Your choice, not mine."

"I'm sorry, Zane. Really. I was young and stupid. I'd give anything to go back."

She started to cry. He was unmoved as she dabbed at her eyes with a fucking silk scarf she untied from the handle of her bag.

"Yeah, well, it's too late for that. We can't go back. Whatever we might have been is gone forever."

Eden's body was stiff and uncomfortable beside him. Zane slipped an arm around her and tucked her into his side. Maybe he was being a cheap bastard to use her that way, or maybe he felt something more for her than he did for Juliet at the moment. Whatever the case, he was definitely using Eden to twist the knife. Didn't make him proud of himself, but it felt good enough he was doing it anyway.

"This is my wife. Eden."

"W-wife?" Juliet's gaze darted between them, disbelief coloring her pretty face. He knew her well enough to know she found Eden lacking. The way Juliet raked her gaze over Eden, her mouth twisting, told him what she thought.

And he fucking hated her for it. His temper started to bubble. "I told you last week I'd found the woman I was marrying. This is her. Eden, Juliet. The ex I told you about."

Eden stuck out a hand. When she spoke, ice wouldn't melt in her mouth. Zane was prouder than hell. He knew it was hard for her, but she was playing it to the max. For him. "It's nice to meet you, Juliet. Zane has told me so much about you."

Juliet made a show of taking Eden's hand and shaking it. Then she turned on Zane, dismissing Eden as if she were nothing. "I came a long way to talk to you. I'd like you to at least listen to what I have to say."

"Call an Uber, Jules. I'm not interested."

Eden palmed his face, dragging his attention down to her. Her pretty eyes were sympathetic. Playing the game. He could have kissed her for it. He *would* kiss her for it if she'd let him.

"It's okay, honey. Let her come inside while she waits. It's chilly outside. We can offer her something warm to drink."

The last thing he wanted was Juliet inside his house, but Eden was right. He couldn't let Eden stay outside any longer, exposed to a potential shooter, and he couldn't leave Juliet on the porch to sit and wait for an Uber. Not that he expected the shooter to show up at his house, but the whole point of protection was taking no chances. And since the shooter had proven he didn't discriminate in his targets, Zane couldn't let Juliet be exposed either.

"You're right, sugar. We'll let her wait inside."

He dropped his mouth to Eden's and kissed her. She stiffened only a second before she softened again. He was doing it to drive home the point with Juliet. He was also doing it because he wanted to.

Because the last day and a half of not being able to kiss Eden, touch her, lose himself inside her, had been hell. Hot need erupted inside him as she kissed him back. He broke the kiss before it got indecent and palmed the back of her head, pressing her to his chest for a moment. When he let her go, he took her hand in his and led her past Juliet so he could unlock the door and take Eden inside.

He didn't look at Juliet. What she thought wasn't the point. The only woman there tonight who mattered to him was Eden.

"ARE YOU OKAY?"

After Juliet's Uber arrived and Zane walked her outside to put her in it, Eden had gone upstairs to change into her pajamas. It'd been a long day and she was tired, but she'd had to go back downstairs and check on Zane. Not only that, but since he'd carried her to bed last night, she wasn't quite sure where she needed to go tonight. She was fine with the guest room, and she needed to tell him so. There was no reason for him to give up his room to her.

Zane stood in the living room, looking out the front window, and Eden's heart turned over in her chest. Did he regret sending Juliet away? It probably hadn't been easy for him even if he'd been angry that she'd shown up unannounced. Eden had given them privacy so Juliet could talk, but whatever she'd said hadn't seemed to matter to him at the time.

Maybe it did now.

He turned at her question and dropped the blind

he'd been looking through. "Yeah, I'm fine. Thanks for going along with everything. I know it wasn't easy."

She twisted the fabric of her pajama pants in two fingers. "You're welcome. I know it meant a lot for you to be able to show her you no longer care. I'm glad I could help." She hesitated. "You don't care, right? You aren't regretting sending her away?"

His eyes widened. "Fuck no. There's nothing she could say to me that would fix the past. Nothing."

"I'm glad then."

"She tried to say we were fated to be together, that she'd had to be with Daniel to make her someone who deserved me." He snorted. "It was all a load of BS. She's unhappy in her relationship because Daniel had an affair. She knows how it feels now, and she's experiencing remorse over what she did. Plus I think she's worried about getting older and starting over. She wants to feel desired again. Guess she thought I'd be an easy way to get there."

"Good Lord, she's already gorgeous. She needs to kick that man to the curb and go find a new one." Not that Eden felt a lot of sympathy for Juliet—none, in fact—but the woman was deluded if she thought there wouldn't be a line of men waiting for her.

"I told her the same thing. Not the gorgeous part," he added. "She's vain enough as it is."

"Does she know you still have her name on your arm?"

"I don't think so."

She was glad.

"I'm going to get it removed. Soon as I can."

Eden twisted her pajamas. "That's good, right?"

"Yes." He strolled toward her, and her heart kicked up. He stopped in front of her, his gaze taking a ride down her body and back up again. He didn't touch her, though.

"I lied about something, Eden."

Her stomach dropped. "Ooohkay."

"Don't you want to know what about?"

She didn't know what was going on with him, but he'd been moodily intense on the ride home. Then Juliet was there, and he'd been more so. Juliet hadn't been the cause, but she hadn't helped his mood.

"If you want to tell me."

He ran a finger down her arm, over the silk of her pajamas. She shivered in the wake of that touch. "I said sex with you was meaningless. I lied."

Her heart throbbed. She waited for him to continue.

He blew out a breath and tipped his head back, exposing the sexy column of his throat as he gazed at the ceiling. "It's not meaningless. It means something." He speared her with his eyes. "But I don't know what."

Her racing heart crashed against the roadblock. It didn't feel good. "Why are you telling me this? If you don't know what it means, why say anything at all?"

"Because I need you to know. I like you, Eden. A lot." He shoved a hand through his hair and squeezed his eyes shut for a second. "I'm not going to change. I'm not going to be a man who risks that kind of hurt again. Seeing Juliet—I felt nothing but relief. I'm over her, for good. It took fucking *years*. I won't do that again. For anyone."

"Then why are you saying *anything*, Zane? I don't need to hear this! I don't want to."

She turned, intent on getting away, but he caught her by the shoulders and pulled her back against him, anchoring her with an arm around her chest. His heart beat almost as hard as hers. His breath ruffled her hair. She knew he'd let her go if she insisted, but she didn't want to. She wanted to feel him close, feel every torturous moment of being held against him.

She would never get enough of that. She leaned back. A tear slipped down her cheek, and she shoved it away with the back of her hand.

"I'm sorry," he whispered. "I want you to know. If I thought I could ever fall for someone, ever risk that kind of hurt again, it'd be you."

Pain spiked in her belly. Anger, despair, fury. She felt them all. She threw herself against the cage of his arms, and he let her go. Eden whirled, not caring that she'd lost the battle with her tears. They ran down her cheeks and dripped onto the silk of her top.

"How dare you?" she demanded. "How *dare* you?"

He reached for her. "Eden."

She slapped his hand away and retreated a few steps, folding her arms over her chest and glaring.

"I'm sorry," he said. "I thought you'd appreciate the truth."

"The truth?" She snorted, emotion whirling through her like a gale force wind. "You wanted to tell me that you like me, *a lot*, but you can't ever *love* me, or anyone else, because Juliet was a bitch who left you for the first guy with a giant bank account? Do you hear yourself?

What that says about *me*?" She smacked her chest to emphasize the word. "You just said you can't ever trust *me* because Juliet left you for another man. *She* was the cheating bitch, but I'm somehow to blame for you not risking your heart again. No, it's my fault you can't fall in love, but now sex isn't meaningless and you like me a lot, so presumably you want me to go back to being the grateful, freckled, *ugly* girl you fuck—"

"No," he gritted, eyes flashing as he took a step toward her. "Don't you dare say that. Eden, you're fucking beautiful. Your tits are perfection. Your ass makes me harder than stone. And your pussy? Damn, honey, I'd walk barefoot over hot glass for another chance at tasting your sweetness. At slipping my dick inside you and feeling the heaven waiting for me there. Yeah, I'd fuck you right this minute if you'd let me. But none of that—*none of it*—compares to how beautiful your face is to me. The way you bite your lip when I'm inside you, the beauty of your eyes, that freckle at the corner of your mouth that drives me wild. The way you looked up at me when you touched my cheek outside. Jesus." He closed his eyes, then snapped them open to answer her glare with one of his own. "You're a fucking beauty queen, Eden. Inside and out."

She could only blink at him in bewilderment, some of her anger deflating. Some, not all. "You literally believe what you just said to me."

"I wouldn't have fucking said it if I didn't," he grated. "But you know who doesn't see you like I do? Who doesn't deserve you and never did? Mitchell fucking Shaw."

Eden flinched. She'd forgotten all about Mitchell. In her emotional outburst about trust and love, she'd never said a word about the man she'd insisted she was in love with. And Zane hadn't either, until now. Which meant he knew—or suspected—the truth.

She lifted her chin. There was no sense in pretending. "No, he doesn't. He deserves Abby and she deserves him. I don't love Mitchell. I know that now."

He shoved his hands in his jeans pockets and nodded. "I'm glad to hear you say it. You're too good to waste your life pining over someone too stupid to even kiss you. You deserve more than that."

Eden sniffed. She was still angry, but it was simmering low now. Because it was draining to be so furious. "So do you, Zane. You deserve another chance at finding your real ride or die. Juliet was never it."

He looked resigned. "Yeah. But how do we ever know? You thought you loved Mitchell for, what, two years? And now you don't. Why? How do you know it doesn't just change one day after you've been with someone for years and years?"

She thought about his teammates today and how happy they'd seemed with their wives and kids. How could he be around all of them and not believe it was possible?

"You don't. But I think love is worth the risk. Your teammates and their wives are happy. Maybe it won't last. But what if it does?" She shook her head. "That's what makes it worthwhile, Zane. The chance it'll last and you'll be sitting on your front porch when you're old and gray, holding hands with the person who knows you better than anyone in the whole world. If you let Juliet ruin that future for you, she wins. She may not ever get you back again, but she still wins because she's determined your entire future. I think that's sad."

He was studying her. Intensely. Then he shook his head as if shaking off a mirage. "We aren't solving this tonight."

She sighed. "No. I'm tired anyway. I wanted to tell you that I can sleep in the guest room. There's no reason to give up your bed for me."

"We can sleep in the same bed without having sex. We've done it before. I like having you and Merlin there."

Eden dropped her gaze to where her toes peeked beneath her pajama pants. "I don't think it's a good idea. I won't be in your house much longer, and I'd rather get used to sleeping alone again."

"If that's what you want." He sounded weary. "But you take the master. Merlin's used to sleeping there anyway. I'll be in the guest room."

"I don't want to take your bed, Zane."

He shook his head. "Doesn't matter. It's not forever, like you said, and I'm used to sleeping in conditions you don't wanna imagine. The guest room is heaven compared to most of the ops I've been on."

She didn't want to sleep in his bed alone, remembering everything they'd done there, but he wasn't going to let her refuse to take the best bed in the house. It wasn't how he was wired. Arguing would do nothing but piss them both off. And she'd still lose. "Okay. Thank you."

There was so much more she hoped they would say, but Zane didn't speak beyond a nod, his jaw tight as he stared at her. She stared back, waiting for something to break the tension.

But nothing would. Nothing except walking away.

Eden climbed the stairs alone, went inside the master alone, pushed the door mostly closed—had to leave it open for Merlin to get in and out—and climbed into bed. Alone.

She thought Zane might follow, might loosen whatever held his jaw tight and say the things he needed to say. But the stairs didn't squeak, and Zane didn't come.

Eden punched the pillow and closed her eyes. It was time to remember what her life was like before Zane. Her heart constricted at the thought. But what choice did she have?

He was so damaged by Juliet that he couldn't see a way out. Fresh tears sprang to her eyes, and she squeezed them shut, trying to make them go away. She'd thought her life was bad a little over a week ago when she'd believed she loved a man who loved someone else.

Turns out that wasn't nearly as bad as loving a man who couldn't love at all.

Chapter Twenty-One

Zane didn't sleep well. He was used to sleeping alone, in rough conditions, with his team nearby. He was used to sleeping wherever he needed to sleep for whatever time he could get.

But after a few nights with Eden cuddled up next to him, he wasn't used to her not being there. Not when she was in the same house, only feet away, in another room. He started to think he'd get a better night's sleep if he dragged himself outside and bedded down in the yard with the night sky above and the cold air leeching away his body heat. He'd be uncomfortable, but it would make sense. This didn't make sense.

He heard scratching on his door during the night, and he opened it to find Merlin sitting on the floor staring at him like he was a dumbass. He thought the cat would come inside. Instead, he turned and sauntered toward the master where Eden was. When Zane didn't follow, he stopped and meowed as if to say, *What are you waiting for, idiot human?*

Zane yawned and scrubbed a hand through his hair. "Sorry, cat, it's not happening."

Not because he didn't want it to. Because she didn't.

Merlin sauntered back and circled his legs, meowing. Zane hunkered down to pet the persistent little beast. "Buddy, she said no. I can't."

Jesus, he was talking to a cat. In the middle of the night.

Merlin finally got the hint and left, disappearing inside the master bedroom. Zane left his door cracked in case the cat came back and crawled into bed. But he lay there with his arm over his head, staring at the ceiling.

Eden didn't love Mitchell Shaw. She'd said as much tonight. Didn't that prove how right he was about love not lasting? Eden had believed she was in love with her boss for two years. Believed it while watching her sister date him, get engaged to him, and plan a wedding. She'd believed it so hard she'd been determined to suffer in silence so her sister would be happy.

She'd either been wrong, or her love had the permanence of an eggshell. Zane didn't like the way that made him feel. She wasn't Juliet, wasn't the sort of woman to tell a man she loved him while dating someone else behind his back, but last week she'd been in love with Mitchell Shaw and now she wasn't.

He thought of his parents. They'd been married for almost thirty-two years, and he knew they'd had problems along the way. He remembered the yelling when he'd been a kid, the way his dad would storm out and leave for hours at a time. He remembered his mother crying. They'd been young when they had him—twenty for his mother and twenty-one for his dad—and they'd gotten married because she was pregnant.

They'd grown into their love, though. He thought of them in Vegas last week, celebrating their daughter's birthday and looking at each other as if there was no one else in the whole world they'd rather be with.

He thought of his teammates. He was less certain about them, but he couldn't deny how happy they appeared to be. Wolf and Haylee and their new daughter were so sweet they made his teeth ache. Saint couldn't do enough for Brooke and the baby that was coming. They'd waited a long time for her to get pregnant. Hell, Muffin had only just gotten a family when he married Alaina and got Everett as a bonus, but there was no denying the dude was head over heels in love with both the woman and the kid. Even if Alaina left him in a few years, Everett would always think of Muffin as his dad.

Zane blew a frustrated breath. What the fuck was he doing imagining the worst scenario he could for his friend and brother? Just because he'd been cursed in love didn't mean the rest of them were.

Maybe you aren't either. Maybe you just have to try. Day at a time, that's all it takes.

Zane flopped onto his side and closed his eyes to shut out the sound of his own voice in his head. He knew better than to believe that voice. He'd listened once before when his gut told him something was wrong with Juliet. But his head, his stupid head, said he was overreacting. That he and Juliet had history and therefore they were meant to be. He'd had *faith*.

He'd believed right up until she'd shrugged off his hug when he went home on leave at Christmas. He'd stood there with his hands at his sides, confused, while she walked around her parents' living room and touched the decorations and talked about all the things she'd been doing since he'd last been home. Then she'd faced him and said the words that had shattered his world—*I don't love you anymore. I love someone else.*

Tonight she'd tried to tell him she'd made a mistake, that she'd been seduced by the lure of an easy life. She'd been terrified of marrying him and following him from Army post to Army post, being cut off from her friends and her family. She'd thought Daniel was the safe choice.

Zane had listened wearily, knowing Eden was somewhere in the house, giving them privacy so Juliet could talk. He'd let her do it, but all he'd wanted was Eden. He'd wanted to be buried inside her, moving his hips to meet hers as she took him all, feeling the hot squeeze of her pussy around him as he made her come apart. He'd wanted a tit in his hand and his tongue in her mouth while she moaned deep in her throat.

He'd gotten none of those things because he was an asshole who had to tell her she made him feel something but he didn't know what it was. He'd been honest, but maybe he should have been silent. Until he worked it out for himself, what was the point? He'd pissed her off and hurt her at the same time, and he hadn't wanted to do either one.

What he'd expected, if he was honest with himself, was that she'd soften in his arms, tell him she understood, and take him to bed so they could shut out the world and be together.

He'd misjudged that situation for damned sure. All he'd wanted was to be with the woman in the next room. As it was, he'd be lucky if she ever let him touch her again.

———

EDEN WOKE to her phone vibrating on the bedside table. She reached for it, her heart pounding. It was Abby. A quick glance at the time told her it wasn't even seven in the morning yet.

"Sissy?"

"Eden," her sister blurted. "I think I'm being followed."

Eden was instantly awake. "What? Where are you? Where is the police officer?"

"It's early. He doesn't get to the hotel until seven. But I was awake, so I decided to get dressed and go pick up some things before heading over to see Mitchell."

Eden ground her teeth together. "Why would you do that? You know you're supposed to stay put until the police get there!"

Abby had been assigned protection since Kate was murdered. She knew it was serious. *What the fuck was she thinking?*

"I know, I know. But I thought it would be okay. It's so early, and I just wanted to run into Walmart and grab some snacks and another sweater. I'm wearing a hoodie. Nobody knows who I am."

Nobody but potentially the person following her. "Where are you *now?*"

"The parking garage at the hospital. I, um, there was a black Tahoe here last night, and it left when we did. This morning, when I went to Walmart, it was there. When I drove away, so did the Tahoe. And now it's in the garage."

"Do *not* get out of that car, Abby."

Eden tried to think. Merlin meowed out in the hallway, and she leapt to her feet, running for the door. Zane stood on the other side, his hair mussed, shirtless, looking like a wet dream. It took him less than a moment to snap to full alertness.

"What's going on?" he demanded.

"Abby. She thinks somebody's following her." Eden gave Zane the details, his face growing darker as she did so. He was clearly pissed. She was pissed too, but right now what she wanted was for him to save her sister from her own stupidity.

"Give me the phone."

Eden handed it over. "Abby. Listen to me. I want you to drive out of the garage. It'll take too long to get to the police station in traffic, so I want you to go to the IHOP near the hospital. You know where it is? Good. I'll meet you there in ten minutes. Do *not* park anywhere you can't be seen by people in the restaurant. Park in front and don't get out of the car. If you can't park, sit there. If you see that Tahoe again, get the plate number. Don't risk your safety to do it, though. Understand me? Okay, good. Now move. I'll see you soon."

He handed Eden her phone and told her to stay online with her sister.

"I'm going with you," she said, in case he thought she wasn't.

A hard frown marred his handsome features, but all he did was nod. "We gotta go now. Get some shoes and a coat."

Eden grabbed her trainers and slipped them on. She didn't have time for a bra or to brush her teeth or comb her hair. She raced down the stairs behind Zane, who'd dragged on a shirt and shoes and looked like a million sexy bucks.

He locked the door behind them, and they hopped into his truck. It wasn't far to the IHOP, but morning traffic slowed them down. Though it was Sunday, that didn't make much difference in the metro area. He hit the button on his steering wheel and called Sky, who answered almost immediately.

"Got a situation, Hacker. Can you get into some cameras for me?"

"Maybe. Tell me what you need."

Zane filled his teammate in. Eden tried to listen while also talking to Abby, but it wasn't easy to pay attention to both conversations. Especially when Abby kept apologizing over and over for being an idiot.

"Sissy, stop," Eden finally said. "You made a mistake. A pretty big one, but you won't do it again. We're on the way. Zane will protect you."

"I know he will. Eden, I've been thinking about all this, and I wonder." She sucked in a breath and whimpered. The hackles on Eden's neck rose at the fear in her sister's voice. "What if it's not about Mitchell and the Allen case at all? Wh-what if it's Trevor?"

Ice formed in Eden's veins, sending a shudder down her spine. "No," she said firmly, though she had no idea. "No way."

She didn't want Abby to fall apart. So much had happened this past week, and Abby didn't need to add fear about Trevor into the mix. She was tired and scared and it was natural she'd look to the most frightening incident of her life for an explanation when the police still hadn't located the gunman. But Eden firmly believed it was something to do with Mitchell. He had far more reasons for someone to hate him than Abby did. Kate had been an unfortunate victim because she'd been in the wrong place.

"You don't know," Abby said. "He's capable of it."

"I know he is," Eden soothed. "But it doesn't make sense. Why would Trevor come after Mitchell? Me? And why would he kill Kate?"

"I don't know," Abby whispered. "But it's the kind of cruel, evil thing he'd do if he had the guts."

Eden couldn't shake the chill that'd crept over her at the mention of Trevor Hagan's name. She hated him for what he'd done to her sister, but he'd spent five years in prison. Why would he do something that could send him back, and for far longer?

There was no doubt Trevor had been a dangerous person. Probably still was. But was he also stupid?

"I don't know why he'd risk it," Eden replied. "But maybe he did. Zane's team can find out where he is. If he's behind this, they'll stop him."

"Okay. I'm at the IHOP. I don't see the Tahoe."

"We're almost there, Ab. Don't worry."

Eden stayed on the phone with her sister until Zane turned into the parking lot. He had her relay instructions to Abby, which were not to get out of her car and to follow him to another, safer space. When they pulled into two parking spots side by side in an almost empty Home Depot parking lot, Zane got out of the truck and went around to Abby's door to retrieve her.

He kept his eye on their surroundings as he hustled Abby and her shopping bags into the back seat and closed the door. Abby cried out and threw an arm around Eden's neck. Eden hugged her hard as Zane started to drive.

"I'm so sorry," Abby said as tears ran down her cheeks. "I shouldn't have left the hotel alone. I-I thought it would be okay if I hid my face."

Eden squeezed her sister's hand. "It's not okay. Not until this is over and the person responsible is in custody. Please don't do anything like that again."

"I won't."

"I'm going to make sure you have around the clock protection," Zane said. "And someone will pick up your car. I wasn't aware the police weren't with you 24/7."

He looked and sounded pissed. Eden was pretty pissed too.

"They pick me up and drop me off," Abby said. "I thought that was okay."

"I wish you'd told me, Ab."

"I didn't think it was important." She shrugged.

"There's been so much going on, and somebody shot at you, too. I wasn't worried about me."

Eden frowned. "I think you know better now, right?"

Abby nodded emphatically. "Yes. Aren't we going to the hospital?"

Zane was driving a different direction, and Abby had noticed.

"I'm taking you back to my place. Once my guys check the cameras to see if they can track down the Tahoe, I'll get you to the hospital. How's Mitchell doing?"

Abby sucked in a breath. "Okay. Not great. He's in a lot of pain, and they're watching him closely, but when he's awake, he knows me. We talk about the wedding." She sniffed and wiped beneath her eyes. "Sorry."

Eden reached back and took her hand again. "No. Don't be sorry."

"He asked about you," Abby said. "If you were safe. I told him you were. I think he'd like it if you visited."

Once she would have clung to that scrap of interest like a precious diamond. Now, she was simply happy that Mitchell was still Mitchell.

"I will, Ab. I wanted to give you all the time with him first. But I'd love to see him."

She glanced at Zane. The only reaction he gave was his knuckles whitening on the steering wheel. But was that good or bad? She didn't know. She didn't know anything since last night.

"He'd like that, though I have to warn you he'll probably want to know about his cases. He's worried about William Allen. I can tell."

"It's a big case," Eden said. "With a man's entire life at stake."

Abby closed her eyes. Her face was paler than usual, her hair lank. She didn't look like the confident beauty she usually was. It broke Eden's heart to see her sister so tired and sad.

"Did you tell Zane about Trevor?" she asked.

"I told him about what Trevor did, yes. I haven't told him about your fear that he's behind this."

Zane's gaze snapped to Eden before fastening to the road again. "Has he contacted you?"

"No," Abby said, sounder smaller than before. "B-but I can't shake the thought he's connected somehow."

"Why would he try to kill Mitchell or Eden? Or Kate?"

Abby bit her lip as it quivered. "Taking my sister and fiancé away from me would break me. That's the only reason he needs."

ZANE TOOK the ladies to his house after following his usual protocol of taking alternate routes and doubling back on himself. The trip took half an hour longer than it should have, but he was confident he hadn't been followed. There were no GMC Tahoes in his rearview.

Once they were inside and Eden was in the kitchen fixing coffee, Zane called Hacker again.

"Got a black Tahoe on cameras in the parking garage and IHOP. I can cross-reference it with Walmart once we get an ID on it."

Zane understood the logic. Walmart was likely to have several black Tahoes in the parking lot, so best to narrow them down first if possible. "Can you see the plate number?"

"Not well. Trying to resolve it now, but they've got a tinted cover over their plates."

Those fuckers were illegal, but that didn't stop people from using them. Not only that, but unless the plate was truly obscured, cops were too busy to randomly pull people over for it.

"Got something else to check out."

"Hit me with it," Hacker said.

"Trevor Hagan." He gave Hacker the rundown on Hagan and what he'd done to Abby, as well as the fact he'd spent five years in prison and gotten released two months ago.

"Holy fuck," Hacker breathed. "Sick asshole."

"Yeah. Hagan was living in Chicago when he dated Abby. But he could have found her here."

"Easily. Her name's in the engagement announcement to Mitchell Shaw along with the date of the wedding." Hacker's keyboard clacked. "Without using any special skills, I have an address and employer for Abigail Mary Hall with a simple Google search. If this motherfucker wanted some kind of revenge, he could find her with very little effort."

Zane didn't like the prickling on the back of his neck. He rubbed it. "I need you to find everything you can on him."

"Looking now. I'll need to dig but—holy shit."

"What?"

"Dude has a net worth of fifty-eight mil, and that's after his houses and part of his fortune were confiscated for back taxes. People think he lost everything, but he didn't. I'm looking at a database that doesn't lie."

"Jesus," Zane breathed. "With that kind of money, he doesn't need to get his hands dirty at all. He just needs to hire it done."

"Helluva risk, though. After five years, I'd take my fifty-eight mil and live the good life on an island somewhere. I damn sure wouldn't risk my freedom to get even with anyone. It's stupid. He didn't do time for Abby, just for taxes. So why go after her?"

"Most people wouldn't. But we aren't sick fuckers who get their jollies controlling and terrifying women." Zane pulled in a breath. "Gotta admit it seems unlikely, but Abby's spooked at the thought this is about her, so we need to check into it."

"Don't blame her. I'll get on it, see what I can find. Shaw's case files are filled with potential enemies, but none stand out as the most likely besides the Allen case and the Benedetto connection."

"Still seems like the most logical conclusion."

"Does to me too. Got word that Kate Vann was wearing a scarf over her hair when she was shot. It was drizzling, so maybe she didn't want to get wet. But it's possible the shooter thought she was Eden from a distance."

That thought slid a chill right down his spine. "Could be. He missed at her place so maybe he figured she'd show up at Mitchell's soon enough and he'd get the chance to finish it."

Zane was chewing on that thought when he heard something that made him stiffen. He couldn't say what it was, though instinct had him drawing his weapon and dropping the phone onto an end table. Glass shattered a second later, and something metallic landed in the center of his living room with a thud. Gas hissed from the canister. Zane grabbed it and lobbed it out the window, then dropped to a knee and sighted down the barrel of his Glock.

Eden emerged from the kitchen, wide-eyed. "Zane—"

"Take Abby into the pantry and lock the door," he ordered. "Now!"

He didn't know if she obeyed or not because, a second later, a balaclava-clad team of men in assault gear stormed his house.

The fight was *on*.

Chapter Twenty-Two

THERE WERE TOO MANY OF THEM. ZANE FOUGHT THE way he was trained, taking out at least one enemy fighter with a shot to the thigh, but he wasn't geared up and they were. They had vests and shields, and they were ready for him.

He couldn't make himself small enough, couldn't avoid their bullets if he tried. But the bullets didn't come. Instead, he was tased, the electricity shuddering through his body, burning every cell until he wanted to scream.

They subdued him as he was coming up again, wrenching his arms behind his back and zip tying them. They did the same to his legs. The zip ties were steel lined. He could feel it, and he knew he wouldn't break free.

Professionals.

But what the fuck were they doing in his house?

He didn't have to wait long for an answer. The men

fanned out, searching the premises, until one yelled he'd found the women.

Two more burst into the kitchen to haul Eden and Abby out where he could see them. Zane's eyes burned into Eden's. She was scared, but she held her sister's hand tight. Abby sobbed and shook, but Eden didn't. Her expression was grim—and furious.

Atta girl.

"Sorry, man," the closest commando said, hunkering down beside him. "Not going to kill you. Not what we're paid to do, but we've got orders to take these two. Respect for what you tried to do. No hard feelings, though I think my guy might disagree."

One man had already exfiltrated with the injured commando, which left four in the room. They'd sent six men against him. Six trained operators.

And he wasn't dead, though he probably should be.

"Who are you?" Zane asked.

"You know the answer. Former team guy. All of us. Pay's better on the outside, though. You ever want to go private, I'll find you."

"If I ever find you, I can't guarantee I'll be as nice."

The man laughed. "Gotcha, bud. Sorry about your windows." He stood and did a circle with his hand to indicate it was time to go. Down the street, Zane could hear sirens approaching. *Not fast enough.*

"Zane," Eden choked out as the man holding her arm swung her over his shoulder and started for the door. "Zane!"

"I'll find you, Eden," he rasped. "Swear to God, I'll find you."

"I love you," she cried.

Then she was gone.

ZANE'S BELLY BURNED, his skull tingled with sensation, and he couldn't sit still. The police had gotten there first, but Saint had been the first of his guys to arrive. Mal was next. Gem, Muffin, Hacker, Harley, Wolf, and Easy weren't far behind. Hacker had heard everything and put out the call.

Merlin was safe. As soon as a cop cut the zip ties binding him, Zane had taken the stairs two at a time, praying the cat was on the bed in the master. It seemed to be his favorite spot, though he sometimes liked the back of the couch and the kitchen windowsill too.

Merlin wasn't on the bed. When Zane called, he poked his nose out from under it. *Thank God.*

Zane had to keep Eden's cat alive and well. She loved the animal, and Zane was pretty fucking sure he loved her. Shitty ass time to realize it, when she was gone and he couldn't say the words back to her. She'd shocked the hell out of him when she'd screamed those words as she was carried away. He'd been too stunned to respond. He'd felt it though, down to his soul. Felt it and wanted to fucking murder everyone who'd been a part of abducting her.

He'd promised to protect her, and he'd failed. *Goddammit!*

Zane had picked up the cat and held him. While Merlin purred, Zane might have had a little bit of a breakdown in the cat's soft fur. Not that he was admitting that shit to anyone.

He was fine now. No, he was fucking pissed as hell.

A team of private contractors had broken into his house, assaulted him, and stolen his girl. He hadn't felt so helpless since he'd been a new Special Forces trainee, learning how to defend himself against enemy attacks. By the time he'd applied to Special Operations and been accepted, he hadn't been helpless in a fight in years.

Mal, Easy, and Gem cleaned up the glass where the team had tossed tear gas into his house. Thank fuck he'd thrown it out before it did any harm.

They'd busted his back door in, too. The frame was mangled, the metal door bent so badly it'd never be right again. Minor problems compared to the biggest one of all.

Who had taken Eden and Abby, and why? They needed to know those things so they could storm in like a fucking tornado and take the women back.

Hacker was on his computer, Saint was on the phone, and Zane was going over everything in his head. They must have followed him, but he didn't know how. He'd been careful. He'd watched his six, doubled back, taken alternate routes, and been certain nobody was there.

The only way they could have followed was a GPS tracker, but they'd had no chance to plant it. Zane had gone to a big parking lot, away from everyone else, and transferred Abby to his truck. Nobody could have gotten a tracker onto his car unnoticed. There'd been no cars where they were. No people.

It had to have been Abby. They'd attached a tracker to her at some point. Not her car. *Her.*

Easy enough to do when she'd been shopping in Walmart. Somebody could have brushed by her, planted the tracker, then sat back and waited. They wanted Eden, or they'd have simply grabbed Abby when the chance presented itself.

"The Tahoe is registered to a private security firm. Gray Horse Holdings. They're based out of Philly," Saint said once he'd finished his call.

Zane was incandescent with anger. It burned a hole in his brain, his belly, destroying everything in its path. The way he wanted to destroy the men who'd taken Eden from him.

"Fucking hell," Mal said. "Let's go knock some heads together and get some answers."

"Not so fast. Just because the Tahoe is theirs doesn't mean it's where they went. Private security. Anyone could hire them. They could have taken the women somewhere in the local area. They could have loaded them on a plane. We don't know, and we aren't taking off for Philly."

Zane's jaw was so tight he thought it'd snap. "What the hell else are we supposed to do?"

"Brother, I know you're angry, and I know you're hurting. I've been there. We all have. But taking off for Philly before we know more could put the women farther out of our reach." He held up a hand as if to say *simmer down* when Zane made a noise in his throat. "That was Ghost on the line. He's getting Ian Black involved. Mendez is aware."

"So Black is going to Philly?"

"Don't know. He might already know something about Gray Horse. If not, he's got people on the ground in Philly. They can check out the Gray Horse site, see what they find. If we're lucky, Black will know how to get in touch."

"Meanwhile, Eden and Abby could be dead," Zane growled. Everything inside him wanted to go nuclear on someone's ass. He couldn't, and that was a bitter pill to swallow.

"I don't think so," Hacker said. "Somebody went to a lot of trouble to hire mercenaries for an extraction. Could have killed them, and you too, and saved a lot of trouble."

Zane took a breath. Hacker was right. He had to stop imagining the worst or he was going to be no good in a fight to get his woman back. Yeah, *his* woman. Eden Hall was his wife, his lover, and by God, he was going to do his best to prove he was the right man for her. That she hadn't made a bad choice when she'd impulsively married him in Vegas.

He'd told her last night in this very room that he felt something when he was with her but he didn't know what it was. *Asshole.* He knew now. And it killed him that she'd had to be in danger for him to realize the truth.

He knew she wasn't like Juliet. She had too much integrity. He was scared, hell yeah, but he couldn't stop thinking about what she'd said to him.

That's what makes it worthwhile, Zane. The chance it'll last and you'll be sitting on your front porch when you're old and gray, holding hands with the person who knows you better than anyone in the whole world. If you let Juliet ruin that future for you, she wins.

"We've got two people with the money for something like that," Zane said, trying to think. "Trevor Hagan and Antonio Benedetto. Jury selection was supposed to start tomorrow in the Allen case, but Eden said the lawyers would ask for a stay due to the circumstances. They'll likely get it, but not for very long. If it's Benedetto, then he wants Eden out of the way so a guilty verdict is more likely. That's the theory anyway. If it's Hagan, then he wants... what? Revenge because Abby left him? Because he wants her back? Wants her to suffer? I don't fucking know."

Easy came out of the kitchen holding up a small disc. "They put an Air Tag in her shopping bag. That's how they tracked her here."

"Fuckers," Mal said.

Zane put his palms to his temples and squeezed. "Fucking hell. I should have checked her out first."

"Dude, you couldn't know. We've been operating under the assumption someone wanted to kill Mitchell and Eden, and possibly Abby, too. You were protecting against shots fired."

"Yeah, but if I'd fucking checked her bags. An Air Tag is too damn obvious. It's not like they put a mini tracker on her body and followed her that way." He'd have needed specialized equipment to check for that. Not the kind of thing he randomly carried around in his truck. In fact, he'd have had to call Hacker and gotten him to scan Abby. That would have left them exposed for far too long.

"Like I said, you couldn't know. Stop beating yourself up," Saint growled.

"Trying," Zane growled back.

Muffin put a hand on his shoulder and squeezed. "Know what you're feeling, man. We'll find her. Hack is right. It can't be about killing her at this point. If it was, why wouldn't they have done the deed and left her body here with yours? Seems like somebody wants her alive."

"But for how long?"

Nobody had an answer to that.

"The marriage," Zane croaked, unable to keep silent a moment more. Not when they were here, doing everything to help. They deserved the truth. "We were drunk. Hurting over our own shit. Seemed like a good idea at the time. So, yeah, I fucking went to Vegas and did something crazy. Crazier than Mal drunk on Jack."

"Thanks, brother," Mal said with a wink. "I'm here for you."

"We're planning a divorce. Except I don't want that now. I want to try and make a go of it. Eden is… She's fucking awesome." He was getting choked up again. "I'm sorry I didn't tell you the truth. Sorry I let you plan a wedding reception because you thought we were a real couple."

"Dude," Wolf said, wrapping an arm around his shoulders and squeezing. "Doesn't matter how it happened, it happened. Every one of us knows what it feels like to fall hard for a woman. And whether or not you believed it before today, it was pretty obvious to all of us you'd fallen when we saw the two of you together the first time."

Zane swallowed the knot in his throat and laughed. "I don't see how. *I* didn't even know."

"Yeah, but the heart knows."

Saint's phone rang and he answered with a clipped, "Rodgers."

They waited, watching for some sign he was getting information they desperately needed. "Okay, thanks. 'Preciate it." When the call ended, Saint was smiling. "Ian Black comes through again. That was one of his staff. Gray Horse Holdings is run by a man named Beau "Horse" Connor. He was a Green Beret, left the service two years ago and recruited former teammates and others who get referred to him through the grapevine. It's still a new operation. Black's people know about them but haven't had any contact before."

"Why've we never heard of him?" Mal asked.

"He keeps it quiet. Doesn't advertise openly. It's word of mouth, referrals. They do off-the-books ops for the kind of people who can pay the price."

"If a Green Beret—or any other SpecOps guy—had shot Mitchell, he'd be dead," Zane said. "And they wouldn't have missed when they targeted Eden."

"True, but what if Beau and his pals didn't do the shooting? They might have been hired after the previous person fucked it up."

"So where do we find him?" Zane itched to go after the fucker, find out if he was the same man who'd spoken while Zane was on the ground. He appreciated being left alive. He didn't appreciate anyone who hired their special skills out to criminals, though. And kidnapping two frightened women from suburbia counted as a criminal activity in his book.

"We call the number Ian's people gave me and leave a message. Say we want to hire his people for a job, and that we were referred by Sam Benson. I don't know who that is, but they assured me that was the name to give and it'd work. After that, we wait for someone to call back."

Zane was ready to explode. "Wait? We can't wait! Goddammit, Saint, it's Eden and Abby's lives at stake here."

Saint's jaw flexed. "I know what the stakes are. That's why we need a good story." He shot a look at Hacker. "Need you to make the call. You know how to sound like a rich prick willing to lay down some coin."

"Thanks, bro," Hacker said. "I think."

They all knew he'd come from wealth, until his dad stole a bunch of money from his investors and fell on hard times. His dad went to prison while Hacker's mother had to go to work to live. Hacker was at Harvard when it happened and had to drop out. He knew how to sound rich because he'd been rich. Until he wasn't.

"Can't we just triangulate the number?" Gem said.

"It's a remote service," Saint replied. "He dials in to check the messages."

"Fuck. I much prefer when we aren't dealing with Special Operators."

"Look, I know it's not ideal, but it's what we've got. Meanwhile, after Hacker makes this call, he'll keep searching for information on Benedetto and Hagan, see if anything pops."

"Yep," Hacker said, waving a hand. "That's me, your friendly computer pro. If it's there, I'll find it."

Zane hoped like hell there was something to find. Because waiting for a call that might not come for days, sitting around with his thumb up his ass and doing *nothing*, wasn't going to work.

If something didn't happen soon, he was going to start busting down doors. Starting with Antonio Benedetto's.

Chapter Twenty-Three

Eden was groggy. She opened her eyes and shook her head as the room spun, which only made it worse.

Abby lay beside her, eyes closed, face pale. Her chest rose and fell as she breathed. *Still alive.*

Eden tried to speak, but nothing happened. Her stomach roiled as she forced herself upright. They were lying on a large bed in a room that was sparsely furnished with a couple of chairs, a small table, and a dresser. It wasn't a big room, but it was warm. She could see a bathroom across from her, and she tried to put her feet on the floor so she could go over to it.

But her stomach rebelled, her head swam, and she had to lay down again. She blinked up at the ceiling, afraid and angry in somewhat equal measure, and tried to recall everything that'd happened. She remembered Zane telling her to get into the pantry with Abby. It wasn't a big pantry, but they'd managed to squeeze inside.

There'd been the sound of shattering glass and men

shouting—then the door was wrenched open, and she and Abby were dragged out by a man dressed in black and wearing a hood. A balaclava. She remembered her heart beating too fast, remembered the insane thought that she was still in her pajamas and wasn't ready to go anywhere, and then being slung over a man's shoulder.

Zane had been on the ground, arms and legs bound, looking murderous. She'd told him she loved him, but he hadn't said the words back. Not that she'd expected it. But she'd needed him to know. After their fight, after everything, she wanted him to know in case she never got another chance to tell him.

He might not believe her, probably didn't, but at least she'd said it.

She must have fallen asleep because when she woke again, her head was no longer spinning. It ached, though. She sat up and waited for the room to tilt, but it didn't. She shook Abby awake. Her sister's eyes fluttered but didn't open. Eden shook her harder, panic flaring.

Abby's eyes finally opened. Her brow wrinkled. "Did I fall asleep? How's Mitchell?"

Eden's heart squeezed. "Ab, honey, we aren't at the hospital. Men broke into Zane's house and kidnapped us."

Eden didn't think it was possible for Abby to grow any paler, but she did. She nodded as if remembering.

"Wh-what do they want?"

"I don't know. I don't know where we are." Eden put a foot on the floor. Then another. When she was standing and didn't feel sick, she shuffled toward the bathroom. It was spacious, with a double vanity, a walk-in shower, and a separate toilet closet. The finishes were nice, too. Marble floors and shower enclosure. Granite counters. Eden finished exploring the bathroom and shuffled over to a door that opened to a closet with nothing in it.

Abby had sat up and now blinked at the room. Eden went to the next door and tried it.

Locked.

"What's happening? I don't understand."

"I don't know. Those men took us, and now we're here. I don't remember how we got here... wherever *here* is."

"Welcome, ladies."

Eden jumped at the disembodied voice. Abby screamed and tried to make herself smaller on the bed. She searched the ceiling and corners from where she'd pressed herself against the headboard. Eden searched too, looking for the speaker. A blue light shone from a Ring camera mounted high in one corner of the room. Eden glared at it, wondering if she could reach it if she moved the dresser. She glanced over at Abby again. Her sister was huddled in a ball, hands over her ears, eyes squeezed shut.

Eden rushed over and jumped on the bed, wrapping her arms around Abby. "It's okay, Ab. I'm here."

Not that she could do anything to protect either one of them. Maybe there was something in the drawers. She hadn't opened those yet.

Abby hugged her hard, hiding her face against Eden's shoulder. Her entire body shook. "It's Trevor," she whispered.

Ice crusted Eden's heart. She whipped her gaze to the camera as if she could see the evil asshole behind it.

"It's been a few years, Abigail. I've missed you."

Eden shuddered as she held her sister. "What do you want with us?" she demanded.

"I don't want anything with *you*, Eden. Abigail, though… I thought about you, Abby. For five long years, I thought about you. Imagined the moment we would meet again. How much you were going to need me."

Abby's eyes were squeezed tight. "No," she forced out. "I don't need you. I don't want you!"

"You will. You've lost so much, haven't you? Your dear friend. Your sister. I'm still here, though."

Abby hugged Eden harder. Her eyes snapped open, and she glared up at the camera. "Don't you dare hurt my sister. If you want me to want you again, you won't hurt her!"

Trevor chuckled. "Who said anything about wanting you to want me? I just want you to beg, Abby. Beg for her life and I might spare it. Or not."

Fear slammed into Eden. Her stomach twisted, her heart dropping like a stone. He was going to kill her. There was no way he planned to let her live. Which meant….

"You shot Mitchell," she rasped.

Abby cried out. Trevor laughed. "My aim wasn't so great, considering he's still alive. Then I missed you at your house that morning. There was really no excuse for that. The big guy made me hesitate."

Eden closed her eyes, more thankful than ever for Zane.

"And Kate?" Abby cried. "Why would you kill her?"

"Because I thought she was your sister." Eden shivered again. He was sick. "Regretfully, she was not. Was she important to you?"

Abby nodded as tears rolled down her cheeks.

"Then it wasn't a wasted bullet."

"You're sick," Abby screamed, voicing Eden's thought. "You won't get away with this! Even if you kill us both, they'll find you, Trevor. Zane and his team will find you and make sure you pay. They're soldiers!"

"Don't antagonize him," Eden whispered. "We need to stay alive as long as possible." Zane said he would find them. He'd sworn it. Her job was to live long enough for that to happen.

"Nobody's finding me, Abigail. I don't leave a trail." He laughed. It didn't sound like an evil laugh, which made it all the more chilling. It was almost an infectious laugh. A happy laugh. Like a gleeful child on Christmas morning. "You'll see. As the days stretch into weeks and the weeks into months, you'll realize nobody's coming for you. They can't because they won't know where to look."

"Why?" Abby demanded. "Why? I didn't have anything to do with your prison sentence. Your lawyers made sure I didn't press charges for what you did. Th-they told me how it would go, how they'd say we were playing sex games, how a jury wouldn't believe me—"

She sucked in a breath and Eden hugged her tighter. "It wasn't your fault. You know that."

"I would have given you everything you ever wanted," Trevor said. "I worshipped you. But you didn't love me enough, did you? As soon as I was arrested, you left. You tried to hide, and then you got *engaged* to another man. You abandoned me, Abby. I can't forgive you for that."

A motor whirred to life. The wall started to separate from the floor, rolling upward. Eden realized it was a shutter as it continued to disappear, revealing glass. Beyond the picture window, water undulated as far as the eye could see. An ocean of water. It looked dark and cold, not the turquoise of a tropical sea. Clouds hung low on the horizon as a splinter of red peeked through. It would be some minutes before they knew if it was dawn or sunset, though.

"Welcome to my island, ladies. I hope you enjoy your stay."

The blue light blinked out and Trevor was gone.

THE MEETING PLACE was a coffee shop in Old Town Alexandria. Hacker had made contact with Gray Horse Holdings. Beau Conner himself was taking the meeting. Zane was on edge. He kept expecting something to go wrong, for Beau to get that prickling sense a special operator sometimes got that told him everything was wrong. He wouldn't show, and where the fuck would they be then?

It'd been over eight hours since Eden and Abby were taken, and time was running out. Might already be gone, though Zane couldn't let himself go there.

Thanks to some assistance from Bliss and her CIA

contacts, Hacker had a watertight background that checked out. He was a rich man looking to hire someone to retrieve his teenage daughter from a drug cartel in Mexico. She'd gone down on spring break and been abducted. He'd paid ransom, but she still hadn't been returned. She was alive, though, because they let him video chat with her every time they wanted more money. He was pissed off they were bleeding him, and worried about his daughter's continued safety. He wanted someone to go get her, and he was willing to pay the price.

"Operator, ten o'clock," Easy said, his voice coming over the headset. Zane watched as a man approached the coffee shop and took up residence on a bench nearby. The lookout, probably. He could be just a dude sitting outside, but everything about his bearing and the way he watched the street and sidewalk said he was trained.

Hacker was inside, working on his laptop and drinking coffee. He could hear them, but he wasn't speaking because they didn't know if Connor was watching him or not. Zane had to admit his teammate looked the part. Bespoke suit, shirt with no tie, open at the neck, cufflinks. Hacker had put on the suit and the attitude that went with it. Channeling his old man, no doubt.

"Sit tight, everyone," Saint said. "Don't move until my say so."

Another man strolled up the sidewalk ten minutes later. He nodded to the man on the bench and then went inside and approached Hacker.

"Mr. Kelley?"

"Yes. Are you Connor?"

There was a hesitation before the man confirmed. "Yes."

"I expected someone older," Hacker said. That was code for he didn't believe the man he was speaking to was their guy.

"It's the one on the bench," Zane said as he watched the man shift so he could see inside the coffee shop. "That's Connor."

"Agreed," Saint replied.

"I'll take him."

"Stand down, Zany. Easy and Gem will do it like we planned. Copy?"

Zane growled. "Copy."

He hated sitting still, but he had to let the plan unfold. If it went right, he'd be face to face with Connor soon enough. If it didn't?

He couldn't think about that. He had to trust his team.

Easy and Gem appeared on the sidewalk, strolling along hand in hand. Two men in love, laughing and enjoying the sights of Old Town on a beautiful fall evening. Connor checked them out, then let his gaze go back to the coffee shop. Inside, Hacker was explaining to Connor's decoy about the predicament his daughter was in. Zane imagined that Connor was mic'd up the way they were, listening in so he could decide if he was taking the job or not.

When Easy and Gem were even with Connor, they

separated and took either side of the bench, putting him between them.

"Hey, get the fuck away from me, queers," Connor said.

"Sorry, man, can't do that."

"Who the fuck are you?"

Zane knew Connor was feeling the stab of a Glock in his side right about then. He also knew where he'd heard that voice before. This morning, in his house, when the man had told him no hard feelings.

It took everything he had not to exit the vehicle and sprint across the street.

"Need to talk to you, bud," Gem said. "About a job you did this morning."

Connor blew out a breath as he raked a hand over his face. "Fucking hell. Knew that was a shitty assignment when we took it. You boys Delta?"

"Not important," Easy said. "You want to get up and come along with us, we can have a private conversation with our team. You want to fight, then we're not gonna make it easy. Got a bead on your boy inside, and the one down the street. Even if you got more sitting around, not a problem."

"All right, where you wanna go?" Connor said, seemingly resigned.

"Nice try," Gem replied. "We know you're mic'd and they're listening. This'll go a lot easier for everyone if you just cooperate. New company like yours doesn't need to get on the wrong side of us or Ian Black's people." There was a hesitation and then Gem laughed. "I see you know Mr. Black. He's aware of the job you did today. Not sure he approves of snatching innocent women from protective custody the way y'all did."

Connor didn't reply. Fucker.

"Let's move," Easy said. "Bring the guy from inside."

"Copy," Hacker said.

Zane leaned back against the seat and let out a breath. The tension wasn't gone yet, far from it, but at least they were making progress. That was something.

Mal put a hand on his shoulder and squeezed. "We won't let you down, Zany. You know that."

"I know."

"Let's drive on over there and pick up Mr. Connor and our gay pals. Meet everyone at the rendezvous point. *Then* we're gonna find out what those fuckers did with Eden and Abby. And *then* we're gonna go get your girl."

"Not gay, you fucker," Easy grumbled in Zane's ear.

"No need to deny it," Mal said. "You make such a sweet couple. So much chemistry. 'Sides, you can be gay in the military these days. I'm sure Jenna and Everly will find new husbands when you and Gem get hitched."

"Mal, you're really too fucking much," Gem said, laughing.

Zane shifted into gear and whipped Gem's big truck into the street, heading for the corner where Gem and Easy stood with Connor. Hacker and the guy with him would go with Saint, Wolf, and Harley. They would meet at the house Ian Black had given them nearby to use and have a private discussion.

It wasn't until Beau Connor got into the backseat

with Gem and Easy that Zane realized why they'd made him drive. Hard to punch a guy when you had to keep your eyes on the road.

"Remember me?" Zane growled, eyeing Connor through the rearview.

Connor dropped his head backward on the seat and blew out a breath. "Fucking hell, can this day get any worse?"

Chapter Twenty-Four

"It was a job," Beau Connor said, spreading his hands. "Client confidentiality has to prevail or nobody else is gonna hire us."

He was sitting at a table with the two men he'd brought to the meeting at the coffee shop and looking pissed. Too fucking bad.

"You busted into my house and took my woman and her sister. It's personal now, asshole."

"Zany," Saint grated.

Zane was ready to choke the motherfucker. "They aren't going to hire you anyway. Ian Black's putting the word out if you don't spill."

Zane didn't know if it was true or not, but he was rolling with it.

"Jesus Christ," Beau said. He shot a look at his guys. They nodded. "This isn't fucking worth it. I got a call from some asshole willing to pay ten times the going rate for this job. He wanted the women, and he wanted to remain anonymous. Means I don't know his name if you're planning to ask."

"Got that," Saint said. "Continue."

"Once the first half of the deposit landed in my account, I didn't ask questions."

"You just took the job without considering what he planned to do with them?"

Saint sounded pissed. He wasn't half as pissed as Zane.

"Yeah. Ten times the going rate. Did I mention that? Fucker paid us two mil to retrieve the ladies and deliver them to him. Got the second half of the money once I turned them over."

The skin on the back of Zane's neck crawled. "Where did you deliver them?"

"Executive airport near BWI. Loaded them on a plane. Dude has his own private island off the coast of Maine. He bragged about it."

"And you weren't curious enough to find out who he was?"

Connor shrugged. "He paid the deposit. Figured he was entitled to his privacy."

"Hack, you got anything?"

Hacker's fingers flew across his keyboard. Then he grinned. "Bingo. Trevor Hagan is from Maine. Grew up in Portland."

Zane's blood froze. He was happy to have an answer, but fucking Trevor Hagan? Made no sense.

"Why did he want both women?"

"Don't know the reason. He said both. We got both."

"How'd Hagan contact you?"

"Look, I don't know if it's this Hagan guy or not. The guy who contacted us called the number a couple of days ago."

"Where would he have gotten it?"

"Facebook? Instagram? I don't fucking know. I have ads running that advertise private security services."

"Jesus," Wolf said. "Fucking Green Berets advertising for business on Facebook. What's the world coming to?"

"Gotta eat, man. We all do."

"You got a number for him?" Saint asked.

"All I got was the number he gave me to call when we loaded the cargo—*ladies*," he corrected when Zane made a noise in his throat.

"Care to share?"

"Do I have a choice?"

"No, but it'd be easier if you just give it to us."

Connor took out his phone and recited the number. Hacker had done something to block his signal, so they hadn't confiscated the phone. Because of that, they weren't worried Connor's people would try to free him.

Hacker typed the number Connor gave him into his computer and waited. "It's a burner, turned off. But the last ping to a tower was eight hours ago. In Maine." He did something on his keyboard, zipped his finger across the trackpad until he stopped abruptly. "Bingo. There's an island a few miles offshore in the vicinity of that tower. Privately owned by Zephyr Industries."

"Is that Hagan's company?"

"One of them."

"You're sure they were going to Maine?" Zane asked.

Connor nodded. "That's what I was told. Confirmed it with the pilot. Wanted the second half of my money and no mistakes. Who's Trevor Hagan?"

"A rich man with boundary issues," Zane replied. "One of those women you delivered to him? He's imprisoned her against her will before. Nearly broke her, but she survived and fought to have a normal life again. She's about to get married, but the guy she's engaged to is in the hospital after being shot at point blank range with a 9 mil a few days ago. You wouldn't know anything about that, amirite?"

Connor looked shocked. "Hell, no. Look, I'll take money to do a job, but I've got my limits. We aren't contract killers. If we're on an op and have to fight, yeah, we'll fight. Not taking money to gun down people."

"Just to abduct women and deliver them to abusive exes."

"You expect me to make people fill out a fucking questionnaire or what? They lie, asshole. You know it and I know it. Somebody's gonna take the job. Might as well be me."

Zane clocked the fucker before anybody could stop him, then stood over his prone body and glared. "That's for fucking busting my windows and mangling my damned door—both of which you can pay for. I'll send a bill."

"You shot my operator. I'd say we're even." Connor wiped blood off his split lip and smeared it on his jeans.

"Not even close," Zane growled. "I'm sending over the bill. You're paying it, or I'll be your worst fucking nightmare. You think you're the only one with skills here? I'll bring the spec ops community down on you, motherfucker. Honor matters. You forfeited yours when you decided money was more important than integrity."

TREVOR HAGAN MADE Eden's skin crawl. And that was before she'd stood in the same room with him. Now that she was face to face with him in his dining room, he made her want to flay her skin from her bones just to stop the uncomfortable sensations rolling across her nerve endings.

After sleeping fitfully in the sparsely furnished room overnight, she and Abby had awakened to a woman bringing in a breakfast tray. Eden had eyed the open door with longing and wondered if she could make a run for it.

The woman had looked straight at her and said, "Run if you wish. There is nowhere to go. Unless you like to swim in shark-infested waters."

Abby had reached for the food, but Eden had stopped her with a hand on her arm and a shake of her head. They'd been drugged yesterday. What if the food was drugged now? The woman removed a plastic fork from her pocket and took a bite of everything. Then she left them alone with the tray and shut the door.

Eden and Abby fell on the food, eating everything. The woman returned a little while later with toiletries and clothing. Eden checked the bathroom for a camera and found nothing. They showered and dressed, and she had to admit she felt better even if the bra the woman had given her was an ill-fitting sports bra. At least it was something.

When dinner time came around, Trevor's disembodied voice informed them they were to dine with him downstairs. Abby's terrified eyes were something Eden would never forget, but she'd squeezed her sister's hand and promised not to leave her side.

Trevor stood when they walked in. He was about six feet tall, with brown hair and blue eyes. He'd have been attractive if you didn't know the kind of person he was. Which Abby had not when she'd first started dating him. Eden remembered her sister's excited texts about the handsome millionaire who showered her with attention and gifts and took her on expensive trips. He'd been good for Abby. Until he hadn't.

"Abigail. Still as beautiful as always. And this is Eden. An interesting face."

He studied her in a way that made her want to run and hide. Instead, she stared back as if he didn't creep her out.

"Not quite as appealing. Shame about the freckles."

Eden's heart constricted. *Zane loves my freckles. Constellations. Galaxies. Entire universes.*

Thinking about Zane made her want to weep. She believed he would come. She had to believe it. But staring out at that stark vista for so long had sown a seed of doubt inside. How would he find them? They appeared to be on an island in the middle of nowhere.

She'd stood at the window, straining her eyes for hours, trying to see land. She had not.

Please, Zane. Please come get us. I need you.

"Where are we?" she asked, ignoring his comment about her face.

Trevor's lips peeled away from his teeth in a smile. "A place where no one can find you."

Eden shivered inside. She hoped her fear didn't show. "But where is that? It has to be *some*where."

"You never mentioned how irritating your sister could be." He directed this comment to Abby, who stayed close to Eden.

"Is she? I never noticed."

Eden could feel Abby's shivers. She'd been worried —still was—about Abby's mental state, but at least her sister hadn't given up entirely. The fact she could clap back was proof of that.

"Sit. Galina's finishing dinner for us."

Abby and Eden exchanged a look before sitting at the opposite end of the table from Trevor. He picked up a glass of whiskey, or so she presumed, and took a sip.

"How did you expect to get away with shooting people?" Eden asked.

Trevor arched a brow. "Have you looked around you?"

"I have. Why?"

He turned the cut glass tumbler back and forth in his hand. Back and forth. Warming the whiskey. "I'm a very rich man. I can hire people to do things for me, or I can do them myself. And when I do them, I can hire people to make the evidence go away." He sipped the whiskey. "You won't find the weapons I used here. Or, indeed, on any of my properties. They don't exist anymore. There is no camera footage either, though the parking garage and Mitchell's house both have cameras. Oh, and your neighbor across the street had a Ring camera on the front door. Took care of that, too."

Eden's belly throbbed with hate and fear.

"I thought the IRS confiscated everything for back taxes." Abby sounded puzzled.

"Not everything. Just the assets in my name. Did you think I wouldn't have offshore accounts?"

"I don't understand then. You have money. Lots of it, apparently. Why risk your fortune this way? Why kill Mitchell or Kate or Eden?"

His eyes were hard. "Because you love them. Because I plan to take *everything* you love before I'm through. Then you'll know what it's like to be alone. To feel despair because nobody's left who loves you."

Eden's pulse skipped higher. Trevor's gaze cut to her before sliding to Abby again. "Maybe I'll fuck your sister before I kill her. She's growing on me. All that fiery red hair, those curves."

Eden's blood ran cold. There was no way she could endure sex with this man after what she'd had with Zane. She'd fight if he tried. Despair crashed through her.

Would she though? Could she? If it was the difference between life and death, she'd have to take whatever happened and pray she stayed alive long enough to see justice done. To see Zane again. She would endure because she had to, and then she'd do everything in her power to rip this man's balls off and feed them to him.

Galina came from the kitchen bearing a platter. There was another woman with her. Younger. This one didn't look at them. She didn't look at Trevor, either. She seemed scared. Before Eden could puzzle it out, she was gone again, having set down her platter and scurried away through the same door.

Eden wondered how many people worked there. How many of them knew that she and Abby were prisoners and not guests? How could Trevor Hagan bring them to this place, and no one questioned their presence or the fact they'd been locked in a room overnight?

Galina and her helper brought more bowls filled with food and a bottle of wine they opened in front of everyone, and then they retreated again. Trevor dug in, piling chicken, vegetables, and bread on his plate.

"You can eat. I'm not going to drug myself. The food is safe."

"But we *were* drugged yesterday," Eden said.

"It was better that way. But you're here now, and you aren't leaving. There's no way off the island. Unless you know how to fly a helicopter. No?" He sliced into his chicken and took a bite. "The island is secure from invasion. There's a radar system, too. If anyone tries to fly in, I'll know. Then I'll take you to the secure bunker beneath this house. The blast doors are rated for a nuclear explosion. Nobody's getting through, and there's enough food and water down there for at least a year. Maybe more. So you see, Abigail, no escape this time.

No cavalry to ride in and save distressed maidens. You're mine for as long as I want you."

He said it cheerfully, smiling as he did so. Then he concentrated on his food. Eden couldn't decide if he was insane or just so fucking rich he thought he could do whatever he wanted without consequence. She'd seen that a time or two working for Mitchell.

Eden shot Abby a look. Her sister was white as a sheet. Eden reached under the table and took Abby's hand. Then she squeezed until Abby looked at her. She tried to impart strength and courage, hope, but Abby's lashes fell to her cheeks and a tear slid toward her chin.

Trevor Hagan had barely gotten started and he'd already broken Abby.

Eden vowed he would not break her, too.

IT WAS FUCKING cold at midnight in the North Atlantic. Zane and his team approached Trevor Hagan's island on a Zodiac. It'd taken far too long to get the operation under way, but there'd been permission to obtain and equipment to gather. They couldn't use HOT assets for the infiltration because those were government owned. They could use Ian Black's assets, though.

Mendez and Ghost had given them a couple days off since they weren't due to rotate out for a while. Mendez had eyed them and said, "Have a nice fishing trip, boys. See you when you get back."

That was the closest to acknowledging the mission

that he would come. Zane gripped the stock of his assault rifle and gritted his teeth against the cold as the boat motored toward the island. He fucking loved General John Mendez. Always would. Colonel Alex Bishop, too. They were the kind of men who could lead an assault against a tank battalion with nothing but butter knives and nobody would refuse to go.

There were nine people on Strike Team 2, and Ian had sent people of his own. Finn McDermott piloted the boat, Jamie Hayes monitored the comm, Roman Kazarov—who could be Mendez's younger doppelgänger—Colt Duchaine, and Jace Kaiser rounded out the team.

They landed on the island on the windward side, which was tricky because of the currents, but the way the house was oriented made their approach riskier from the leeward side. Finn—former Irish special forces, or Sciathán Fianóglach an Airm—navigated the rocks like the pro he was and landed them on a sliver of sand between two rocky outcrops that could have torn them to bits if his skill was less sure.

They abandoned the boat for pickup by a different team later and trekked inland on foot. If all went to plan, they'd locate Eden and Abby and exfiltrate by air when Ian sent a combat helicopter to scoop them from the landing pad Hagan had built on his roof.

The house was lit up like a beacon, even at this late hour. There were motion sensor lights, alarm systems in three concentric rings that had to be neutralized before continuing, and two trained Belgian Malinois attack dogs. The Malinois would be easier to deal with than the alarm systems. Finn McDermott and Jamie Hayes both carried tranquilizer guns and would take the dogs out when they charged. They wouldn't be hurt, but they would be stopped before they could do damage.

"Approaching first alarm," Hacker said in their ears. "I'll need a few minutes."

Zane hated the time it was going to take, but what choice did they have? While Hacker worked, logging into the combat computer that was connected by satellite to the internet, then infiltrating the alarm's central nervous system so he could disable the sirens and set the cameras on a loop, Zane went over the house plan in his mind.

Ian had managed to get a copy. Trevor Hagan had bought the island years ago and started planning for his compound long before he'd gone to prison. There'd been a house, along with a network of caves, but he'd had the house demolished and started again. The caves were part of his nuclear fallout bunker. One thing they could not afford was for Hagan to retreat behind those blast doors with Eden and Abby.

Zane thought about the layout of the house, the rooms they'd decided were most likely where Hagan would keep his prisoners. There was a section labeled *guest rooms* on the plan while the others had different labels: office, gym, staff quarters, library, etcetera. The guest rooms consisted of three rooms, each with ensuite baths. Two rooms had balconies. Only one didn't, and that was the room they would attempt to breach first.

If the women weren't there, they'd try the other two. But first they had to get to the house undetected, and that was going to take longer than any of them had thought as the minutes stretched by and Hacker still hadn't disabled the first alarm.

"Got it," he finally said. Zane swore he heard a collective sigh of relief.

They ghosted past the first perimeter and headed for the second. That one took almost thirty minutes to disable. Twice as long as the last. Zane's gut twisted with impatience as they moved to the last perimeter.

Hacker set up and got to work. Zane couldn't feel his feet anymore. He wasn't sure Hacker could feel his fingers as he typed and grunted softly to himself.

"Taking longer than I thought," he said. "This guy's good."

Not what Zane wanted to hear.

"Wait—what's that sound?" someone said.

That was the only warning they got before the dogs emerged from the darkness at a full run.

Chapter Twenty-Five

The sound of sirens blaring woke Eden. She bolted upright in bed, heart pounding. Beside her, Abby stirred. Her sister had drunk far more wine than Eden thought wise, but Trevor kept offering fresh bottles and Abby kept accepting glasses. Each bottle was opened in their presence, so Eden didn't think it was drugged, but she'd stopped drinking long before they were escorted back to their room. She wanted her wits about her.

Needed them. She had to be ready for whatever might happen, whether it was Trevor trying to fuck her or kill her or, much better scenario, Zane arriving to rescue her.

She'd tried to impart the same philosophy to Abby, but her sister was too scared and craved numbness. Eden couldn't judge her for it.

"Wha's happening?" Abby slurred.

"I don't know." Eden jumped out of bed. She'd kept on the clothes she'd been given earlier, down to the socks. She did not have shoes, though. The shutter had rolled down over their window again at some point in the evening so there wasn't much to see. The bathroom window, a large porthole on one wall, was black, which meant it was still dark outside.

The sirens kept sounding, loud and insistent, and Eden went over to drag Abby from bed. "We have to be ready."

"For what?"

Abby swayed on her feet, grabbing Eden to hold herself upright.

"I don't know. For anything. Ab, please try to focus."

The bedroom door swung open, and a shape filled the entry. "You two. Come with me."

It was Galina's rough smoker's voice. The Polish woman was devoted to Trevor, though Eden didn't know why. Eden had tried to persuade her to help. That suggestion had been met with peals of laughter. Suggestions Trevor would be in bigger trouble than ever once caught had resulted in a harsh growl and a threat of violence. Eden hadn't done that again.

She thought about refusing to go with Galina, but the woman leveled a pistol at them. At least that's what Eden thought it was as dim light from the hall glinted off the barrel. "I said move."

Eden had to drag Abby, who cried and threatened to be sick if they didn't stop moving. "Ser'sly, Edie, gon' puke."

"Down those stairs," Galina said. "Hurry. And keep her quiet."

"What's going on? Are we being attacked?"

"Shut up."

There was a crashing sound at the end of the hall in the direction they'd come. Eden strained to see anything, but it was too dark. There was some kind of emergency lighting on the floor, kind of like in an airplane, but no other lights.

"Go," Galina ordered. "Or I will shoot you where you stand."

Eden hesitated. It sounded like booted feet coming toward them. Many booted feet. That had to be a rescue, right? What else would it be?

Excitement churned in her belly. Zane was coming for her. Like he'd promised. She *knew* it. Believed it. Felt it.

She opened her mouth, then closed it. If she screamed, Galina might shoot her. But if she didn't, would they end up behind Trevor's blast door that he'd promised nobody could get through?

Abby moaned and swayed. Galina grabbed her arm and tried to shove her into the stairwell. Abby retched, the air smelling like sour wine as she threw up on Galina's torso and dropped to her knees.

"You stupid girl," Galina cried.

"Zane! We're here! Zane!" Eden screamed.

"No!" Galina tried to grab her, put a hand over her mouth, but Eden jerked backward, pulling Galina off balance. She tugged, trying to bring Eden with her, but she must have slipped in Abby's vomit because she kept going back into the stairwell. For a moment, she seemed suspended in midair. Then she screamed as her body dropped from beneath her. The sound of her tumbling down the stairs would be imprinted on Eden's brain for the rest of her life.

Boom, thunk, thunk, thunk, thunk, boom, crunch.

"Eden!"

She turned, her eyes blurring with tears. Abby knelt nearby, crying, retching, gasping. "Zane? It's really you?"

Strong arms wrapped around her, catching her against his hard chest. He smelled like smoke and gunpowder and steel, and he wore the same face covering the men who'd taken her and Abby from his house wore. His skin beneath the balaclava was covered in greasepaint, but the rain-gray eyes were his.

"It's me, Eden. It's me." When his mouth landed on hers, she knew she wasn't dreaming. Zane's lips, Zane's tongue, Zane's electric kiss. It was *him*. Her man. The man she loved. She clung to him, weak with relief and tense with fear they weren't safe yet. She might not feel safe again for a very long time, but being in his arms was a start.

"I love you," she said, clinging to him. "You, not Mitchell. I-I was wrong about my feelings. You were right. I chose him because he was unavailable. He was the safe choice. Easier to love someone you can't have than to put yourself out there for real."

"Eden. Jesus." His fists tightened in her clothing. "I love you. You make me believe again, honey. This tattoo is going away. Covered, erased, I don't fucking care, but I won't wear her name on my body anymore."

His head lifted as he peered into the darkness. Then he reached up and dropped goggles over his eyes that she hadn't noticed before.

"We have to go, baby. Chopper's on the way."

"Abby—"

"Mal's got her. I've got you. We're getting you out of here."

"Wait! There was another woman, Zane. I don't know her name, but she didn't look like she wanted to be here when she served us dinner earlier. She wouldn't make eye contact and she looked scared."

"Saint, you hear that. Copy."

Before Eden could protest, he swung her into his arms and started booking it back the way he'd come. They took another set of stairs up. When the door opened, cold air whipped inside, chilling her all the way to her marrow. Eden buried her face in his neck, trying to stop her teeth from chattering.

"I know it's cold. I'm sorry. We'll get a warm blanket around you soon as we get you in the chopper."

"It's okay. I'd rather freeze out here with you than spend another second inside that house."

Zane had pulled his balaclava up, but he pressed a kiss to her forehead anyway. "Not long now. Hear it?"

In the distance, the sound of a chopper beating the air separated itself from the wind's howl. It got closer and closer as more people appeared on the roof.

It wasn't until they were inside the metal beast that Eden looked at the faces that weren't covered. There was her, Abby, and the quiet woman from dinner who sobbed into her hand. *Thank God.*

"Where's Trevor?" she asked as a chill that had nothing to do with the frigid night settled in her bones.

If they didn't catch him, if he got free, would Abby ever be safe? Would she?

Zane exchanged a look with someone, then dipped his mouth to her ear. "We tried to take him. He was waiting for you and Abby inside the shelter. He hadn't closed the doors, and Gem and Wolf went after him. He fired at them. No choice but to return fire. He's dead."

Eden squeezed her eyes shut. Was it wrong to feel relief? Maybe so, but she did. "Good," she whispered. "I'm glad."

"So am I. Did he hurt you? Either of you?"

"No. Well, maybe Abby. Mentally, I mean. She's sick because she was drinking. She couldn't cope." Tears welled. "I was scared, but I knew you'd come. I kept telling myself you would. It got me through. And you did. You really did."

He squeezed her to him. "So long as I've got breath in my body, Eden, I'll come for you. Wherever you are, whatever happens, I'm there."

She sniffled and cupped his jaw. "My ride or die for life, huh?"

"For life, Eden. On my honor."

―――

THE HELICOPTER TOOK them to the airport where a private jet waited to return them to the DC metro area. Zane carried Eden onto the plane and settled her in a chair, sitting beside her and buckling them both in.

She held his hand, clinging to it, and he put an arm around her, stroking her hair.

"Is it true?" she asked, gazing up at him.

"Is what true?"

"You said I made you believe again."

He dropped a kiss to her temple. He'd shed the balaclava when they'd gotten on the chopper. "You do."

She smiled. "I'm glad."

"So am I."

She dozed with her head against his chest, only waking when they reached their destination. He took her and Abby home, where Merlin waited for them, meowing insistently when they walked inside. Eden laughed and picked him up, cuddling him and cooing nonsense. Zane imagined her doing that with their child, and he almost couldn't breathe. He wanted that vision someday. They hadn't even talked about children, but he could see it with Eden. Cats and dogs too. A house with a fenced yard where they could play.

"What?" she asked when she turned to find him watching her.

"Nothing, baby. Just happy to have you home with me."

"I'm happy, too."

They got Abby settled in the guest room. She was asleep instantly. She'd have a helluva hangover tomorrow, but for now she was out like a light.

Eden cuddled Merlin again, then set him down and stepped into Zane's waiting arms. "I missed you."

He kissed the top of her head. "I missed you, too."

They stood that way for a long while, then he took her hand and led her to the bedroom. It was the middle of the night, and they were both tired, but somehow they ended up in the shower together, scrubbing off the grime and sea salt that'd blown into their hair and clothes.

"You're so fucking pretty, Eden," he said, cupping her wet breasts in his hands.

She smiled shyly. "I'm still skeptical, but I'm trying to see it your way."

He skimmed fingers down her body, over the flare of her hips. "You get me going in ways nobody else can. You think you aren't confident, but you're brave and bold and ballsy. Your sister got drunk. You stayed sober so you could *think*. If you wanted, you could join up with me and go on missions. Think I could get the general to sign off on it."

She laughed even as she shivered at the way he touched her. "No, thank you. If tonight was any indication, it's too damn cold. And late. Why can't you schedule your rescues at more decent hours?"

Zane laughed with her then tugged her wet, naked body against his. "I want you, Eden. I need to make love to you to remind myself you're here. That you're okay. But it doesn't have to be tonight. You've been through a lot."

She grasped his cock and he groaned. "I need you, Zane. When I thought that man..." She swallowed and he felt himself start to growl deep inside.

"Did he threaten you, baby?"

The worst of it for him was when the dogs attacked and the alarm sounded. Finn and Jamie had tranquilized the dogs before they'd done damage and the team had stormed the compound. Zane had been frantic until he'd found her. And now she showed fear for the first time since then, and it killed him.

"He said I had an interesting face but too bad about the freckles. Later he said I was growing on him and he planned to fuck me before he killed me. I was scared, Zane. But I didn't let it show. I was determined not to let it show."

Zane was incandescent with rage. He reminded himself that she was here, safe in his arms, and Trevor Hagan was dead. He only wished he'd been the one to pull the trigger.

"I'm sorry I wasn't there sooner. Fucking kills me you were scared and I wasn't there to help."

Eden cupped his face and stood on tiptoe to kiss him. "You saved me. He didn't get a chance to hurt me. I'm fine."

Zane kissed her, his heart hammering with the knowledge he'd almost lost her. He turned off the shower, dried her off and then himself, and carried her to the bed though she protested she could walk.

When he was buried to the hilt inside her, her legs wrapped around his hips, their mouths tasting and seeking, he thought his heart wouldn't be able to contain all he felt. He'd thought he loved Juliet, but that was a youthful love brought on by mutual loneliness and obsession.

This love was more. It was new, but it was right.

"I want to stay married," he said when it was over and they lay curled together, his arm around her, her leg thrown over his.

She propped herself on an elbow to look at him. "I do, too."

"You told Abby. I have to tell Mia and my parents."

"Will they be upset?" She looked apprehensive.

"No. Because once they meet you and see how much I love you, they'll be happy I found you. Mia pointed out in Vegas that I never brought another woman home after Juliet. I think she worried I was lonely. My parents never said anything, but I know they've wondered if I'd find someone, too. Told my team tonight as well."

"They already know. Remember the party?" she teased.

"Yeah, babe. I mean I told them the truth. Like you told Abby. I also told them I wanted to make a go of it with you. I was asking them to risk their lives to help me get you back, I owed them the truth."

She smiled. "I love you, Zane."

"Love you, too, Eden." Her eyes drooped and he knew she was fighting sleep. Merlin jumped on the bed and sauntered up to Eden's pillow like he owned it. "Go to sleep, babe. Your cat's ready for bed, and so am I."

"'Kay."

He kissed the tip of her nose. "I'm bringing you coffee and breakfast in bed tomorrow. And every morning I'm home."

"You don't have to do that, Zane."

"I do. You own me, Eden. Body and soul. Ride or die. Spoiling you for saving *me* is what I mean to do."

"Mr. Perfect," she sighed.

"Only for you, honey."

"That's all I need."

TWO MONTHS LATER...

THE CHURCH WAS DECORATED with poinsettias, red ribbon, and greenery everywhere. Candles flickered with warm light. Eden stood beside her sister, who looked absolutely amazing in her white dress, and watched as Mitchell made his way up the aisle.

He walked hesitantly, but he walked. Two months ago, they'd wondered if he would live. He'd fought hard to recover, and he'd managed to return to work much faster than anyone expected. He'd even successfully argued the William Allen case. Now he was at his wedding, his face shining with happiness as he walked toward the woman he loved.

Joyful tears pricked Eden's eyes. She did love Mitchell, but not the way she'd once thought. She loved him as the brother he was about to officially become. She loved him because Abby did.

Abby had been seeing a therapist since everything that had happened with Trevor, and she was doing well. Eden hadn't realized she hadn't seen one the first time Trevor had kept her prisoner. Abby had confessed it the next morning after their rescue, and Eden had suggested she needed to find someone. Eden still worried, but she was confident Abby was on the right track.

Especially with Mitchell, who loved her to distraction and would be there for her no matter what.

The shooting was officially unresolved. Kate's death,

too. Trevor had said they would never find weapons, and they hadn't. The only thing connecting him to the shootings was GPS location information for the rental car he'd used. A man with the money he had could have bought a car, but he'd rented one and driven it to the parking garage, Mitchell's house, and hers. The car had been there at the time of the shootings, but without a weapon, and with the suspect dead, there was no further action to be taken.

The official story was that Trevor had taken his own life. The woman who'd been pulled off the island with Eden and Abby was someone he'd groomed through a few dates, like he had with Abby, and then taken to the island where she couldn't escape. She'd had plenty to say about Trevor's methods. Eden thanked God that Zane and his team had found them when they had, or it could have been so much worse.

Abby and Mitchell said their vows while Eden tried not to cry. She caught Zane's gaze. He looked at her like she was the most important thing in the world to him. That look still had the power to make her stomach bottom out in the best of ways.

She smiled. He smiled back. Butterflies swirled. She'd never known she could fall so hard for a man. Never known she could feel so confident and beautiful either. But she did. Zane's love did that for her.

He'd had the tattoo covered. Juliet had never called again, but Mia had told them that Juliet and Daniel seemed to still be married. They still lived in the same house, anyway. Zane had shrugged and said he didn't care. Eden didn't care either, but she felt kind of sorry for the woman who'd been stupid enough to let a man like Zane Scott go. Then again, thank heavens she had because now he was Eden's, and she wasn't ever giving him up.

After the reception was done and Abby and Mitchell departed for their honeymoon in Hawaii, Zane helped Eden into her CR-V and then got behind the wheel. They'd taken her car because it wasn't as far up for her to climb in her bridesmaid dress.

"Are you sorry we didn't have a big wedding?" he asked when they were on the road.

Eden yawned. "No. Are you?"

"Considering I never thought I'd get married, no. But if you wanted one, I'd give it to you."

She reached for his hand. "After everything I had to do to help Abby pull off her dream wedding, I'm cured of the idea. Besides, I much prefer that we bought a house instead of spending that money on a ceremony."

Zane lifted her hand to his mouth and pressed a kiss there. A shiver ran from where he kissed all the way to her core.

"I love our house."

"So do I."

They'd found a sweet little house in Mystic Cove, where Ryder and Alaina and Noah and Jenna lived. They'd thought they would have to wait since Zane still had a few months left to pay for Mia's tuition and Eden was saving for law school, but they'd happily discovered a house they could afford. Especially when Mitchell informed her she'd be getting one of the firm's scholarships for next fall.

She loved being close to her friends, especially when Zane and the team went on missions. She and Alaina and Jenna got together with the other women frequently, and sometimes she went and stayed with them and their kids. Merlin went too. The kids loved him. Surprisingly, he loved them as well. Or at least he tolerated a lot more than she'd thought he would.

When they pulled into the driveway, joy suffused her at the sight of their house decorated for Christmas. There were lights on the cedar tree in the yard, lights on the roofline, and red bows on the carriage lights. A potted cedar sat by the door, also with a bow and lights, and once they walked inside and turned on the lights there, the Christmas tree would fill the front window with color.

"I'm going to miss this when we go to Arizona for Christmas," Zane said with a sigh. "It's not even cold there."

"I know, but we'll have many more Christmases in this house."

He smiled. "You're right."

When he walked around to help her out of the car, he didn't let her feet touch the ground. Instead, he carried her to the front door and unlocked it with one hand while holding her against him.

"What are we doing?" she murmured.

"I'm carrying you over the threshold, babe."

"You already did that when we moved in."

"I know. But you seem to like it, so I'm doing it again. Plus, you've got that sexy dress on, and I plan to strip you out of it when we get on the other side of the door."

Eden shivered and laughed. "Being married to you is never boring."

"That's the plan, babe. I'm never giving you a reason to leave me."

"I'm not leaving you, Zane. Ever."

"I know. I just like to hear you say it."

She cupped his cheek and kissed him softly. "Then I'll say it as often as you want me to."

The door opened and he carried her inside. Instead of stripping her, he carried her to the couch and sat down with her in his lap, then reached over and flicked the switch for the tree. They sat in the soft glow of the lights, his cheek to her forehead, her arms around his neck.

"Welcome home, Mrs. Scott."

There was nothing in this world better. Home, family, love. She had them all. The future was bright and beautiful thanks to this man. Apparently, getting married while drunk in Vegas was the best decision she'd ever made.

Viva Las Vegas.

Epilogue

HOT HQ

ALEX "GHOST" Bishop obeyed the summons to appear in Mendez's office. When he walked inside, he stopped short. Ian Black and Samantha Spencer sat across from Mendez. The billionaire mercenary and his CIA handler? Not what he'd been expecting.

"Alex," Mendez said. "Have a seat."

Alex did as he was told, eyeing the three of them and wondering what the hell was going on.

"I'm not going to beat around the bush," Mendez said. "You've been a great second for me at HOT. Hell, I thought when I retired, she'd be yours to command."

A pit opened in his stomach. He'd thought that, too. He didn't say anything, though. He'd learned not to fill the silence with words. Waiting meant someone else would speak and you'd get to the truth faster.

"I want you to retire," Mendez said. "Put in your papers and leave HOT."

Alex felt his jaw drop. "Sir?"

Mendez sighed and raked a hand through his salt-and-pepper hair. "I'm sorry, Ghost. I know this isn't what you expected. It's not what I expected, either, if I'm honest."

"It's not as bad as all that," Ian Black said. "You look like someone kicked your puppy."

"Kinda feels that way after everything I've done."

He'd run ops to clear Mendez's name when Congress had ordered HOT to stand down. He'd done it against orders and illegally, but it had been worth it in the end. HOT got their commanding officer back and stopped a plot to kill the president in the process.

"We need your talents elsewhere," Sam said. "This comes from the president, I should add."

That sounded a bit better, though he was still processing the shock. "What do you want me to do?"

"We want you to go private. Recruit your own people. And we want you to set up shop in Alabama."

"Alabama?"

"There are things happening down there that need close attention," Sam said. "Discreet attention."

"Non-military attention," Mendez added.

"You mean you want me to set up ghost ops," Alex replied. "No ties to the military, no ties to HOT—but with hand-picked operators who know the drill."

"Sounds about right," Ian said.

Alex didn't have to think about it a moment longer. "I'm your man, then. When do we start?"

HOT Hon...

Who's HOT?

Strike Team 1

Matt "Richie Rich" Girard (Book 0 & 1)
Sam "Knight Rider" McKnight (Book 2)
Kev "Big Mac" MacDonald (Book 3)
Billy "the Kid" Blake (Book 4)
Jack "Hawk" Hunter (Book 5)
Nick "Brandy" Brandon (Book 6)
Garrett "Iceman" Spencer (Book 7)
Ryan "Flash" Gordon (Book 8)
Chase "Fiddler" Daniels (Book 9)
Dex "Double Dee" Davidson (Book 10)

Commander
John "Viper" Mendez (Book 11 & 12)

Deputy Commander
Alex "Ghost" Bishop

Strike Team 2

Cade "Saint" Rodgers (Book 1)
Sky "Hacker" Kelley (Book 2)
Dean "Wolf" Garner (Book 3)
Malcom "Mal" McCoy (Book 4)
Noah "Easy" Cross (Book 5)
Jax "Gem" Stone (Book 6)
Ryder "Muffin" Hanson (Book 7)
Zane "Zany" Scott (Book 8)
Jake "Harley" Ryan (HOT WITNESS)

SEAL Team 1

Dane "Viking" Erikson (Book 1)
Remy "Cage" Marchand (Book 2)
Cody "Cowboy" McCormick (Book 3)
Cash "Money" McQuaid (Book 4)
Alexei "Camel" Kamarov (Book 5)
Adam "Blade" Garrison (Book 6)
Ryan "Dirty Harry" Callahan (Book 7)
Zach "Neo" Anderson (Book 8)
Corey "Shade" Vance

Black's Bandits

Jace Kaiser (Book 1)
Brett Wheeler (Book 2)
Colton Duchaine (Book 3)
Jared Fraser (Book 4)
Ian Black (Book 5)

Tyler Scott (Book 6)
Dax Freed (Book 7)
Thomas "Rascal" Bradley
Jamie Hayes
Finn McDermot
Roman Rostov
Mandy Parker (Airborne Ops)
Melanie (Reception)
? Unnamed Team Members

Freelance Contractors

Lucinda "Lucky" San Ramos, now MacDonald (Book 3)
Victoria "Vee" Royal, now Brandon (Book 6)
Emily Royal, now Gordon (Book 8)
Miranda Lockwood, now McCormick (SEAL Team Book 3)
Bliss Bennett, (Strike Team 2, Book 2)
Angelica "Angie" Turner (Black's Bandits, Book 3)

Books by Lynn Raye Harris

The Hostile Operations Team ® Books
Strike Team 2

Book 1: HOT ANGEL - Cade & Brooke

Book 2: HOT SECRETS - Sky & Bliss

Book 3: HOT JUSTICE - Wolf & Haylee

Book 4: HOT STORM - Mal & Scarlett

Book 5: HOT COURAGE - Noah & Jenna

Book 6: HOT SHADOWS - Gem & Everly

Book 7: HOT LIMIT ~ Ryder & Alaina

Book 8: HOT HONOR ~ Zane & Eden

The Hostile Operations Team ® Books
Strike Team 1

Book 0: RECKLESS HEAT

Book 1: HOT PURSUIT - Matt & Evie

Book 2: HOT MESS - Sam & Georgie

Book 3: DANGEROUSLY HOT - Kev & Lucky

Book 4: HOT PACKAGE - Billy & Olivia

Book 5: HOT SHOT - Jack & Gina

Book 6: HOT REBEL - Nick & Victoria

Book 7: HOT ICE - Garrett & Grace

Book 8: HOT & BOTHERED - Ryan & Emily

Book 9: HOT PROTECTOR - Chase & Sophie

Book 10: HOT ADDICTION - Dex & Annabelle

Book 11: HOT VALOR - Mendez & Kat

Book 12: A HOT CHRISTMAS MIRACLE - Mendez & Kat

The HOT SEAL Team Books

Book 1: HOT SEAL - Dane & Ivy

Book 2: HOT SEAL Lover - Remy & Christina

Book 3: HOT SEAL Rescue - Cody & Miranda

Book 4: HOT SEAL BRIDE - Cash & Ella

Book 5: HOT SEAL REDEMPTION - Alex & Bailey

Book 6: HOT SEAL TARGET - Blade & Quinn

Book 7: HOT SEAL HERO - Ryan & Chloe

Book 8: HOT SEAL DEVOTION - Zach & Kayla

HOT Heroes for Hire: Mercenaries
Black's Bandits

Book 1: BLACK LIST - Jace & Maddy

Book 2: BLACK TIE - Brett & Tallie

Book 3: BLACK OUT - Colt & Angie

Book 4: BLACK KNIGHT - Jared & Libby

Book 5: BLACK HEART - Ian & Natasha

Book 6: BLACK MAIL - Tyler & Cassie

Book 7: BLACK VELVET - Dax & Roberta

The HOT Novella in Liliana Hart's MacKenzie Family Series

HOT WITNESS - Jake & Eva

———

7 Brides for 7 Soldiers

WYATT (Book 4) - Wyatt & Paige

7 Brides for 7 Blackthornes

ROSS (Book 3) - Ross & Holly

———

About the Author

Lynn Raye Harris is a Southern girl, military wife, wannabe cat lady, and horse lover. She's also the New York Times and USA Today bestselling author of the HOSTILE OPERATIONS TEAM ® SERIES of military romances, and 20 books about sexy billionaires for Harlequin.

A former finalist for the Romance Writers of America's Golden Heart Award and the National Readers Choice Award, Lynn lives in Alabama with her handsome former-military husband, one fluffy princess of a cat, and a very spoiled American Saddlebred horse who enjoys bucking at random in order to keep Lynn on her toes.

Lynn's books have been called "exceptional and emotional," "intense," and "sizzling" -- and have sold in excess of 4.5 million copies worldwide.

To connect with Lynn online:
www.LynnRayeHarris.com
Lynn@LynnRayeHarris.com

a BB f g ⓞ

Made in United States
Orlando, FL
24 October 2023